THE LONG SHADOW

Anne Buist is the Chair of Women's Mental Health at the University of Melbourne. She has over twenty-five years' clinical and research experience in perinatal psychiatry, and works with protective services and the legal system in cases of abuse, kidnapping, infanticide and murder. Her *Natalie King* series of thrillers is published by Text.

THE
LONG
SHADOW

ANNE BUIST

TEXT PUBLISHING MELBOURNE AUSTRALIA

textpublishing.com.au
textpublishing.co.uk

The Text Publishing Company
Swann House, 22 William Street, Melbourne Victoria 3000, Australia

The Text Publishing Company (UK) Ltd
130 Wood Street, London EC2V 6DL, United Kingdom

Published by The Text Publishing Company, 2020

Book design by Imogen Stubbs
Cover images by Peter Chadwick / Trevillion and Arcangel
Typeset in Sabon by J&M Typesetting

Printed and bound in Australia by Griffin Press, part of Ovato, an accredited ISO/NZS 14001:2004 Environmental Management System printer

ISBN: 9781922268709 (paperback)
ISBN: 9781925923285 (ebook)

A catalogue record for this book is available from the National Library of Australia

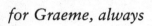

for Graeme, always

THE THERAPY GROUP AND THEIR FAMILIES

Isabel (Issy) Harris
Her son, Noah
Her husband, Dean, corporate troubleshooter

Sophie Barclay
Her son, Tom
Her husband, Lachlan, political candidate
Lachlan's father, Gordon, member of parliament
Lachlan's mother, Grace, charity worker
Lachlan's brother, Matthew (Matt), farmer

Teagan Moretti
Her daughter, Indiana
Her father, Joe, ex-political candidate/greengrocer
Her mother, Donna
Her brother, Joshua
Her boyfriend, Jed

Róisín Rearden
Her daughter, Bella
Her partner, Al, local newsagent
Her father, Conor, hospital shop steward

Kate McCormack
Her daughter, Ruby
Her husband, Brian, local barman
Her brother-in-law, Chris, local doctor/political candidate

Zahra Sorouri
Her daughter, Raha
Her husband, Massoud, local doctor

The baby killer is going to strike again. Soon.

Five women sat looking at me, waiting. I was aware of the shuffles from our children next door, the ticking of a clock that was three hours slow and the hiss of the coffee urn in the kitchenette. And of my hand, holding the note I was supposed to read out, beginning to shake.

It was my first time running a mother–baby therapy group—my first session. My supervisors back in Melbourne would have said: 'See, Isabel? That's why you need to interview participants before you take them on.'

Interviews hadn't been an option. We'd only been in town a week, and Yvonne, the child-health nurse, with the long neck and darting eyes that reminded me of a chicken, hadn't been available until this morning.

'I run a group sometimes,' Yvonne told me when I arrived at the small house that was the town's child health centre, set in the narrow road behind the main street's three shops. Her look suggested that it was she who ought to be running this one, not some jumped-up junior psychologist. 'The GP and I put this lot together for you.'

She'd taken me through the files—three minutes for each

of four clients and a quick read of the fifth before we'd been interrupted by the first woman, Sophie, arriving with her son Tom. The Sydney law graduate who had married into the Barclay family—sheep and politics. If she was anxious, as Yvonne had indicated, her smile was masking it well. 'Is it okay if I call you Issy?' She didn't wait for an answer.

Yvonne took the children, my own son Noah included, into the room next door, where babies were usually weighed and measured; during my groups it was being turned into a playroom. This left me in the bigger meeting space for the mothers; half a dozen plastic chairs with faded cushions organised in a circle, a few beanbags had been thrown in the corner and a whiteboard was pushed against the wall, one wheel looking precarious. The room had an air conditioner, but it was turned off and the room was stuffy, with a smell of talc, cleaning fluids and mould. My thighs were stuck together; I wished I was wearing my thin cotton trousers from Bali but they were a ten-hour drive away in Melbourne, along with my friends and family. I risked being labelled a wimpy city-girl if I turned on the aircon; besides, the control wasn't in the wall holder.

The start was less than auspicious. The women hadn't said more than a curt hello to each other as they arrived and there was a definite sense of them not wanting to be there. I figured it was my nervousness combined with country wariness of talking about emotions. Later, I wondered if there could be more behind it.

I waited until Teagan Moretti arrived—ten minutes late—before suggesting we all introduce ourselves. Pregnant Teagan. Indigenous; with *issues* according to Yvonne. There was an undisguised message that they went together. It was unclear if the baby's father was going to stick around—

Yvonne seemed to think this was no surprise either.

Starting a group in a small country town was always going to have its challenges, but they kicked in early.

'*We* already know each other,' Teagan said as she pushed a chair back and pulled out a beanbag. She looked at me from under her spiked red fringe and fiddled with the stud in her lip. Her T-shirt, decorated with a hand-sewn image of an owl with round yellow irises, strained over her bulge.

'What exactly is this group for?' Kate's arms were crossed. Reluctant mother, reluctant group participant. A solid woman with muscle to match the baby weight, short brown hair and fierce eyes. Her T-shirt was only half tucked in; she looked like she hadn't checked the mirror before leaving home.

'To help us be the best possible parents.' Sophie, the politician's daughter-in-law, jumped in before I had a chance. 'Isn't that right, Issy?' Her lemon silk dress—great fit, no puke stains—made me regret the Bali trousers a little less. My post-pregnancy bump still hung over them even though Noah was a toddler now.

'Motherhood can be daunting,' I said. Sophie frowned. Did I sound patronising? 'Fun sometimes but also hard work. Constant demands, and a lot of our own stuff to deal with because things from the past—our own childhoods—come to the surface. It's a pretty fertile environment'—I tried a little smile: no response—'for problems like anxiety and depression.'

Sophie took out a notebook and paper; one woman at least prepared to play along. Kate glared—arms still crossed over her chest. Teagan got up to make herself a coffee. My final two clients weren't any more engaged. Róisín, whose name I didn't know how to pronounce and the oldest by probably ten years, curled a strand of hair around her finger; she looked as much depressed as anxious. Zahra, the Persian doctor, appeared bewildered. She had suffered from post-partum psychosis and just returned after an admission in Sydney; 'Never seen anyone get so sick so quickly,' Yvonne had told me in a conspiratorial tone. 'They had to give her shock treatment.'

That was the point where I handed out the pens and paper for the getting-to-know-you exercise. 'Write down something about yourself, about how you are as a mother, that worries you,' I said. 'Something other people don't know. We'll put the notes in a bag with no names attached.' My own note included.

Sophie asked for clarification and then repeated what I had said to Zahra, who I was pretty sure had understood the first time.

'We all wish to be good mothers,' Zahra said softly in the slightest of accents, as she bent to the task. 'And good people.'

'No names, eh?' said Teagan. 'So, could we write something we'd like people to think was from someone else?' If it was a joke, nobody laughed, but Teagan was already putting the note into the bag.

The first five contributions generated some useful discussion about universal problems. Sleepless nights; the idea of 'good enough' parenting that I had contributed. But I was conscious of a growing feeling that something wasn't right about the group.

Then I pulled out the last note. About the baby killer.

It was surely just a melodramatic attempt to stir up the group—or me. It seemed to sum up where my life had taken me: out of my depth, to places I didn't want to be. I probably should have laughed. But I couldn't overlook the possibility that there was a serious issue underlying it.

The silence was becoming awkward. I cleared my throat. Squashed the unease.

'I'm not going to read this one out.' I folded the piece of paper; looked around the room for any indication someone knew what was going on.

Teagan was checking her phone. Sophie waited, tapping her pen on her notebook. Zahra smiled hesitantly then looked down, hands fidgeting with the already-crumpled white top that hung over her jeans. Róisín turned away, distracted by a squeal from the playgroup; Kate was looking at the clock.

'This group is about our anxieties, and about trust. The author of the note has shared her motherhood fear, as I asked, and I want to honour that. But I am concerned that...it falls outside what we can address productively in this group.'

'Not like we can talk about much in here anyway,' Teagan muttered, eyes on the phone in her hand. Sophie shot her a look of irritation. Everyone else was looking at Kate. She kept her gaze steady.

This tension hovering around Teagan: some small-town dynamic? A racial thing? Or just my own anxiety?

'Yvonne didn't tell you?' Kate smiled without humour. 'I'm a cop.'

I could think of trickier challenges to my authority— maybe a professor of psychology in the group—but it was line ball.

'While Kate's here,' I said firmly, 'she is off duty. Short of a situation where anyone is actually at risk, everything else stays in this room. Are you okay with that, Kate?'

Kate caught my eye. Hesitated, then nodded.

'If the person who wrote the note would like to talk, I'm happy to discuss it with them in confidence.' I paused. 'Okay, moving on.'

I returned to the standard first-group discussion topics—expectations of motherhood, where they diverged from reality and the impact. I set homework: write down any negative self-talk you notice; think of a positive message to yourself and jot it down somewhere you'll see it often during the day. I outlined a plan for future sessions; Sophie suggested they all take it in turns to bring morning tea, and there was a murmur of agreement.

By the time they left I was exhausted; plenty about the dynamics and individual client issues to work on before next week's group.

But it was the note, and the ominous *again* and *soon* that dominated my thoughts.

We had arrived in Riley a week earlier. The final stage of the drive, after Dubbo, was stretched out over a monotonous two hours into the glimmer of the sun setting on the horizon. The only sound was car wheels on tarmac. Noah was asleep and we'd given up on the radio because the reception was so bad on most channels. The channel we could get was discussing something to do with dipping sheep; I wasn't even sure what that was. The occasional patches of cultivated land—wheat and cotton—disappeared completely, replaced by large paddocks where the only sign of human presence was a wire fence on either side of the road and occasional groups of incurious livestock.

As we drew closer the roadkill ramped up. Kangaroos on the verge, legs stiff in the air; older fragments decayed, picked over by crows. We narrowly missed one ourselves when a large grey bounded onto the road in front of us. Dean swerved instantly, despite the long day behind the wheel, but he was still visibly tense half an hour later.

There was little to announce Riley itself, just a dark line of trees in the distance: a gash, with Riley on it, that cut through the centre of the landscape. Trees clumped on either side of a river that was a slow shallow ditch in the dry season and a flood plain when it rained up north. Treacherously unpredictable, we'd been told, like many things in this part of the world.

A billboard welcomed us to *Riley and the Great Outback*, 2,500 residents enumerated under the beaming face of Gordon Barclay—Sophie's father-in-law—and a proclamation: *A National Party seat for twenty years.*

Travelling slow, we passed the hospital that Dean— the Red Adair of hospital administration stuff-ups—had been sent here to fix. We had left the town itself before we crossed the river. At the bridge, what looked like a large brown and white owl swept in front of us with a human-like scream to attack a smaller bird that thumped down onto our windscreen in a shower of feathers. Its dying eyes were fixed on mine as it slipped down the car bonnet. The unsettled feeling stayed with me all the way to our new home.

The house stood on a flat plain ten kilometres from town; a sad, dust-covered weatherboard owned by the Barclays with a shed, water tank and carport. Clumps of trees at the rear delineated a winding creek bed. The land further west was classified as outback, but even here it looked as if nothing was meant to survive in the cracked landscape except wispy eucalypts that would explode and vanish if a bushfire should ever sweep through.

We drove over another bridge, a structure that looked like it had been built for stock, its boards creaking and rattling under the weight of the car. The flood indicators beside the stock bridge went up to three metres. Now there was barely a trickle of water.

The cottage was separated from the paddocks by a

sagging wire fence. No one had lived there for a while, judging by the scattered pellets of animal droppings on the veranda, but inside it was neat: dusty living room with a faded green couch and threadbare chairs, kitchen with a gas stove attached to a large cylinder, bathroom and three small bedrooms with floral curtains. A trapdoor from the pantry led to a large area under the house that could have been renovated into a games room. Now it was just a big space full of old tools and machine parts with a door into the shed.

'A chance to sample country living,' said Dean as we celebrated our arrival the first night, soaking in the quiet remote beauty that was foreign to us both. There were more stars in the sky than I had ever seen in the city haze.

'Let's see if we can find the Southern Cross,' I said to him on impulse, grabbing his hand and leading him out onto the dry earth that might once have been a front garden. I lay on my back and allowed myself to be dazzled by the shimmering silver dots. Dean frowned as I made a dust angel but then gave in and started laughing. Heads together, dirt in our hair, we made up our own versions of warrior gods and giant wombats—and Dean's dust angel was left imprinted on the ground as a mirror image of mine.

That first night, I slept with real hope of a new start. It was beautiful enough that I wasn't worried about the distance from town or the complete absence of mobile reception. There was a land line; it would be fine.

Now, after Dean had dropped Noah and me home and returned to the hospital, I was taken back to the sense of foreboding I'd had on our arrival. I started dinner and thought about the weird baby-killer note. My mind—blank then—started racing with possibilities.

Another prickle of muted dread ran across my skin. I looked up from a mound of chopped carrots and—

Where was Noah?

A surge of panic, a flashing memory of brown and white, pulse racing, dry mouth, a knot in my throat. The persistent thought behind it that I mustn't slip, that I had to fight against the anxiety that had crippled me after Noah's accident...

There was a snuffle from under the bed—the sound of a two-and-a-half-year-old trying not to giggle—and I felt a surge of relief that nearly knocked me over.

When I'd finally got him to sleep, and dinner cooking—it had taken me a minute to remember the gas bottle needed to be turned on—I sat on the veranda with a cup of tea, staring across a dusty landscape mottled with shadows as the sun hovered on the horizon, a few kangaroos grazing in the distance. One, a large grey, stood on his hind legs and appeared to look straight at me. Not a bad neighbour to have, though the farmers probably thought otherwise. His ears flickered as a sound like a dog's bark came from the nearby trees. I stood up and peered into the dusk light. Were there dingoes around Riley?

The baby killer is going to strike again. Soon.

It was my first group. I didn't want to dismiss the note as a hoax, and my reaction as out of proportion anxiety, without considering what it meant. And it might tell me a bit more about the women—or one of them—who, browbeaten or otherwise, had decided to attend.

What did it mean by striking *again*? Had there been a suspicious baby death recently in Riley? Why on earth *would* anyone write it? To see how I would react when it was read out? To test the rules I'd put in place? It seemed unlikely there was a real risk—how would anyone in my group have this information anyway, and why put it in a note?

I could ask each of them if they had written it, of course, but I was pretty sure they'd deny it and there was nothing to learn from that. My work as a psychologist relied on people telling the truth, at least as they saw it.

I took out my own note about good-enough parenting and put it aside, then flattened each of the other notes on the table in front of me.

All that matters is my child, but how do I know what's best for them? I had thought Róisín, Sophie or Zahra. Róisín was clearly child-focused, Sophie seemed competitive, needing to be best; Zahra would be trying to make sense of what was important and what wasn't.

Me = crap mum had to be Teagan or Kate; either of them might have used those words.

Why didn't anyone tell me motherhood was so hard? Any of them.

All children deserve the best chance. Probably Sophie; bigger-picture stuff that the others were too stuck in the here-and-now to imagine. Maybe Zahra, if she wasn't too unwell.

And then, the warning note. Was that Kate the cop, with some kind of confidential information she wanted to get out there? If that was the case, it could get her in strife—there were less traceable ways to leak something than in a group of five.

Nobody else was likely to have real information, unless perhaps they'd been involved in the other baby death—if one had even occurred. In which case, why not just tell the police? There were anonymous hotlines.

Sophie. I thought I'd picked up from her a need to be in control—keeping her from trying to run the group might be as much a challenge as stopping Teagan disrupting it—in which case she'd have told the police if she knew something. I couldn't see Sophie making it up.

One of the women could have *thought* it was true: Zahra because she was still psychotic and delusional? Or Róisín, who had the look of a woman beaten down by life. Was her depression serious enough to lead to delusional thinking? I didn't know much about either of them yet, except that the letter from the Sydney mother–baby unit in Zahra's file left no room for doubt as to how unwell she had been.

Teagan; delivering a bomb so she could enjoy the fallout? She had done this several times through the course of the group. Behaviour that, along with Yvonne's reference to 'issues' could be consistent with borderline personality traits, or even disorder. Unstable emotions that ricocheted around her life and inside her relationships. Was there intergenerational trauma in her family?

I shivered, acutely aware of the stillness and absence of traffic noise, and admitted to myself that Teagan's owl T-shirt had creeped me out a little after the incident on the bridge last week. A few days' isolation and my anxiety could take hold if I didn't keep the reins on it.

Still, there had been an undercurrent in the group, a wariness I had sensed that could have been more than just uncertainty about attending, or sharing secrets with a cop.

I saw Dean's car blowing up dust in the distance as he returned from work. I wouldn't be able to discuss it with him. As the therapist, I was bound tighter by the privacy rules than any of the group participants. But he was dealing with the hospital—he'd know important history.

'In your hospital brief was there anything about unexplained baby deaths?' I asked as we ate dinner.

Dean's cheek muscle flickered. His hand paused in the air before transferring a forkful of curry to his mouth. 'Why?'

It was an obvious enough response. But I knew my husband. He was holding something back—and he was worried my anxiety was returning.

'Just a throwaway line I overheard.' I was pretty sure I sounded calm.

Dean took time to finish his mouthful. 'No recent baby deaths I know of.'

I didn't think he was lying, but nor was I convinced he was telling the truth. I lay awake for a long time, listening to silence broken occasionally by the bleating of distant sheep. Wondering what the note meant—and what my husband was hiding.

The town of Riley amounted to two tree-lined streets, set back from the road to Sydney. Dubbo was the nearest big town, nearly two hours south-east. The highway continued west to Cobar and Broken Hill, mining towns that, along with the local copper mine, kept the train running. It had long since stopped taking passengers and the newly painted red railway station on the main Riley street now housed a museum and small café. The only new building, a medical clinic, stood beside the postage-stamp-sized park; beyond it was the hospital, then the river.

Opposite the railway line there was a line of shops, most of which had closed down. Only a newsagent, takeaway and supermarket still operated. A faded flower and plant shop, an auto-repair shop and a movie theatre that looked like it hadn't been patronised since the 1950s sat on the small cross streets that led to the second Riley boulevard. This street, neater than the shopping strip, was where the child health centre sat tucked among the solid white-and-blue painted library, the council offices (flying both the Australian and Aboriginal flags), a post office and the police and fire stations.

The Riley Arms was on the corner of the main shopping

street. It had wide return verandas on two storeys and a blackboard out front with the day's specials. In our second week, Gordon Barclay, the MP, was hosting a welcome there for Dean.

'This is a company town—the hospital is at the core. It's a chance for locals to hear what I'm doing,' Dean had said, 'and for Gordon to show he cares. You don't have to come.'

I did, though. I was spending more than enough time alone with Noah, miles from anywhere.

The main street was deserted save for one corner, where a group of Indigenous men and women were engaged in a lively conversation as a bunch of children ran around their legs. Behind was a building I had previously dismissed as closed down. Now that I looked more closely, I saw a neat sign over the door: Local Aboriginal Land Council. The windows were covered with more colourful, less formal messages; *Wongaibon Nation at Work* with food-group posters and faded photos of people swimming in the river and gardening.

A gawky teenager was sitting on a post by the door while two young children tried to drag him in their direction; as Dean and I walked past, I saw Teagan bump the teenager off and beat the giggling younger children to claim sitting rights. A woman in a bright red dress and matching glasses— Teagan's mother?—seemed to be telling them off. They didn't look like they were planning on welcoming Dean.

The Arms was an old-style pub with an uneven bare floor, sticky in spots, a long wooden bar-top, and shelves lined with glasses and a sparse selection of liquor.

Dean ordered a neat scotch and was told they didn't do shots: 'Community decision.' Dean let them add soda.

I guessed that a Cosmopolitan would be asking too

much. Even if cocktails weren't on the restricted list, it didn't look like the pub ran to cranberry juice. 'Dry white wine? Thanks.'

A footy tipping board was in prime position—rugby, not AFL. There were a few framed black and white photos of racehorses—apparently once a year there was an event in Riley—and a couple showing ancient cricket matches. In a series on another wall, floodwaters lapped at the door of the sandbagged hotel, a rowboat navigated between roof tops and an army helicopter was winching people to safety: *Floods of 1990*. The river was at least five hundred metres away, and currently the muddy brown stream was four metres below the bridge. It was hard to imagine.

Kate the cop was behind the bar with her husband, a stocky man with stubbled jowls. Just then he was laughing with affection at something she'd said, although Kate seemed oblivious. Their eighteen-month-old daughter, Ruby, was wearing a tutu and laying down the law in an oversize child pen. I dumped Noah in with the other kids, then turned back to scan the room.

About fifty people were there, packed in. Almost a big enough crowd to lose myself in—and I wanted to keep the boundaries up. Dean didn't understand my concerns about socialising with clients: 'I'd socialise with my plumber, and he's seen a lot more of my dirt than any psychologist.' The blokey streak ran in his family—his father was a football icon from the seventies and his brother Kieran had played briefly for St Kilda.

Gordon Barclay hadn't arrived, but Dean pointed out his wife Grace and sons Lachlan and Matthew, standing with Sophie from my group, and steered us towards them. I nodded, keeping my expression neutral, but Grace Barclay greeted me with a warm smile. A slender woman in her late fifties, dark hair and eyes, olive skin and high cheekbones. Maybe Italian background, I thought. In her pearls and heels, she seemed like a model—a stereotype—of the establishment politician's wife.

'I'm so pleased you could make it,' she said with the surprising hint of an American accent. 'We didn't know if you would be able to come, given the young one.' Grace smiled over at Noah. I wasn't sure if she was referring to tonight, or to coming to Riley in the first place. Her arm gently touched mine. 'It's lovely to have you here—don't hesitate to ask if there's anything I can do to make things easier.'

Easier? Her tone, reassuring, just made me wonder if there was something that should worry me.

'I was about your age when I came here from the States,' she continued. 'I found the loneliness the biggest problem. We'll have you over soon, hmm?'

'It'd be lovely to have you visit.' Sophie had joined us. I thought of the Sophie-types I'd known at school; all that poise, confidence and certainty—and a need to express it that always made me uneasy. Under that she was anxious, or so my psychologist-self told me. In equivalent circumstances, I retreated inward.

Grace was called away; one of her sons appeared to want to leave, or maybe just not hang out with his family. After a short exchange that looked more like a conversation you'd have with an adolescent than a man in his twenties, he went to the bar and ordered a beer.

'That's Matt, my brother-in-law,' Sophie told me in a tone that said she'd noticed the body language too.

After Dean settled me at a table and headed off to network, several people took the opportunity to introduce themselves. They all knew who I was. Information got out quickly in small towns, which made me think again about that unsettling note. If I had read it out loud everyone in town would have known about it by now.

A woman was in the process of telling me in forensic detail about her anxiety disorder and how 'bars therapy' had helped her, when I was rescued by a thirty-something man with sandy hair. He looked a little like a friend of my brother's who, when I was little, would be left to dink me on his bike or hand over lollies to shut me up, and who never seemed to mind. Medium height—a few centimetres taller than me—open-necked white shirt, neater than most of the other diners. He smiled at the woman and asked if he could have a word with me. 'I'm Chris McCormack, the GP here. I'm Brian's brother.'

'The publican?'

Chris nodded: he was Kate the cop's brother-in-law.

'Do you need to have a word with me about anything in particular?' I said.

He smiled—grey-blue eyes with a streak of humour. 'I do.' He dropped his voice. 'To survive in small towns, *never* talk shop after hours, and especially avoid Mrs Jackson's generalised anxiety disorder.'

I smiled back. A fellow professional. And without the superior air some medical doctors affected.

'Have you worked here long?'

'Since I graduated—far too long, probably.'

'You come from round here?'

'Dubbo. I got into med school on a rural fellowship,' he said. 'Can't blame that, though—I've done my time now.' A grin. 'I like the country.'

'So, what's the secret of loving Riley?'

'Get involved when you can.' He shrugged. 'And be prepared for the times'—he glanced towards the Barclays—'you find you're still on the outer.'

Just like high school, then.

'Are you the GP that referred the women to my group?' Sharing of 'relevant background' was certainly permitted within professional protocols, and if the first group was anything to go by, I was going to need all the help I could get.

Chris nodded. 'You'll find a few of them or their families here tonight. My sister-in-law for one.' He grinned. 'Getting her to attend anything about feelings was no easy task, I can assure you.' I thought of Kate the cop and her crossed arms. He was probably right that she needed the group but I wasn't sure I would thank him for it. I wondered what leverage he'd used.

Chris went on: 'That's Teagan's dad, Joe Moretti, over there.' He nodded to a thick-set balding man sitting alone, nursing a beer. He had a distinctive nose, more retired boxer than Pinocchio. No sign of Teagan's mother—the woman I'd seen in the red dress and glasses?—or of any other company. Joe caught my eye and stared back without smiling. 'I'll help you keep an eye on her.'

'She's a handful,' I agreed.

'Well, not surprising, really. Difficult family history.'

I wasn't given a chance to ask anything more. But I made a mental note to look in her file before the next group.

Lachlan Barclay, Sophie's husband, was on his feet calling for our attention. He was clean-shaven, mid to late twenties, with his mother's glossy dark hair and olive complexion. He looked like a model in an ad for multi-vitamins. Sophie, standing beside him, looked as if she'd been grown in the same pod. The brother, Matthew, was standing at the bar with a beer and still scowling. He was the farmer and Lachlan the future politician, I figured.

'My father has asked me to start the meeting,' Lachlan said. He thanked the publican for hosting, talked about how important it was to hear the locals' views, and thanked them, too, for coming. As he was introducing Dean, an older man came through the doors. Beefy and balding, sunspots dotted over the crown of his head, he stood in the doorway beaming. Lachlan stopped and everyone turned to look. Gordon Barclay's photo seemed to be several years out of date; he was older than his wife by ten years at least. He shook hands with several men near the entrance. I couldn't hear what he was saying, but there was a laugh and he slapped a younger man on the back before shaking hands with Dean—one of those grips that goes on too long, with his left hand tight on my husband's arm, eyes firmly focused.

'Don't let me hold you all up, folks,' he said into the microphone that both Lachlan and Dean had stepped back from. 'I see my son's doing a great job—the same great job he'll soon be doing as your new National Party member.' He gripped Lachlan's shoulder, then turned to Dean. 'But of course we're all wanting to hear what Mr Harris here is going to tell us, about making sure our hospital stays right where it is. Dean?'

Dean looked more at ease than Lachlan. It didn't surprise me; I'd seen him keep his cool in more charged situations than this—once in front of a bereaved family aiming to torch the hospital he was representing. Like a lot of big men, he knew how to use his physical presence to his advantage. But he also had the surprising capacity to come across as slightly dorky and rather earnest, a look that disarmed people, me included. That versatility had served him well in his last posting, in Auckland, which involved a sexual harassment scandal and a more complex set of racial tensions. It had still taken him eighteen months to sort out, though. I hoped the problem in Riley was going to be a quicker fix.

'Thanks. Lachlan. Gordon.' He nodded to the Barclays. 'And to you all who have been so welcoming to us.' He looked to me and everyone else did likewise. Noah took the opportunity to call out '*No!*' to Kate's daughter as she grabbed a toy. There was a ripple of laughter.

'Things may seem a bit different after having one man running the hospital for twenty years,' continued Dean, 'but now that he's moved on'—*been* moved on was what Dean had told me—'I'm just overseeing the process to get his successor in place, making sure you get the best possible person to look after the hospital, hopefully for another twenty years or more.'

Someone put up a hand. 'There's no truth to the rumour you're closing the place down?'

'Absolutely not,' Dean replied. His smile was all schoolboy. I felt some pride as I watched his magic win over the crowd, while conceding that the locals might have cause to be concerned.

'The hospital is here to stay, Michael,' said Gordon. 'I know how important it is to you all, and I say: long may you continue to have your babies there and be cared for in your old age.'

Dean spoke further about the role of the hospital in the town and gave an overview of what he'd be doing: more than just selecting a new manager. He'd be 'making sure it was running efficiently, not only to provide the best possible service but to keep it off the radar of the bean counters who were targeting the underperforming rural hospitals'. Lachlan—encouraged, I thought, by a nudge from his father—told the group that Dean would be happy to answer questions.

'What about employment at the hospital?' In the crowd I could just make out a man in his early sixties, good looking in an older-guy sort of way. 'You're big on this "fair and equitable process" but what does that actually mean, hey?'

There was a murmur, and someone close to him said in a loud whisper, 'Not now, Conor.'

Conor ignored them and took a step closer to Dean. Dean was the same height and probably thirty years younger, but Conor had tattooed arms like rocks under the T-shirt. 'You say the hospital is the heart of the town? Didn't see a lot of heart for Eric Anderson.' The recently departed CEO.

'I'm sorry, I didn't catch your name, sir?' said Dean. 'If you have a grievance about Eric's departure, I'd be happy to talk after the meeting.'

'I have a grievance against you being here. And we never had any need for a therapist here either, until your wife wanted a job.'

Chris McCormack put his hand on my shoulder and whispered, 'It's not personal; the hospital's a sore point for him. He works there, and so do his son and daughter.'

It really was a company town. And I was married to the person who might be responsible for the company—the hospital—closing. Never mind Dean's denials.

Lachlan Barclay cleared his throat. 'Mr Rearden, Conor, we'd like to keep things positive. No one's planning on closing the hospital.'

Rearden. Róisín, the older woman in my group, was a Rearden; was Conor her father? The same black hair—

Róisín had just let the grey in. I had read she worked in hospital administration.

'And how can you be so sure of that?' One of Conor's mates this time.

Lachlan looked around, as though he'd forgotten his lines.

'Reckon the other candidate might want to have a say too.' The interjection came from the publican, Kate's husband Brian. I looked at him more closely: dark tufted eyebrows over intense eyes; a laconic smile. Older than his doctor brother, and not much alike in looks.

There was another awkward silence. Gordon was not happy.

Lachlan managed a smile. 'Of course. Chris, perhaps you'd like to say a few words?'

He was looking towards me—or rather, towards the local GP, who was still beside me—and pointing to the microphone.

Chris smiled easily. 'No, no, that's fine Lachlan, Gordon.' He nodded to them. 'As my brother says, I've lived here eight years, grew up nearby, been involved with the party, and I'm currently the branch president. I've always said I'd stand for preselection when Gordon chose to step down.'

Did this mean everyone voted National here? Probably best if I kept my Greens-voting inclinations under wraps.

I couldn't read Grace's expression. Lachlan looked awkward. Sophie looked like she'd swallowed a prune. Matt, Lachlan's brother, was smirking.

'You all know me and my story,' Chris continued. 'Probably birthed a few of your kids and jabbed the rest of you. After I lost my wife you helped me get through a bad patch. You know I'm a strong supporter of keeping the

23

hospital up to date. I would be pleased to represent your views, and I'm always open to having my own changed.'

There was a ripple of laughter, and Chris smiled. I was left wondering about his wife's death. He couldn't be any older than thirty-five.

Lachlan took over again and asked for other questions. This got the locals onto road upgrades, the internet and what was being done about managing floods; the last had been two years earlier, though nothing like the 'horror of 1990', which was apparently still fresh in everyone's minds.

'My brother died,' one woman said. 'I know they say he shouldn't have driven into floodwaters, but there needs to be more depth gauges on the back roads.'

It seemed a ludicrous idea with blue sky and sunshine every day so far, and the land dusty and parched. Gordon finally intervened and wound the evening up. The crowd clapped politely and moved either to the bar or the door. I was feeling like making for the latter; quite aside from the mixed welcome, Noah was cranky. I could wait for Dean in the car. Just then he spotted me and came over.

'I see you've met our local doctor.' Dean nodded at Chris. I felt a flicker of tension; Dean was always territorial around me, but I sensed there was something else. Dean had told me the longstanding GP—presumably Chris—was the linchpin of the hospital's viability. I wondered how much Chris knew about the problems, whatever they were, that Dean was here to sort out.

'I was about to suggest Isabel drop in and see me one lunchtime.' Looking at me, Chris added: 'I understand you're willing to take on more work? I have a few thoughts.'

'Okay,' I said. 'But I'm not going to be here long enough to do anything that requires follow-up.'

Dean smiled his scout grin as he dragged me off to say goodbye to the Barclays, then we walked to the car with Noah wriggling and grumpy because it was so long past his bedtime.

'That,' I said as soon as we were in the car, 'was a little rough. Conor Rearden—what's his problem?'

'What a loser,' said Dean. 'No one gets to have a job for life.' He paused. 'Conor's a union man. My guess is he's got some nice deals going down at the hospital. Small town, people do each other favours, especially if someone else is paying.'

'The Barclays seem to think that can continue.'

'They might think that. You saw: young Lachlan has opposition,' said Dean.

'You mean Chris? At least he was friendly—the rest don't want me here.'

'Welcome to my world.'

'Still think you'll be done by Christmas?'

'Jesus, not this again.' Dean banged his hand on the steering wheel. 'I'll be done when I'm done, all right?' Noah started to cry. I distracted him with his comfort toy and stared ahead all the way home.

Dean gave Noah his bath. While I put him to bed, Dean sat outside and poured himself another beer.

Coming out onto the veranda I thought I heard something. 'Did that sound like a dog to you?'

'There's no neighbours. What would a dog be doing out here?'

'It could be dingoes, or domestic dogs gone feral.'

'Iz. Really?'

'Dean,' I said, and stopped. I didn't know where to start.

'We're staying until I get this done,' he said, mouth in a grim line.

I hadn't been going to ask about returning to Melbourne; but then Dean's anger wasn't really about my reluctance to come to Riley. He still hadn't forgiven me, and he wouldn't talk about it.

We were both sick of me saying sorry; he knew damn well how guilty I felt every time I looked at Noah. He could see for himself that I could hardly bear it when Noah was out of my sight.

What would I tell a client? Not to repeat the same patterns. I'd challenge her, too, if she persisted in telling herself it didn't happen often, or that it just needed time.

I said I was tired. By the time he came to bed I was asleep.

A couple of days later, as promised, Grace Barclay sent us a dinner invitation. Dean raised his eyebrows when I showed him the elegant card, the kind of thing you'd send for a wedding.

'Supping with the devil. Should be entertaining.'

We'd just finished dinner on the veranda and I was washing up as Dean dried. I still hadn't got used to living without a dishwasher, let alone being so stingy with the rinsing water.

'But Gordon was behind you coming here, right?'

'He'll wait till he sees how it goes before he claims responsibility, but yeah. Nothing happens in this town without Gordon approving it.'

'Wasn't the old manager the problem?'

'Still is. His legacy, anyway. Eric ran the hospital via handwritten notes—no system, no routine copies, no proper money trail. How he ever survived an audit...probably because no one was too fussed about a tiny country hospital and...pretty obviously there's been a political dimension.'

'So Gordon...?'

'Supported Eric. As did Athol Broadbent; retired doctor,

still on the board along with the new doctor. Happy little club, well past its use-by date. No one wants to upset the Barclays.'

'So, why did you get called in now?' I was not generally interested in the details of Dean's work—but that was because I usually didn't know the players.

'The Opposition's been calling out inefficiencies in the health system.'

'And Riley was one of them?'

Dean nodded. 'Big time.' He put the dishtowel down and yawned. 'Also: bed time. Remember you'll need to organise a sitter for Noah. For this Barclay dinner?'

I hadn't been separated from Noah since the accident. I could see the appeal of a social occasion that didn't revolve around sleep routines and cracked nipples, but it was not as strong as my fear that something might happen to him.

I thought about the argument we would have if I said I couldn't go, or if I rang Grace to ask if we could bring Noah. Dean was right. I needed to get a grip. I'd ring Yvonne, the health centre nurse; I thought she'd be happy to get some extra dollars, and in country terms she didn't live that far from us.

With no internet and no mail delivery this far from town, I established my own routine: two or three times a week, I picked up the mail from the post office then hit the café at the railway station for free wi-fi. On the first visit I opened a hand-delivered envelope with 'The Harris family' typed on it, to find a package of dog poo. It took me half an hour to calm down.

When I thought about it, it was pretty obviously a juvenile response to the pub meeting or, more broadly, the perceived threat that Dean posed to the town. *Nothing to do with me.*

How, though? The private mailboxes were not in sight of the desk and there was easy street access, but they needed a key. You couldn't just stuff something through a slot. I asked the postmaster who might have had access, but he looked bewildered and tried to convince me *I'd* put it in there. I was in danger of being accused of bullying if his expression was anything to go by. I gave up.

There was a shaded, fenced-in area on the station platform that worked as a safety pen for Noah while I had coffee and facetimed my family. Specifically my mother, with whom my fraught relationship was now in an uneasy new phase: distant girl–angry, unwell mother. The postpartum psychosis she'd suffered for many years after I was born was something I was convinced for a long time that I had caused. I understood her better now, I thought; I accepted that she hadn't been rational when she tried to hold a pillow over my face. But fraught was how things remained.

My calls to friends were briefer. Angelica, my best friend since the age of six, had different problems from mine. Seemingly the biggest was that her favourite coffee shop had changed hands. She was between relationships and, like most of my friends, hadn't had children yet; since my time away in Auckland, I had felt myself drifting away from them all. In Auckland I had been part of a mothers' group—here I'd be running the group, and the mothers were my clients. It was like I was watching the town from somewhere on its outskirts.

On my second visit to the Railway Café Noah decided he wanted to check out some mining relics in the tiny museum attached to the coffee shop. I judged them robust enough to withstand a two-year-old's attentions and wandered over to the history section where there were some moth-eaten albums of old newspaper clippings. I browsed through the section on the floods: some of the same photos I'd seen in the pub.

The year after the floods, the most exciting thing that happened was Joe Moretti winning the shire pumpkin-growing competition. But what I found in the subsequent year books—from twenty-five years earlier—was considerably more gripping. I stared at the headlines.

'BABY-NAPPING HORROR' and 'BABY-NAPPED PARENTS DEMAND ANSWERS' appeared in December and 'MORETTI BABY STILL MISSING' in January the following year.

The third article summarised what had happened: Donna Moretti had given birth to Joshua the previous day. When her husband Joe came to take her and the baby home, a nurse found he was missing from the nursery. A police search failed to find the baby or any clue as to who'd taken him. There was a photo of a distraught Donna: a gangly woman, all elbows and hands, and a mess of dark hair around a face with sharp features and big eyes, very like Teagan's. Joe was stony-faced and distinctly younger—I could just recognise the man I had seen at the town meeting from the nose, which must have been broken and badly repaired before he became a father.

A fourth article dated a month later was headed 'MISSING BABY: REMAINS FOUND'. After an anonymous tip, the remains of an infant presumed to be Joshua Moretti had been found on the banks of the river.

My doctoral thesis was on infanticide; I knew the most likely scenario here. Had anyone—Teagan's mother?—ever been charged? I had studied dozens of infanticide cases and all the neonaticides—death in the first twenty-four hours—had been committed by the mother. None of the murders had involved anyone I knew. Of course, this murder might have been committed by someone other than the mother, in which case it wasn't infanticide.

I thought about the tension in my group; Chris's throwaway line about the Morettis' family history; my sense that Dean was keeping something from me. And about the baby-killer note. Was Joshua's death the one it was referring to? Hard to make sense of it if Teagan's mother had been responsible—unless Teagan was worried about how she would react to her grandchild.

For the first time in a long while, I felt suffused—and invigorated—with purpose. These women, Sophie aside, had grown up in a small town that would have been shaken and shaped by this tragedy. Becoming a mother was hard enough. A background illustrating the dark side of motherhood and the intense vulnerability of infants would weave tentacles around every decision they made. No one knew that better than I did.

Better late than never: before the group met again I set up one-on-one interviews with the participants. Kate was up first. After dropping off Dean I had time for a quick coffee, and went into the little shop in the hospital that sold snacks, flowers, gift ideas and emergency personal items for patients. Beside the charity box (donations for flood gauges) was a community computer that looked about ten years old.

The coffee, instant, was worse than the stuff in the child health centre. The white-haired woman who served me was about five foot nothing and must have been eighty-five.

Jeannie, said her name badge, and *Not Tech Savvy*.

'You're from Melbourne, aren't you?' said Jeannie. 'You won't like the coffee. City people don't generally, Melbourne folk especially.'

'Oh no, it's good.' I took a gulp; it was worth it for Jeannie's smile.

'You've worked here a long time?' I asked.

'Oh yes, dear. Been volunteering ever since Charlie passed. My husband, twenty-seven years. We first came here in '56; Charlie was with the railway. Was only meant to be for three years.'

'So you were here when the baby was taken,' I said, as much to myself as her.

'You've heard about that? Yes, I was. Right here at the hospital.' Jeannie shook her head. 'Donna...well, I've never seen a woman so distressed. And Joe too, though with men it's different, isn't it? They go all hard and angry and try to *do* things. And sometimes there just isn't anything *to* do.'

'It must have been hard for you all,' I said.

'We were devastated. The police interviewed everyone here.' Jeannie sighed. 'Not that it helped. Least of all Donna and Joe.'

Jeannie stopped to attend to another customer—Róisín, the oldest client in the group; the one Yvonne had flagged as being anxious. Was she Conor Rearden's daughter? I thought I saw a resemblance in the long fine nose and regular features.

'Hello, Isabel.'

'Hi...Ah, I'll see you later in group, right?' Had she noticed the way I'd avoided saying her name?

I had the sense of a brief internal conversation as she fumbled in her bag to pay for a bottle of water then scuttled away. As if she wanted to say, 'Please be my friend' and some inner voice replied, 'You can't trust her.' I thought she'd be a challenge to help; she didn't seem to let the drawbridge down for long.

Jeannie said, 'You're the psychologist aren't you?' She didn't wait for an answer. 'You'll have your work cut out for you with young Teagan. Can't have been easy for her growing up with all that in the background, and of course—'

'I read the articles,' I said. 'It didn't sound like anyone ever found out what happened.'

'No, well the papers couldn't say it, could they, dear?' said Jeannie. 'Local boy reported on it—works for the council now. We were all upset enough, without airing dirty linen.'

'Who did the police think was responsible?'

'Oh, it was Donna, we all knew that. I imagine the argument with Joe upset her; perhaps she dropped the poor little mite.'

'Oh?'

'He'd been drinking. Domestic violence they call it these days, but back then it was just men drinking and behaving badly. His father was the same.'

Causes of infanticide fell into several categories, including a subgroup associated with a violent partner. But Donna could have had postpartum psychosis like Zahra, the Persian doctor in my group. It was rare—one in six hundred births—but a mother's separation from reality put her and her baby at risk.

'No winners really, were there?' said Jeannie, as I rescued one of the pink furry *It's a girl* toys she was selling. Noah had been about to share his chocolate drink with it.

•

Kate arrived a few minutes after I got to the health centre, wearing baggy denim shorts and a sleeveless T-shirt that emphasised her arm muscles. Ruby was dressed in pink with a bow in her hair. I was amazed she allowed it to remain there. She smiled when she saw Noah and promptly swiped his toy. Noah for once didn't seem fussed.

'This shouldn't take long. I just wanted to get a bit of background,' I said, as we got ourselves tea. Neither of us was up for the instant coffee.

'On?' Kate sat down, not looking at me.

'You and Ruby,' I said. I wanted to add, '...and anything you can tell me about the Moretti case or any other baby killer you know about', but I wasn't going to be able to go there.

'Ruby's doing fine.'

'She certainly looks like she's growing well,' I said. 'I love the outfit.'

Kate's eyes narrowed. 'My mother-in-law makes all her clothes.'

'Tell me about Ruby, and the pregnancy.'

Kate hesitated, then seemed to decide to not mess around. 'It was fine. She wasn't planned. Brian or his mother take her when I'm at work.'

'And your parents?'

'My father dropped dead when I was a teenager. Mum's still going but...there's a few kangaroos loose in the top paddock.' She tapped her head; I turned a snort of laughter into a cough. 'I was an accident. They were both into their forties when they had me; I reckon they didn't actually know how babies were made.'

I took her through a checklist of depressive symptoms. She had the lot, though she downplayed the suicidality. 'I just wish sometimes I wouldn't wake up in the morning, okay? But I wouldn't do anything, wouldn't do it to Brian or Ruby.'

Next were questions about parenting—her own experience and her thoughts on how she was doing now. 'Ruby doesn't really need me, anyone can do it,' she said at one point, which was probably the most telling statement— both of her own lack of confidence as a mother, and her need to distance the child. I hoped it was only her avoidant attachment style—the non-nurturing, promoting-play-over-comfort style of mothering. Otherwise it might indicate she was planning on not being around.

'Anything you enjoy?'

'Work.'

'Did you always want to be in the police force?' Perhaps it offered a sense of belonging and maybe order that was missing in her family.

'Umm...' Kate looked surprised at the question. Like she hadn't given it much thought. 'Well, since the Moretti baby was killed, I guess. That was pretty much the biggest thing that's ever happened to Riley. Other than the flood; they both put us on every news channel in Australia. I was too young to remember the floods, but I was five when Joshua went missing. The cops came to our school and it was more exciting than anything that had ever happened in my life. Except maybe when Matt Barclay called me a dyke and I punched him.'

Kate's eyes had more spark than I'd seen before. She hadn't really answered my question, but she'd given me a lead-in to talk about the kidnapping.

'Do you think the town's history is impacting you, now that you're a mother?'

'Because Teagan's having a baby? Teagan's always been stirring things up, the little moll...I mean, you can hardly blame her; she's had to fend for herself forever.'

I didn't want to gossip about Teagan. 'Do you want to tell me which note was yours?'

'Nope. You said it was anonymous.'

If she hadn't written the baby-killer note—I doubted she'd risk her job to no benefit—I figured she was the *crap mother* or maybe the *motherhood is hard*.

Kate looked at me pointedly. She *did* know something, but I didn't think she was acting like the author of the note would. More like she wanted to run me down to the station for questioning.

'What did that note say? The one you didn't read out?'

It hadn't occurred to me anyone would ask. 'Why?'

'It spooked you,' said Kate. 'So, I got to thinking what would have done that. If someone had said they were planning on topping themselves, I don't reckon you would have let us go without quizzing us all first.'

I nodded slowly.

'So I figured maybe it was too personal.'

'Which, if that was the case,' I said slowly, 'I'd hardly be likely to tell you now, would I?'

'But,' Kate continued, 'you said the note was about anxiety. What wouldn't you want to tell us? Something sensational? Unsubstantiated?'

'I really can't say one way or another, because...'

'Didn't expect you would,' said Kate. 'But there's something I can tell you—and this didn't come from me, right? Confidentiality?'

I nodded.

'Let's say that maybe…just maybe…the police received an anonymous tip. About babies being in danger.'

I realised I was holding my breath.

'It would hardly be something anyone would take seriously, right?'

'Well, maybe not,' I agreed, feeling my tension level drop.

'Unless,' Kate continued, 'they said something that was credible. Like some fact about the original kidnapping and murder of the Moretti baby, something the general public didn't know.'

Kate fixed her eyes on mine. I felt unable to look anywhere else. 'Think very carefully about what you were told. If it was a threat, you need to report it. We're taking this seriously. Knowing you kept a confidence isn't going to comfort you much if a baby dies—and you could have prevented it.'

Kate and I were still staring at each other when Sophie arrived, dressed in royal blue and bearing muffins. Her son Tom had most of one spread across his face.

'Did I interrupt? They're still warm.' Sophie put down the plate. 'I've made little ones for the children.'

Noah had already seen them; Yvonne, hot on Sophie's heels, took charge of the small plate and promised to minimise the mess.

'It was so nice meeting Dean,' said Sophie. She went on to list his praiseworthy qualities until Róisín arrived, at which point she casually threw me a lifeline: 'Hi, Ro-sheen.'

Róisín smiled vaguely and spent ten minutes separating herself from a very clingy Bella, who was the same age as Noah. Teagan arrived late again, but we were still organising muffins and drinks. Zahra didn't arrive at all. Her husband had rung Yvonne to say that she wasn't well enough and asked me to drop by after the group. Yvonne said she'd mind Noah.

Sophie was getting a lot of 'you didn't make them, did you?' about the muffins, and promised us all the recipe. I had plenty of time for cooking. In the last week we'd had honeycomb cheesecake, pineapple soufflé and pavlova with tropical fruits. The fruit and veggie section of the supermarket wasn't a great source of exotic ingredients, but the canned-fruit aisle filled the gap.

I had thought a lot about this group—partly because I didn't have much else to think about. Noah was great, but not twenty-four seven; and the hours Dean was working, there was never much time for conversation. Priority one, of course, was to try to help these women. They had some common issues, some specific issues, and some issues I had no clue about yet. We would get into all that, but gently. I had run through my material several times and printed out handouts.

But the note continued to gnaw away at me and now, with the warning from Kate, I was even more determined to find out who had written it. If there was a real threat, the author needed to share what they knew with the police; and if not, there was something going on with the writer that needed to be addressed. I read the note again. I wasn't obliged legally or ethically to report anything this vague. The police letter apparently contained a lot more information. And I couldn't see how a police interrogation of the innocent women would help their mental health.

It was possible my note-writer was the same person who had written anonymously to the police. With the exception of Róisín, who would have been fifteen, no one in the group was old enough to have kidnapped the child themselves; and fifteen-year-olds didn't tend to make great crime queens. They were more likely to be protecting someone. Or scared of them.

Or, of course, they could be doing no more than relaying gossip that had leaked from the police or the informant.

Kate's husband the publican, for one, was surely privy to most of the town's gossip. That was what Dean would tell me, but I needed to be sure. And I needed to know if there was any danger to Noah.

I pulled out the pens and paper I'd bought in town. The newsagent was Róisín's partner, Al, and he'd seemed a little bewildered as to why I needed them. *Those kids are too young to draw*, he'd repeated three times.

The women's assignment was to sketch—stick figure was fine—the animal that best represented them as a mother. After that, they were to draw the animal that best represented their child (not necessarily, I said, a baby version of the mother animal) and finally their partner.

Teagan grabbed a pen and got down to it, Sophie and Róisín started drawing obediently, with studied care. Kate looked at me like I couldn't be serious.

'Farm animals, maybe?' I suggested to her. 'Jungle? Birds? Um…sea life?'

I didn't draw myself because I needed to keep a distance from the group; but if I had to, nothing felt quite right. A mother hen felt too old and fussy, a horse was unable to encompass their offspring in a way that would have to be inherent in any representation I did. Noah, with his cheeky joy and ceaseless activity, was a monkey for sure. For Dean… maybe a racehorse? I wasn't sure why that came to mind. A bear was more his physical shape.

I let Sophie present first. 'I'm a butterfly,' she said. 'Ever since becoming a mother I feel I have to flit here, there and everywhere.'

Wanting to flit away, more likely. Next to it was some sort of fluffy animal—a ferret?—and on the other side a puppy dog.

'What breed?' I asked. There was a big difference between a poodle and a rottweiler.

'Lachlan? Oh, he's a collie, I think. Lots of energy and ideas, loyal, and very responsible. And Tom's a baby fur seal: the cutest, cuddliest animal I could think of.'

'Not so easy to cuddle if you're a butterfly,' said Teagan. It was an astute observation, and the women laughed. Sophie looked stricken so I added, 'I wonder if it makes it tough for you sometimes, doing so much?'

Sophie paused. 'I…well…I suppose so.' I wasn't going to push it, but I thought Sophie was probably spending a lot of energy on being what others expected rather than on what she wanted. If she even knew.

'Your collie can herd up your baby seal for you,' said Teagan.

Sophie smiled tightly. 'Unless he's off in the water.'

I let this go. I didn't want to picture a baby seal swimming away in case it started to look like Noah.

'It kind of shows how difficult it can be bringing a new family together, doesn't it?' I said. 'A farm dog happy on land, a seal in water, an airborne insect. Yet I imagine you have quiet times when there is harmony together.'

This generated some discussion. Kate's expression showed she thought the idea that what we had drawn might in any way represent reality was completely barmy.

'Motherhood can be destabilising, can't it? Do any of you feel like that?' I said.

'You become something better, don't you? I think it gives me a sense of purpose in life,' said Róisín. She smiled, more naturally than earlier. With her dark eyelashes, clear complexion and long dark hair, now pulled roughly into a ponytail, she could be quite beautiful.

41

'When you're pregnant, people come up and touch you,' said Teagan. 'Like the baby's the only thing that matters.'

'Wait till after you've had it,' said Sophie. 'It's even worse: suddenly it's like you're not there at all. Another muffin anyone?'

'I'm a whale,' Teagan said, grinning. The picture was startlingly good; water from the animal's blowhole seemed to lift off the page. 'Guess pretty soon I'll feel like a cow. Baby? I reckon she's going to be a little pussycat; kind of looks like that on the scan.' There was no picture for the father of the child. But she drew what looked like a possum, wide-eyed and wise, in a tree over the whale and cat. 'That's Mum looking over us, you know?'

Like from Heaven? Or from somewhere interstate? I really did need to look at her file.

'If you have a boy you could call him Jonah,' said Kate.

Teagan's more concrete approach to the exercise opened up some talk about the physical changes of pregnancy, and how they had reacted to them. No big surprises.

Róisín went next, holding her drawing so we couldn't see. She furtively looked at the group as she spoke, as if trying to gauge their reactions. 'My partner is a lion. The male lion—sleeps a lot, lets me do all the worrying and growls occasionally.'

Everyone laughed. Presumably they all knew Al, the taciturn newsagent who'd sold me the pens and paper. Róisín's take suggested she didn't get him—or the needs of a toddler—any better than he got her.

'I'm a cat,' she continued.

I glanced at her drawing. Róisín's cat was asleep on a mat...with one eye open. A good choice; cats were self-contained. But she had drawn Bella as a fish in a bowl. 'I kind of just watch her, wondering,' said Róisín.

A cat with a fish. I moved on to Kate before Teagan could say anything.

The sketch was basic. The dog, she explained, was a St Bernard. Brian: loyal and trustworthy. There was something touching in her blunt description. 'Ruby's a monkey; friendly, smart, independent.' I thought of the wide-eyed child in her elaborate outfits and wasn't quite so sure. 'Me as a mother? A tortoise. I pull my head in when it gets too hard.' I had a mental picture of a documentary I'd seen—hundreds of tiny tortoises rushing across the sand and being picked off by seagulls. Kate's shell would be mostly about keeping an emotional distance.

'Slow and steady,' I said. 'Okay, seems like there are some really different types of mothers. We've got busy like Sophie, cautious—Kate—watchful, like Róisín, and all adapting to physical changes like Teagan is now. I'm wondering when we think of ourselves like this, are we missing anything? Is there any other animal, as a mother, you would like to be, even in part?'

'Lioness,' said Teagan immediately. 'Protective.'

'At least the females stay awake more,' said Róisín under her breath; the others smiled. She seemed a little startled that they had even heard her.

'In *The Lion King* they were rather noble, don't you think?' said Sophie.

'Disney?' Kate mumbled. 'For God's sake.'

'What does it mean to protect your child?' I asked. 'All of you.'

'Well, Tom's starting to crawl, and he loves buttons,' said Sophie. 'I'll need to keep him away from little things— and, umm, watch out for forks in the electric socket.'

Impression: Sophie doesn't think too deeply if she can help it. No obvious paranoia—or kidnapper fears. She could have written the note, but I couldn't see her writing a letter to the police. She'd get her family to talk to the hierarchy. Or bring in private security.

'Keeping them from experiences they're not equipped to handle,' said Kate. 'But Jesus, it doesn't mean keeping them in cotton wool.'

Impression: Kate knows there's a threat out there—she's aware of the warning letter to police—and she thinks the risk is pretty small. Tutu or not, she's a 'let the kid learn from her mistakes' type of parent.

Róisín took a long time to think about the question. 'For me, Isabel, I want to protect Bella from everything. I worry about…I mean, it's not like we can trust…Even here in Riley not everyone's the same as us—' Her eyes went to the empty seat and I was glad Zahra wasn't there. Before I could work out how to assure Róisín that different didn't mean dangerous she had pressed on. 'The thought of anyone harming her, picking on her at school, of her getting sick… it makes me feel ill. It's surely the one most important thing mothers have to do. Al isn't sure it's a good idea, but I want to homeschool her. The world is just…It's not a nice place.'

Impression: I felt better about the fishbowl. Róisín wants Bella in there to keep her safe. If she believed there was a genuine risk, then anxiety would drive her to do something. She was the best candidate to be the note-writer, though I felt she was too preoccupied with her own anxiety to be issuing warnings to anyone else. I'd also checked her handwriting in her file—long loopy letters. A good match for the note that had said *All that matters is my child, but how do I know what's best for them?*

Which left Teagan. Kate was watching her closely. Was it because she thought Teagan had written the note in the group—and perhaps also to the police?

'Drugs,' said Teagan. 'I sure as hell don't want my kid to go through what I have.'

Impression: Kate is disappointed. I'm not so sure. Teagan's protective hormones aren't in play yet.

She'd homed in on an obvious issue that parents worry about—just not parents of little children. But Teagan wasn't a parent yet. She probably had lots of fears that she pushed away. It was easier to do that when the baby wasn't there in front of you. She could have written the note in the group to get attention, but that wasn't plausible as a motive for writing to the police.

Which left the missing mother—Zahra. Missing because she was unwell, the same reason she could have written the note in the group, and also written to the police. If so, were her fears delusional...or based on something? Like something one of her patients had told her. Something real.

After the group, another interview: Sophie. I watched her with her son, Tom. He was a cute kid, but serious. Sophie was trying to get him to build a tower; he was keen to play, but couldn't quite get the idea. He was after her approval and knew he'd have to succeed at the task to get it. Finally, he put one block where it was meant to go—and beamed when she piled praise on him.

'I've only lived here two years,' said Sophie. 'Lachie and I met at uni in Sydney; he was in first year ag sci. I was the older woman.'

She laughed self-consciously. She was twenty-seven now; like me, they'd married relatively young.

'We were both in Amnesty,' Sophie continued. 'A group of us came to Riley for Easter. Never imagined I'd end up here!' She laughed again; it sounded ambivalent. 'He proposed after his final exams and next thing I know, here I am.' Big smile. Tom looked up, frowning.

'I'm a city girl too. It's different.'

Sophie paused and for a moment I thought I might get something more authentic, but off she went again, ponytail swinging. 'Grace has just been the most brilliant mother-in-law I could ever hope to have. Her family were lawyers…'

I learned about Grace being on the hospital board, about her charity work and the resulting Order of Australia. Sophie was part cheerleader for her mother-in-law, but I sensed also part competitor for Lachlan's loyalty. In between the fabulous work Grace did through the hospital shop and end of year fete, and a bemused riff on how much Lachlan loved the country, she'd remarked in passing that it wasn't easy living with your in-laws.

'Did you work before you had Tom?'

'No, I finished Law but never did articles. I've thought of doing a course instead so I could practice. We can afford it, but…' She shrugged.

'Lachlan's going into politics.'

'Yes.' Toothy smile. 'I guess we'll spend some time in Sydney then. I mean, we have to live here to represent the constituency, but it doesn't mean we have to be here *all* the time.'

Sophie's parents and her brother were lawyers. They hadn't pushed her in that direction, but she hadn't thought too hard about alternatives.

We returned to the routine part of the interview: the symptom checklist, parenting. I sensed that her answers, while not lies, weren't always the whole truth. The ponytail swung back and forth with each response. Tom watched her warily.

'Oh yes, I worry. Don't all mothers?' And 'No, it's not like I'm depressed or anything.'

'So…what do you hope to get out of the group?' I didn't believe her denials but I didn't want to press her on them: I needed her to connect to her motivation.

For a moment she looked startled. 'Oh…well, being a

first-time mother is like having L-plates isn't it? Only there's no instructor in the car with you.'

I thought Sophie found vulnerability hard at the best of times. She wouldn't have wanted to be vulnerable in front of Grace, who she needed to impress.

I asked her which note she had written. She frowned for a moment, then laughed. 'I'm trying to remember. I didn't really have a secret…I think I said something about children deserving the best.'

That was the one I had guessed was hers. Which pretty much confirmed what Kate—*Motherhood is hard*—and Róisín—*All that matters is my child*—had written. No way could I see Zahra using the word 'crap', which put the *crap mother* in Teagan's hands, where it fitted comfortably. And left Zahra as the author of the warning note.

Sophie was still talking about how wonderful Lachlan was.

'Seems to me, Sophie, that you're trying really hard. This—being a mother—is important to you, right?'

'Of course.' She looked automatically to her son. He was watching Noah. 'Go on Tom, you can do it, crawl over to him.'

'But,' I continued, 'as we talked about in the group, *all* mothers don't enjoy it *sometimes*. Doesn't mean they aren't good mothers. Just that when it's not easy, motherhood can be everything from boring to terrifying to completely overwhelming.'

'Yes, of course,' said Sophie, still looking towards Tom. 'What's hardest for you?'

Sophie paused. 'Being me, I think.' She laughed. I waited. 'I've always felt I had to be perfect. My parents expected me to get A's and to be honest, it wasn't all that hard, but…

it wasn't always enough. For me.' She shrugged. 'I had anorexia nervosa.'

Haltingly, she told me about her diagnosis at nineteen. Before she'd started dating Lachlan. I pushed gently and she opened up a little. 'They sent me off to get "fixed" and I think I lost more weight, just to show them I was in control of…something. Something they couldn't make me do. Stupid, right?'

She'd seen a therapist but wanted to believe meeting Lachlan had cured her; perhaps he had provided the incentive. Now she wanted to be perfect: perfect wife, perfect mother.

'Just remember, you're aiming for good enough—not perfect,' I said.

'That was your note, right?'

I nodded and Sophie smiled. I figured she needed to end the interview having regained control.

After Sophie had gone, I took a quick look at Teagan's file. Yvonne looked over my shoulder. Because Teagan didn't have a baby yet, the file consisted of blank pages and a short note from Chris. What I was looking for was there under family history; father—alcohol abuse, mother—deceased (probable suicide). The first thing I thought was *then this isn't the killer the note referred to.*

'Alcohol involved,' said Yvonne with a distinct tone of disapproval. 'Open finding—she drowned in the river. Suicide or accident, take your pick. Not long after she had Teagan.'

Poor Teagan. She really had had a rough start to life.

I left Noah playing under Yvonne's eye and went out to the car—where someone had written a message in the dust on the back window: *Go home.*

I stood staring at it, feeling the knot in my chest. All of my group except Zahra would have passed my car on their way in and out. I looked up and down the street: no people and no security cameras. Small towns didn't like newcomers of any sort; I wondered if Zahra had also received messages like this—or worse.

I took a brisk walk in sunshine which I no longer felt warmed by. The only person I saw was a bloke in a beaten-up truck with a bumper sticker that read *Buy a Bale*.

Zahra's house was a neat weatherboard with a recently mown lawn and the start of a veggie patch along the side fence. A woman I assumed to be Zahra's mother, dressed formally by Riley standards in a tailored suit, greeted me at the door.

'She had a bad night. Perhaps she is not taking her medication.'

Zahra herself couldn't manage a smile. Psychotic or sedated? The doctor I'd seen in New Zealand had prescribed me antidepressants to help my panic attacks, and even at low doses I had felt like a zombie; then therapy had started helping so I'd stopped taking pills rather than try alternatives. Zahra's medication was stronger—antidepressants, antipsychotics and a mood stabiliser, according to the file Yvonne had shown me. But if she wasn't taking them, and wasn't sleeping, her illness would get worse.

'We missed you in the group,' I said, sitting beside her on a sofa draped with colourful rugs. 'How are you feeling?'

Zahra looked down at her hands. Long white fingers, one fingernail bitten to a reddened cuticle.

'Anything in particular worrying you?'

'My mind is like syrup,' she said finally, with a hint of a smile. 'I worry that I might never feel like myself again. I have tried studying—in Iran I was a paediatrician but here I must sit your exams. I can't recall what I read.'

'It's too early,' I said. 'You know that—you're a doctor. Give yourself time. Do you have any thoughts like before? Worries about people harming you or Raha?'

'My husband says I thought he was poisoning me, but

51

this is not true. I just did not like the medication they gave me in the mother–baby unit. It feels like it is bad for me.' Her illness winning out over her knowledge.

'Are you taking your medication?

'Massoud says I must.' Zahra's husband was also a doctor.

'Do you feel you need to?'

Zahra sighed. 'There are so many things I do not remember. My husband...and Doctor McCormack, they both tell me things that I did. It is hard to believe what they say. There is no memory of much of it.' She looked at her six-week-old daughter, who was being rocked by her grandmother. 'I see pictures of her when she was born, but have no recollection of this.' She paused. 'Raha means freedom.'

'Can you talk to Doctor McCormack about the medication? It takes time, but if what you're on doesn't suit you, there may be an alternative.'

'I worry for Raha. For our future here.'

'What sort of worries?'

'These are real worries, you understand? Some are from the past, the memories of when my parents were standing up to the regime in Iran, the worry about what might happen to them. But also about being in Riley, whether people will trust me, about whether I can work again. About...Teagan.'

More gossip? Racism? 'Why?'

'She makes trouble for my husband.'

'How?'

'She makes up lies. Because she wants drugs. My husband would not give them to her, because of her baby. She says she will tell the College. Makes problems for us.'

This sounded real rather than delusional; also, I wouldn't have put it past Teagan, though I suspected a lot of her attitude was just talk. Was she using? Getting drugs for a boyfriend? Teagan was linked through family ties to a murder and a suicide: Zahra had plenty of fuel for anxiety.

'She is not well. Her family, too,' said Zahra. 'Her father...I do not think he should be helping her.'

'Why not, Zahra?'

Zahra wouldn't meet my eyes. Because she was hiding something? Or because she thought I might see too much... based on a psychotic premise? I was feeling increasingly comfortable with my hypothesis that she was the author of the note.

'You don't have to worry about Teagan,' I reassured her. 'You need to focus on yourself and your family.'

It was clear there was a sense of despair in the molasses of her mind. No surprise: as psychosis settled, depression was common. I took her through a risk assessment. I believed her when she said she would never hurt Raha, but her assurances about her own safety were less robust.

'Perhaps your mother and husband could keep your medication, for safety?' Her mother was nodding.

Zahra shrugged. 'If they want.'

'Raha needs you,' I said, 'and you will get better. This doesn't last forever, it just seems like it will.'

'It's hard, being a mother,' she said as I went to leave. 'But this of course, you know.'

She looked at me, like she really knew.

'Yes, Noah can be a real handful. Two-year-olds don't stay put like babies do.'

'No.' She looked down at her hands again. 'And they like water so much, don't they?'

53

~

I held myself together just long enough to walk back to the health centre, collect Noah and put him in the car before the cracks in my mind sheared open.

I'd had a month without a panic attack and two months without diving into despair, convinced I was the worst mother who'd ever lived and that I didn't deserve a child. Now the tears were running down my face as I drove. Noah frowned from his car seat. 'Poor Mummy,' he said, and I started sobbing. Then Noah started to cry.

I had to pull myself together. I was the grown-up. All the books said the same thing; I knew it intuitively anyway. I was the one that had to reassure him, not vice versa.

'It's okay, Noah,' I said. 'You didn't upset Mummy. Mummy will look after herself, sweetheart, and she'll look after you too.'

He looked doubtful.

It had been nearly a year ago. Bored and homesick in Auckland, I'd joined a mother's group and finally made a few friends. Noah was older than their children, but it worked okay. We were having lunch at Sylvia's. I was halfway through my second glass of wine when Sylvia said the words that would haunt me for months to come: 'Was that a splash?'

Noah had been in the room next door—playing happily the last time I had looked, which had been...when? Now the sliding door was slightly open. So was the pool gate.

I was beside the pool without knowing how I got there. There was a small dark shape on the bottom. Not moving.

I don't think I screamed. I was fully clothed when I went in after him.

It was twenty-four hours before we knew Noah was going to be okay—and even then there was always the possibility of subtle hypoxic brain damage affecting motor, sensory and intellectual development. He'd inhaled some water, so he was treated for a lung infection and kept in hospital for three days, during which time my father rarely left my side. Dean was in and out. Partly because of work, partly because he hated sitting around doing nothing. I imagined him taking out his anger and despair on the equipment at the gym. Then, after we were home, after the relief of Noah's surviving, it was me who had to face the fallout.

I had always thought myself a pretty sensible person: calm, rational. My mother had spent most of my childhood with a variety of ailments that I came to understand were psychosomatic, as well as depression and anxiety. She'd say, 'I wasn't really well enough to have you, you know.' I was only eight when she took too many pills 'by accident' and I had to call the ambulance. My father was effusive in his praise for his 'wonderful, smart, quick-thinking daughter'.

Now I had to face a very different version of myself. One I didn't trust. And one Dean didn't, either.

It was mostly in the looks that said *All you had to do all day was keep him safe.* My father tried to soothe me, telling me it was an accident. The best Dean could do was: 'He's okay, thank God' and 'You won't let it happen again'—always with an implied *will you?*

I'd seen a therapist in New Zealand, for the panic attacks that started whenever I put Noah in the bath or drove past a swimming pool. It helped to reduce the sheer terror and the immediate, searing pain. So did time. But every time I thought of the incident, or someone raised it, my heart raced and I felt I was going to be sick. And whenever Dean and I argued, I saw the same expression in his eyes: *You nearly killed my son.*

I had Noah tucked up in bed and Yvonne settled in front of *Bondi Rescue* with a notebook of instructions before we left for the Barclays'. We arrived a little after seven-thirty. Half the journey seemed to be along the driveway up to the Barclays' sprawling two-storey mansion. I'd half-expected it to be surrounded by greenery, but even Gordon Barclay couldn't get water from a dry creek bed. There were plenty of trees, though—all natives—and stables, set slightly apart from the house. We passed a liver-chestnut mare and a bay gelding drinking at a trough. Warmbloods, I thought, with a twinge of regret for lost childhood dreams. I wondered who the rider was.

The interior designer, I was certain, had been Grace. The entertaining area opened to an internal courtyard of angles, lights and reflections with a fountain sculpture in the middle. On the other side was a spectacular cactus garden and the rooms themselves were high-vaulted ceilings with huge paintings. They might have been important and valuable—I couldn't tell.

Grace was in a cream silk dress with a red brooch and matching scarf. She brushed her lips past my cheeks in greeting and offered sparkling wine from a silver tray held by one of her staff. I was pleased I had worn my one decent dress. I was almost back to pre-baby weight, and it was an old favourite in a brilliant blue that brought out the colour in my eyes. I had my hair loose the way Dean liked it; he had his arm around my waist.

'Don't you look the perfect couple,' Grace said, smiling. My mother sometimes said the same thing.

Dean made the right noises about the house and Grace introduced us to the other guests; Sophie and Lachlan, inevitably; Massoud and Zahra Sorouri, less predictable and even less welcome, though Zahra was looking better—I noted from a distance that she even managed to make Dean laugh—and Athol Broadbent, the retired doctor and hospital-board member, with his much younger Filipina wife, Luningning—'just call me Lu'. She was his second wife, Sophie informed me. 'Six months after his wife died, he just came back from the Philippines with her.' Matt arrived late, about as enthusiastic as he had been at the pub meeting, and made no effort to engage with anyone.

Sooner than I had ever seen before at a gathering and the first time ever at a dinner party, the genders separated. The men disappeared; I imagined them all smoking cigars and talking about...what? Stocks and bonds? I wondered what Massoud would make of it.

'Gordon's old school,' said Grace, as if she could read my mind.

The conversation felt strained—but then we were essentially strangers, and two of them were my patients. Grace kicked off with a discussion I would have found interesting under normal circumstances, but with Zahra and Sophie present, I had to constantly worry about anything I said.

'What sort of psychological framework do you subscribe to, Isabel?'

'Um, I'm eclectic I guess. Loosely Jungian—father of psychology and all that—but mostly these days we practise Beck's CBT.'

'Jung and Freud are a bit passé now, are they?' asked Sophie.

'Well, they gave us a good base to understand motivation.'

'When I was growing up,' said Grace, 'it was all about blaming the mother, which I have to say was hard to take. But the tabula rasa concept is preferable, don't you think, to the current craze for everything we do or say being put down to genes?'

I wasn't sure what I thought because I'd never heard of tabula rasa.

Zahra saved me. 'Blank slate, yes?'

The theory that behaviour is mostly not determined by genes but learnt: a good deal closer to Freud's take than to current popular wisdom.

'There's a lot of evidence for at least some predetermination,' I said.

'That makes sense to me,' said Sophie.

'Nonsense.'

Sophie's face fell at the rebuke from her mother-in-law.

'There have been people whose parents were illiterate, living in the jungles of Papua New Guinea, who've gone on to be doctors, pilots...'

This was one fight I didn't want to be part of. I turned to Lu and engaged her in conversation, which was tricky—she was very shy—until I found she was, of all things, a dressage fan. 'Grace competes, you know,' she told me, as she produced a picture on her phone—it could have been anyone on the meticulously presented horse. 'State championships.'

After watching *International Velvet* at least twenty times as a kid I had dreamed of being in the Olympic three-day event. Showjumping was my passion, but I had spent many hours watching Angelica coax a horse between carefully placed letters on an arena. Lu, once started, was unstoppable. Our one-way conversation kept me at a professionally appropriate distance from Sophie and Zahra. Zahra said very little.

When we went in to dinner, I thought maybe Grace had some sense of my need to keep myself separate. I was seated with Gordon on one side, Athol on the other and Dean opposite. Halfway through the gazpacho they were back to a conversation about the hospital that must have begun in the drawing room.

'Everyone expects things to be new and shiny. But equipment used to be built to last. Waste of money replacing things that are working perfectly well,' said Athol.

'But some things are done differently now, Athol, more efficiently,' said Grace.

'Thing is,' said Gordon, waving his soup spoon, 'it's what people expect.'

'You mean voters,' Athol said with mild distaste.

'Voting is how they tell us what they expect. They're not going to put on a three-piece suit and make a speech at one of your board meetings.'

'They may want things,' said Dean, 'but who pays?'

'That's what taxes are for,' said Lachlan. 'If this was a city hospital we wouldn't be having this discussion.'

'City or country, taxpayers expect their money to be used efficiently.' I could see that Dean was stirring the discussion to see what floated to the surface.

'Grace's charity work keeps the hospital going,' said Sophie.

'Only a small proportion of what is needed,' Grace said. 'How are you going sorting things out, Dean?'

'Slowly.'

'No need to be cagey,' said Gordon. 'You're a bit of a star, I hear.'

'It has been a long time since the processes at the hospital were reviewed,' said Dean. 'I'm identifying what needs to be done to bring them into line with best practice.'

'So, it won't mean much change?' said Lachlan.

'I wouldn't assume that.'

'But no job losses, right?'

Dean paused. 'Ultimately, that won't be my decision.'

'We can't have job losses.' Lachlan looked to his father. 'We said—'

Gordon's look silenced his son. 'No problem to us.' He put his glass down. 'I've been in this business a long time. Seen too many politicians go down because they skimmed off the top and took freebies. I make sure our accountant has every receipt, that every expense is documented. Accountant at the hospital should have done the same.'

Matt's expression suggested that the impression Gordon was giving—of being a tight-arse—was an accurate one, and a source of tension. Also a contrast, it seemed, with how Gordon let Eric run the hospital. But then, Gordon wasn't on the hospital board. I flashed a look at Grace but if she was worried, or thought her husband unsupportive, it wasn't evident.

Gordon continued. 'We'll wait and see what you recommend.'

'This will be soon, yes?' Massoud asked.

Dean shrugged. 'I'm expecting to be finished by February.'

I had wanted to be home for Christmas. Eight weeks away.

Massoud looked concerned. 'This is not good for people.'

'What isn't, Massoud?' Grace asked.

'There is too much worry in this town. It is not a good... vibe? No, I think it is a stronger word I need than this.'

'Massoud, no.' Zahra pulled on his arm, speaking softly and urgently.

Massoud turned and spoke briefly in what I assumed was Arabic or Farsi. Then he turned back to the table. 'I think important people like you must act.'

'Spit it out,' said Gordon, pouring himself some wine, then passing the decanter to Dean.

'I know, they worry about their jobs. But I am speaking of something more. A threat.'

'Threat?' Sophie asked sharply. I looked at her carefully as she put her hands together and smiled tightly.

'The tragedy, with the baby—'

'But that was years—'

'...yes, long ago, this I understand. Is it possible that the person who killed the baby is still here?'

There was dead silence. Even Grace seemed to be struggling to find an appropriate way of dealing with this.

'Who the fuck'—Gordon put his wine down with a thud—'told you that?' In contrast to the words and body language, his tone was oddly mild. No, *even*. A pool of red discolouration appeared around the glass.

Zahra looked like she was about to grab her baby and run, with or without Massoud. She didn't need this type of stress. Nor did I.

61

'I apologise for Gordon's language,' said Grace. 'I understand why this is a frightening idea, but it does seem unlikely.'

From the other end of the table, Gordon shared a grim look at his wife. 'I need to know who's spreading this bull. The town doesn't need to panic for no reason. Kidnappers returning after twenty-five years? Ye gods, what's next? Martians?'

'We have heard the police received information they have not shared,' said Massoud, arm around his wife. 'For me, for Zahra, we need to see something being done about it.'

A voice within me seemed to speak of its own accord. 'I've heard something similar.'

Silence again. Dean looked at me as if I'd turned into one of Gordon's Martians.

'Morettis, eh? Stirring the pot again.' Matt Barclay spoke for what I thought was the first time all evening.

'Regardless,' said Sophie, sitting still and straight. 'The town needs some reassurance.'

'The Morettis haven't ever recovered,' said Grace. She moved up behind her youngest son, hand on his shoulder. To the rest of us she smiled sadly. 'Poor Donna. It was such a tragedy. I don't think Joe was able to…move on.'

'Okay,' said Gordon. 'I hear you, all of you. I'll deal with it. I'll meet with Sam—Sergeant Keller. They might not have worried so much about bla—' Grace coughed loudly. '…Indigenous people then, but times have changed. And you…' He was pointing at Dean. 'You need to make sure that any cost-cutting doesn't compromise safety.'

The remainder of the dinner was strained. When Zahra and Massoud's baby started crying they took the opportunity to make an early exit and, with our babysitter as an excuse, we weren't far behind.

As soon as we started down the driveway, Dean said in a low voice, 'What was all that about?'

'If you mean me backing up Doctor Sorouri, then it was the truth.'

'Didn't you think perhaps you should have told me?'

'I couldn't. Confidentiality.'

'Didn't stop you blurting it out over dinner.'

'I didn't say what I heard or where I got it from. The point is I'm not the only one who's heard it.'

Dean sighed. 'Gordon will deal with it.'

Gordon had seemed more concerned about how the rumour got out than whether there was substance to it.

Still, now I knew that Zahra had heard about the letter to the police—and Sophie, too, more than likely. Sophie's demeanour was too controlled to suggest she was hearing about this for the first time. Either of them could have written the note in our group based on gossip. Depending how widely the rumours had circulated, so could Róisín.

'We don't know if Gordon can do anything,' I said, trying to sound reasonable. 'Nor the police, who've been sitting on the information. If they don't know who killed the first baby, how can they stop it happening again?'

Dean shook his head. 'Iz, listen to yourself. Does it sound like a sane idea to you that someone who killed twenty-five years ago would suddenly strike again? Some kind of silver anniversary present?'

Maybe not, but someone appeared to have threatened it. And who said they were sane?

We drove the rest of the way home in silence.

After I dropped Dean at work the following day, I stopped off at the hospital shop. I used the ancient computer to send an email to my mother—easier than a protracted phone call.

Jeannie had purple tips in her white hair today. She brought me a coffee I hadn't ordered and sat down to chat.

'How's your group going, dear?'

'It's nice for new mothers to have a chance to talk.'

'When I had children there was none of this postnatal support, we just got on with it.' She thought for a moment. 'Or didn't.'

'Donna Moretti?'

Jeannie made a small gesture of acknowledgment. 'Mothers can do terrible things you know, dear,' she said. 'Though in Donna's case I doubt she meant to. She wasn't *bad*.'

Should I be talking about this? It was common knowledge, I supposed. 'What I can't understand is what happened to the baby…Joshua. How did she get him out of the hospital?'

Jeannie frowned.

'Did any strangers wander in?' I asked.

'No dear, though the police at the time did have some theory about an outsider.' Her expression made it clear exactly what she thought of the theory. 'We know everyone here. It was just a normal day; my daughter's toddler had a temperature, he ended up having his tonsils out, then he was right as rain; anyway, I came in late, just before Joe and Donna had their argument. He went off, but not long after…well, I heard Donna scream. We all did, and it wasn't a scream anyone ever wants to hear; no woman at least.'

I looked down at Noah, feeling vaguely nauseated, unsure if it was the coffee or the thought of him going missing. Or worse.

'So Joe wasn't still with Donna? When she screamed?'

Jeannie started fussing with the layout of the soft toys on the display stand beside her. 'No. They'd been fighting like I said…here in the foyer.' She waved outside the door beyond me, with a small blue bunny in her hand. 'He stormed off like he had ants in his pants and Donna went back to her room.'

'And *then* the nurse found Joshua was missing?'

'That's right,' said Jeannie. 'The police came straight away. Tracker dogs, all that, quite a drama. But it was much later they found the child, poor thing.'

So Joe had left before Joshua was discovered missing. Left in a hurry. Had their argument been *about* Joshua's death? Had he taken the baby—his body—to protect his wife?

'Did you hear what they were arguing about?'

'No, dear.' Jeannie shook her head. 'Just occasional words. But I can still see them standing there. What happened after…it kind of fixes things in your mind, doesn't it?'

'Was Joe carrying anything?'

'Oh. Yes, I believe he was,' said Jeannie. 'She was supposed to be going home that day. He had her bag, to take to the car.'

Her bag. A bag big enough for a dead newborn? I shivered. All the same, it sounded too organised for postpartum psychosis. If Donna had been psychotic, she wouldn't have been able to maintain the façade, even if Joe had been cool-headed enough to make up a story and dispose of the body.

Of course, parents did sometimes kill their children—my doctoral research had left me in no doubt about that—and sometimes they hid the body afterwards. But not when the child was only a day old, while they were still supported by the hospital staff. Nor did they generally pull themselves together so quickly to hide the body, or at any rate to hide it that well. If Joshua's death was an accident the same would hold true.

Unless, perhaps, longstanding prejudice against Donna in the town meant she and Joe had developed a well-oiled routine of banding together against the world.

I tried one last question. 'You said they brought tracker dogs. Did they...do you know if they checked out Joe's house? His yard?'

'Oh yes, dear. Dug up his garden too—all the vegetables he'd planted. Joe used to have the best pumpkins and tomatoes in town, but after Joshua, he lost interest. Never grew another one.'

Jeannie kept talking—she was president of the local branch of the Country Women's Association; they really did need some young blood—but I was only half-listening, wondering how to dump the coffee. I heard about how the gift shop earned money for the hospital—'I'd guess sometimes five hundred dollars in a week, but I couldn't be sure, I'm not the one who counts it'—about the medal her husband got in the war, the year the floods had kept her isolated on her farm for a week, and how she used to grow prize zucchinis but now stuck to chrysanthemums.

I left the coffee. I suspect I wasn't the first to do so. But I bought two bunches of her chrysanthemums.

As I left the hospital, I saw a new poster on the community noticeboard: Gordon Barclay's face next to that of the local police sergeant, Sam Keller. There was going to be another town meeting—a chance to 'discuss concerns regarding safety at Riley hospital'. Presumably the outcome of the Barclays' dinner. Scheduled on a Saturday night with only two days' notice, which might discourage people from attending. On the other hand, if there was a decent turnout it would be a clear message that the town was concerned.

Dean wasn't keen on me going. 'I've got to be there, obviously,' he said as I was packing Noah's bag, 'but it'll only get you worried.'

'Not as worried as I'd be sitting here wondering what was being said.'

I didn't add that I couldn't trust him to report the whole story; that I could only trust him, in fact, to downplay my concerns. I'd told him about the dog poo in our postbox and he'd said, 'Kids.' He'd wiped the *Go home* graffiti off the car without mentioning it.

I could see his point. I'd been a lot better in the last month or two; I guessed he didn't want me to go back to being housebound and unable to sleep.

The pub was full when we arrived; it was lucky I'd eaten because there were no tables. I popped Noah in the playpen—Kate's daughter, Ruby, and a boy of about three I didn't recognise were already there—and joined the throng at the bar to order a glass of sauvignon blanc.

I spotted most of the group—Kate was pulling beers; Sophie was with the Barclay clan; Róisín and her partner Al—slumped shoulders and a morose expression—were huddled in a far corner. With them was Conor the union man, who clearly was her father, and a heavy, tired-looking woman I assumed was her mother. The cluster of dark-haired men and women aged from late teens to late thirties sitting at beer-laden tables with their partners or friends could have been Róisín's siblings. Matt Barclay was joking with one of the younger men in the group. Teagan was sitting with her father and a group of Aboriginal men and women. They were talking quietly, heads lifting occasionally to check if anyone was listening, or maybe to make sure proceedings hadn't started. One of them was the gangly young man I had seen in the street—I'd thought he was a teenager but I now realised he was probably Teagan's age—with a big smile, almost as many piercings as Teagan and a better selection of tattoos. I wondered if he was the father of her child. He seemed primarily interested in checking out who was turning up. Massoud was with Chris, the GP who'd chatted to me at the earlier event. No sign of Zahra.

Gordon—with Lachlan standing awkwardly beside him—welcomed everyone and called up Sam Keller to the landing at the base of the staircase. I had pictured Sam as looking a bit like Gordon—big build and blustery—but he was tall, thin and weathered, with a nervy look. I suspected he'd be more comfortable driving teenage drunks home than investigating a kidnapping or murder—or a threat of either. Lachlan stepped back.

'I think you all know why we're here this evening,' said Gordon. 'Sam is going to set your minds at rest.'

Sam cleared his throat, his Adam's apple seeming to track the length of his neck. 'Thanks Gordon. Everyone knows that twenty-five years ago, the Moretti family had their baby taken from the Riley hospital, and the body was found a month later. The case remains open. I see Teagan Moretti here, about to have a baby herself, as well as her dad, so I want to remind you all—it's on the record—Joe and Donna were cleared of any involvement.'

The group around Teagan nodded. The tattooed young man whispered in her ear and she shoved him away, but with a smile. One of the older women pushed him in the other direction and whatever she said made them nod in furious agreement.

The man in front of me said to his wife in a low voice, 'Never trust those hot-blooded eye-ties.'

'Her lot were pretty bloody hopeless, but,' his wife whispered back.

'Both sides had form,' said someone else.

I wondered if that meant routine strife between neighbours or if the 'form' was more serious. It was normal to try and make meaning of the shocking, the horrible and senseless things that happened in the world, but so often it segued into victim-blaming. I was pretty sure Donna's Indigenous heritage played into the attitudes—and was uncomfortably aware that I might have fallen into the same trap before coming to Riley and meeting Teagan.

'A month or so back,' Sergeant Keller continued, 'we

came into the possession of'—couldn't police ever say anything directly?—'an anonymous letter that referenced the Moretti tragedy. Just to be safe, I turned the letter over to forensic experts and we're keeping an eye on the hospital. Things are different than they were back then—we've got CCTV and Mr Harris agreed to have two nurses on in the ward any time there's a baby there. But it's only a precaution. There's nothing to worry about.'

'You telling us someone's made a threat towards the hospital? Towards the babies?' interjected Brian McCormack from behind the bar.

'Nothing specific, Brian,' said Sam.

'Was it the same person who tipped you off as to where my son could be found?' It was Joe Moretti.

'No telling that, Joe,' said Sam.

'What did the letter say?' Teagan this time. She was on the edge of the chair, hand tight on the can of Coke in front of her. The tattooed guy held her other hand.

'Just saying that the hospital was important and that our babies needed it to be looked after properly.'

Sophie turned to Lachlan and said something that made him frown.

'Maybe it's someone with mental problems?' said the man in front of me. 'Like, unhinged then, after the floods and now because we've got the drought...?'

Sam laughed drily. 'Well, it's a theory. But...'

'Police must get crackpot letters all the time. Why are you taking this one seriously? This meeting, guards at the hospital...'

'There are no guards, just...' But there was a buzz in the room, and Sam changed tack. 'There was an item of information included in the letter about the Moretti case that wasn't widely known. So we're not dismissing it, and if anyone here knows something about the letter, we're asking them to come forward. The person who wrote it can possibly help our enquiries.' He looked around the room and added, 'To be clear, that information had not been made known even to the Moretti family.'

Joe and Teagan's expressions suggested this was true— and that they weren't impressed. I watched Kate clock their reaction. She looked thoughtful.

'So, what the hell did it say?' Teagan tried again.

Sam shook his head. 'I'm not in a position to share that information, Teagan.'

I felt Dean's eyes on me and forced a smile. I wasn't feeling especially reassured.

'Someone knows something!' It was Joe again, words slightly slurred. The group around Teagan nodded. One called out, 'Something you not telling us, Sam?'

'Sounds to me like it's all about this hospital review,' said Conor. His arms were crossed and he was looking defiantly at the police sergeant.

Sam was unimpressed. 'Conor, what we discussed with you needs to...'

I looked at them both; I figured the police had interviewed Conor about this. And he hadn't been happy.

'I'm just saying what we all think—the hospital ain't broke, it doesn't need fixin' and these people who think they can tell us what to do should just bugger off back to where they came from.'

Conor was looking at Dean as he spoke. My desire to return to Melbourne with Noah was becoming more like a plan.

Dean stood up. 'I can assure you that the government

has given every indication they intend to continue the current funding of the Riley hospital. My concern is that we make best use of that funding. In the interests of everyone in the community, not just hospital employees.'

'Just promise us now that no jobs'll be lost and I'll shut up.'

'Conor,' said Gordon, 'this isn't the time for politics.'

'It's always time for politics. *Gordon.*'

Joe stood up, swaying a little. 'Same as back when Joshua went, eh Gordon? Is it Doctor McCormack you're trying to stop this time?'

What did he mean? I flashed a look at Chris—Dr McCormack. He was shaking his head, expression grim. *This time.* Who or what had Gordon been stopping last time?

'This is about keeping our community safe,' said Gordon firmly. 'Mr Harris has assured me there will be no decline in safety measures at the hospital.' He paused and everyone looked at Dean. Joe's expression suggested he was unimpressed; ditto Conor Rearden, whose tatts rippled as his fingers drummed the table in front of him. Gordon went on. 'Sam, you have more to say?'

'Thank you, Gordon, yes I do.' Sam looked serious, pausing to make sure everyone was paying attention. 'I know quite a few of you have young kids. Please be aware that this note is meant to get people upset, pure and simple. *Maybe* it was written by whoever killed Joshua Moretti twenty-five years ago. More likely it's someone using information they got hold of somehow to stir up trouble.

'But there is no reason to suggest they would do anything. What seems clear is that this person's got a grievance with the hospital funding. Mr Harris and Mr Barclay are happy to talk to them any time. I'll repeat, we do not believe there is a credible threat to anyone's safety.'

Conor was still looking angry as the crowd broke up. Joe was pulled away by Teagan and her boyfriend.

If Dean was right about Conor, and he or his union mates were involved in kickbacks, he had enough motivation to stir things up and try to get rid of Dean. Could he have been involved with Joshua's disappearance, though? Matt had moved to the bar, but was watching the tensions between his family and the Reardens. If I'd had to put a name to the expression, I'd have said confusion; the moment he caught my eye it changed to a scowl and the little boy out of his depth disappeared.

Sophie was looking tense; her forced smile evoked a slightly crazed clown. Who knew what her baby Tom would make of that—he was unlikely to find it reassuring. She batted Lachlan's hand away from her upper arm and walked off. Chris McCormack came over to join me.

'Welcome to the downside of small towns.' He looked tired. 'When are you coming to see me about that extra work? I usually take a lunch break between twelve and one.'

All I wanted to do was go home. I promised Chris I would visit. I turned to get Noah and found Sophie was there to collect Tom. She looked worse than I felt.

'Are you okay?' I asked.

'No, I'm not.'

The image of her in our interview—smug, in control— flashed before me. Her expression now was a long way from that: a mix of vulnerability and frustration. Sophie needed that feeling of control, and right now she didn't have it.

I thought back to that conversation. We'd talked about the notes we'd written and she'd guessed which note I had written in the group—yet she'd struggled to recall which one she herself had written. I realised that I'd been hoodwinked: Sophie knew perfectly well who'd written which note—she'd worked it out in her mind so she could claim one that was neither mine nor, in fact, her own.

'That day in the group. You wrote the note that I didn't read out.'

Sophie looked flustered, but only briefly. 'You needed to know. I wrote it because I didn't want this warning'—she waved her hands wildly and then spoke in a hiss—'to be *covered up*. Like they've just gone and damn well done.'

I felt a small flutter of anxiety start up in my stomach. 'What do you mean covered up?'

'*You* haven't seen the letter that was sent to the police. If you of all people...' Sophie stopped abruptly. 'I'm sorry, I don't know what's gotten into me. I had a bad night last night, not much sleep. Sorry.'

If you of all people. I felt the panic rising but I took deep breaths and focused on the task at hand. *Noah's right here. He's fine.*

But I couldn't watch Noah every minute of the day and night. Just what did the warning letter say?

'Sophie, I need to talk to you.' As she left the pub and walked to her car, I rushed after her with Noah in my arms.

'I'm in a hurry. I have to—'

'It won't take long.' I leaned against the driver's door. 'What did you mean?'

Sophie's earlier vulnerability had given me an exaggerated sense of my own power. She squared her shoulders. 'I didn't mean anything. Would you mind getting off my car?'

For a moment I was fourteen again, back at school and the class mean girl was about to destroy me in front of all her friends. Olivia Doyle. Back in Year Nine her bullying had gone on for weeks—notes on my locker, on the whiteboard, texts—until eventually I'd thrown up over her shoes. Which didn't, of course, improve the situation. Thank God it was before Facebook.

Noah pulled tightly into me, perhaps frightened by Sophie's bared teeth, and something shifted.

'I understand why you wrote the note in the group. You felt it was unfair that you knew and the others didn't—you got the information from your father-in-law, right?'

Sophie was staring at me, not trying to interrupt. I pushed on. It really didn't matter if I got the details wrong—I just wanted to give her an out.

'You wanted to warn us. You're a mother...and you'd studied law, worried about the repercussions if something did happen.'

Sophie's expression turned smug but I rattled on: 'Whatever. I just need to know what you meant by me *of all people*.'

She looked less smug now; more torn. 'Look, it was a typed letter sent from Sydney. Just like the letter that tipped the police off back then about where the Moretti baby's body was.' Her expression said: *so not some drunk local crackpot*. 'I can't recall the exact words. But it was political, so naturally Lachlan and I were worried it was about us... or, more to the point, Tom.'

'When did the police get the note?'

'About six weeks ago. Lachlan had just formally announced his political intentions...so there was the uncomfortable similarity to...well, twenty-five years ago. When Joe Moretti was running against Gordon. But...it was also targeting anyone involved in the hospital review.'

I thought of Joe's comment about Gordon stopping Chris McCormack. Last time it was Joe whose political career had been halted by the person who had taken the baby.

Six weeks ago was about the same time that Dean had accepted this job.

On the way home I was mostly quiet while Dean talked about Conor. 'Just a hot-headed old-school union blowhard,' he said. 'There is *nothing* to worry about, Iz.'

After Noah was in bed and we were sitting on the veranda, I looked out into the dusk light, imagining silent ghosts hovering in the stillness until there was that odd barking sound again. It made me think of baby Azaria and the dingo. I pictured it dragging her off. The moon was already high in the sky, the light eerily bright; the dark shadows beneath the trees all the more forbidding. I shivered. It wasn't cold, but the saying about someone walking over your grave made sense in a visceral way it never had before.

There was danger. I felt it. Just because I didn't know where the danger was coming from didn't mean it wasn't there.

What sounded like a cockatoo shrieked somewhere behind the house; a flock of them had disappeared into the dark shape of a distant clump of trees an hour earlier. I'd checked Google, and dingoes had been eradicated from the region long ago. Kangaroos and wombats might be aggressive if backed into a corner but they weren't going to seek us out. Snakes couldn't get through doors. Spiders could be watched for and avoided. That left humans.

My anxiety was a familiar companion, but this was something else. Anger perhaps. We didn't get angry in the house I grew up in—it might have upset my mother, and there were already plenty of other things that could do that. I had watched my father smoke and drink to deal with her instability. I studied psychology as much to make sense of my parents as myself.

I loathed confrontation but had never reflected on why— what deeper childhood fear, if any, I was avoiding. It would take years of psychotherapy to sort that out—not the short-acting, in-the-moment, cognitive behavioural therapy I had been trained in.

In five years of marriage I had backed down on every issue that had come between me and Dean.

Auckland with no friends and no work? Nearly two years there.

Sell the car I loved, an old VW Beetle that was a gift from my grandmother? It made sense—but I had given in rather than participate actively in the decision.

Clothes, hairstyle...nothing to rock the boat. But then I hadn't really minded. I hadn't *wanted* to rock the boat. I loved Dean and he made me feel safe. I wanted to make him happy in return.

Dean finally figured out something was wrong. He looked over. 'You okay?'

'No, not really.'

'What? Noah?'

'Noah's fine.' I wasn't looking at him, didn't want to be weakened by that perpetual hint of accusation. 'Dean, we need to talk.'

'Oh-o. Sounds serious,' he said. 'I'll get another drink. Want one?'

'No.'

Dean came back with an open stubbie. 'Okay, hit me with it.'

'I want you to look at me,' I said, turning my chair. 'And I want the truth.'

Dean looked at me warily.

'What did the letter to the police actually say?'

There was a long silence. Dean was going through options. He could say that he hadn't seen it and hope I bought that. It might even be true. Or he could attack.

I knew which he would go for.

'Jesus, Iz, not this fucking thing again.'

My hand clasped one of Noah's favourite little toys in my pocket. I need to be reminded of him.

'What does it say, Dean?'

'You heard Sergeant Keller. No need for anyone to have details.'

'But I do need to know. And not only what it says, but when you first heard about it. It came before we arrived in town. Did you ever consider that it might have been warning us—you—to not come? Threatening your...*my* son?'

'Look, Isabel, I don't know what you've heard,' said Dean, 'but that's bullshit. Do you really think I'd put Noah in danger? After what we've been through with him? For Christ's sake, what sort of father do you think I am?'

I blinked tears back. 'I know you're a great dad, Dean. But that's not the point. *You've* made a judgment about *our* safety—about the safety of our child—without even talking to me.'

Dean shook his head wearily. 'Iz, you've not exactly been yourself, have you?'

I won't let him do this. I closed my eyes; held on to the toy. 'I need to know what it said, Dean.'

'Okay, okay.'

I opened my eyes as Dean threw his hands in the air and slopped beer onto the deck. 'Sam Keller emailed me a partial transcript.' He pulled out his phone and scrolled; pushed it in front of me.

I took a breath. Keller had taken out the confidential information and left the remainder of the message. The email was dated the day we arrived in Riley.

Healthcare is about people not big business. Save money? Then lose lives. If one death can save many then I'll be getting another [deleted]...to bury another baby in.

I handed him back his phone, and sat looking out across the paddocks. A few bats were leaving their roosting sites.

The shadow of a bird circled and dived. Moments later there was the same shrill noise I'd heard from the attacking owl on the day we arrived in Riley. The image of the dead bird slithering down our windscreen flashed before me.

I wondered about the detail the police had redacted. Something about what the killer had used as a shroud, I supposed. Or a tiny coffin.

'Happy now?' Dean said. 'Better for knowing? No. Just more anxious.'

'You really don't read that as a specific threat to Noah? Even after the dog shit and the message written on the car?'

Dean winced—he probably hoped I hadn't seen the message. 'You heard Sam,' he said. 'It's just someone using the town history, that's all. They don't like the fact that I'm turning over stones—and there's a fucking big rock with a lot under it. Maybe outright theft on top.'

'The point isn't whether this guy is an actual killer or just knows something about what happened to Joshua Moretti. The point is they are *threatening our son*.'

'Don't you think you're being a tad hysterical?'

'Look, there's other stuff.' I thought of Zahra. She had heard or read something more than the rumour about a police note—something about Joe, more than likely. Then there were the vibes I felt in the group, vibes that weren't about me being nervous or my clients reacting to the warning to police. 'Stuff I've been told in confidence. Nothing... definite. But this is what I do, Dean. I'm a psychologist. Something is wrong. You'll have to trust me.'

'Oh, right. So I just tell my boss, sorry we're leaving town because my wife has a bad feeling? When I explain you're a *psychologist, Doctor* Harris, well, of course he'll understand perfectly.'

I was standing now. I clutched the toy and took two deep breaths. 'I'm going back to Melbourne in the morning. You can either come with me or drop me off at the airport. Take your pick.'

Dean now stood up too. He was twenty centimetres taller than me and thirty kilos heavier. I didn't think he'd hit me, but looking at the anger on his face, I was shaking.

'You want to issue ultimatums?' he hissed. 'Here's one for you. Take my son and I'll make sure the cops pick you up before you get halfway to Dubbo. You really think they're going to give Noah to a mother that nearly...' he stopped.

He didn't need to say anything more.

In the days that followed, it felt as though the temperature dial had been turned down. A cold front drove away the hint of approaching summer, bringing a grey sky and a dullness to the light so that the gash where the river cut through the landscape appeared dark and forbidding. The clouds threatened rain but delivered nothing more than a dampness in the air that made the dust stirred by the wind stick to my skin.

I stayed in bed all Sunday, listening to Noah's shrieks of delight as Dean threw him up in the air, the giggling over his night-time story. Dean brought me breakfast but I didn't eat it, nor the lunch that followed. I kept thinking about Noah's accident, reliving it as clearly as if it had happened the day before.

I hadn't known how deep the pool was when I plunged in to rescue him—instead of diving towards the shape at the bottom of the pool, I must have jumped. At any rate I sank without air and instead of saving my son I came gasping to the surface without him.

I could make him out, there on the bottom of the pool, but I was hyperventilating so badly that when I put my head back under to dive down to him, I couldn't do it.

I don't know how long I trod water, gasping and floundering—Sylvia told me she had been right behind me, so it can only have been a few seconds—but it felt like an eternity. And in those seconds, my child could have died. I failed three times as a mother: not watching him, not ensuring he couldn't get out of the house, and then, worse, not being able to save him when I had the chance.

It was Sylvia who dived in, fully clothed, and came back up with my unconscious child. It was one of the other mothers who helped Sylvia get him out of the pool and another still who called an ambulance. Sylvia was still giving him mouth to mouth when they arrived; I was sitting on the edge of the pool with no recollection of how I had got there, shaking in terror. The medics bundled me into the back of the ambulance with Noah but I was more hindrance than help. I was still hysterical when Dean arrived at the hospital an hour later—no longer screaming, instead frozen with shock.

After our fight, on the third day of almost complete silence between Dean and me, I was home alone with Noah. A car came over the bridge and onto the plain: Grace's smart white BMW, which I'd seen around town. I had tried to think up an excuse to visit her, some way of finding her at home without Sophie about. I was drawn to her; I could see why Sophie might want to emulate her. Grace would know better than anyone if there was a real threat to my child. She was tough and smart and she knew this town. I pictured her on her warmblood—black jacket and top hat—and there was something reassuring in the image of a person I admired inhabiting my own childhood dream.

And I really needed to know who wrote the letter to the police. Whatever Dean thought, I saw the note as targeting him—and therefore Noah.

She looked at our car. 'That's your husband's car isn't it—you drive him to work and then bring it home? Would you like a loan of one of our farm cars?'

'That's a lovely thought, but we're managing,' I said.

'Well, think about it if you're still here during the summer rains. This place is lower than the town. It's not wise to be here without transport.' She looked back towards our only exit—the stock bridge. 'I'll see if Gordon can get someone to look at that rickety antique.'

She must have seen me flinch. Grace squeezed my hand. 'I've brought these. Just out of the oven.'

Over English Breakfast made with teabags—I felt sure the Barclays would use a teapot—Grace, Noah and I ate warm scones heaped with raspberry jam and cream.

'It was Gordon's mother's recipe,' said Grace. 'I humour him sometimes. At Thanksgiving, we have pumpkin pie.'

I wondered what else she humoured him about. What she would have done had she been in my situation.

'So how are you settling into Riley?' she asked.

'It's had its challenges,' I said cautiously.

Grace looked at me. 'I imagine that's an understatement.'

'I hadn't known...about the Moretti baby,' I said. My eyes went to Noah, who was playing happily with some pans he'd hauled out of the kitchen cupboard. Grace followed my look.

'They are so precious,' she said softly. 'And so dependent.'

'Did you worry for Lachlan, when he was a baby? Given they never caught who did it?' It had occurred to me that Grace's position then was similar to mine now.

Grace shook her head. 'No, the police may not have charged anyone, but...I knew Donna. She...had her problems.'

I remembered what I'd heard at the meeting. 'Trouble with the law?'

'Her family...There was a lot of trouble with alcohol in the town back then. Now there are a few controls. Donna's mother also had, ah, a weakness for men, I guess you'd say. Quite a few children, to quite a few fathers'—she made a gesture that seemed to say she wasn't judging—'and after Joshua was born...'

Grace stopped, and I waited until she continued. 'I'm not a doctor of course, but I thought...well, Donna seemed closed, anxious. Not herself. I know all mothers worry, but this was different. I'm talking about before the child was taken.'

The timing was right for postpartum psychosis. It was the most dramatic and potentially dangerous mental illness for new mothers, and it usually showed up in the first week.

'And afterwards?'

In a woman psychotic enough to kill her child, the psychosis would subsequently become full blown.

'Poor Donna,' said Grace, looking as though she really felt it. There wasn't anything quite like the death of a child to unite parents. Or divide them.

'Until Joshua...after his body was found Donna was heavily sedated, then Joe just took her away. In retrospect we understand he covered up the child's death, hid the body, to protect her. He had a friend in the police force...perhaps they didn't look at the case as hard as they could have. Mental illness...he's old-school Italian and there's a lot of stigma. And prejudice about Indigenous people.'

A mate in the right place, police incompetence or indifference…they all played a part in Grace's version. I knew the police had dogs check Joe's property, though. They had made some sort of effort—unless maybe Joe's mate knew that wasn't where the body had been disposed of.

'He took her away?'

'I'm not sure where she went initially, but later we heard she and Joe were with his family down south. Griffith, I think. After Joshua had been found and buried. They returned when Donna was pregnant again. They seemed to think another baby would make things better.'

My eyes met hers and we shared the thought without saying it. Having a second child didn't magically fix things. Untreated mental illness tended to get worse, not better. I wondered about her temporary disappearance—maybe a stint in a psychiatric hospital? But even if she had been treated, Donna had probably stopped the medication when she was pregnant again, with Teagan—and the pregnancy itself would have been a stress factor. Any postpartum psychosis would have been likely to recur, especially with this birth following so soon after the other.

'If she did kill Joshua—and Joe was complicit—what do you make of the recent warning to the police?'

'Joe Moretti…' Grace carefully scraped the crumbs from her scone into a tissue. 'He hasn't ever really forgiven Gordon. Joe was in no fit state back then to do the work needed to win an election, but he resented it, resented Gordon. Now Lachlan, too, I suppose. I can imagine the letter to the police as a wild, probably drunken, release of anger at the hospital for not keeping his child safe from Donna all those years ago. If it hurt Gordon and Lachlan, that would be a bonus.'

It made as much sense as alcohol fog and unresolved

anger was ever likely to make. If Joe had disposed of Joshua's body, he'd have known what the baby had been found in. It might not have occurred to him that the police hadn't released this information.

'Not to warn Dean off?'

Grace smiled knowingly. 'It's hardly done that, has it? If they scared him off, I assume his company would just send someone else.'

If it had been up to me, that was exactly what would have happened. In Grace's scenario it was probably Joe who provided the tipoff about the body's location twenty-five years ago. That made sense—closure for both himself and Donna. I wondered about the Sydney postmark; but it wouldn't have been that hard to organise.

'Just a man with a grudge and a poison pen,' Grace added.

'But...what's Joe's motivation to stir all this up again unless he wanted the killer caught?'

Grace flashed a look at me, then covered it up with a smile. I tried to pinpoint what it was. Pity?

'The older I get,' she said slowly, 'the more I think people are able to distort memories, to recall the past the way they wish it had been, rather than the way it was.'

She was right about that. But it didn't convince me that Joe had written the note.

'You're on the hospital board, Grace. Is anyone particularly invested in the hospital's survival?'

Grace went to the bin to tip her crumbs in before she replied. 'I run the charity—we hold fetes, social evenings to raise money for the hospital—which, incidentally, is why I'm here; I'm hoping you'll bake something for the Christmas fete. We're raising money for new medical equipment, even if Athol doesn't think it's needed.'

She sat back down. 'The hospital runs at a loss. It's why the Liberals aren't supporting Gordon on this. They want bigger regional hospitals that are cost-effective, so they want to close us down and put the money into the Dubbo hospital. But that's two hours away. We'd lose a crucial community resource, and most of the staff would have to move—it would be the death of Riley. The ALP has the same view. They have to tread carefully with the unions, of course—and Conor Rearden is, to say the least, a vocal union rep—but quite frankly they don't get a look-in here. This is Nationals territory.'

'You don't think he could have written the letter to stir up trouble for political reasons?'

'Conor?' Grace shook her head. 'Conor's all hot air. I could see him turning up at the police station or organising a protest, but to write to them? Not his style. Besides—'

I sensed she wished she had stopped earlier. I waited her out.

'I know Conor had nothing to do with what happened to Joshua Moretti.'

'How can you be sure?' I asked. Even if he hadn't kidnapped the boy he might know something.

'I was with Conor at his house.'

I must have gaped.

Grace gave a terse laugh. 'No, nothing personal. Gordon was doing a deal with him, about how the party would work with the unions, and he, Gordon, was in Sydney that week and needed some paperwork dropped off. Right at the time Joshua Moretti went missing.'

'But that can't have taken long.' I wondered what the time window was.

'Gordon and Conor doing business is never simple.' She laughed. 'At least half an hour, more like an hour. I went from Conor's to pick up the takings from the café and when I arrived at the hospital, they'd just realised Joshua was missing.'

Conor was the best suspect if I wanted the Morettis to be innocent—which, I realised, for some reason I did. But he hadn't been there, any more than Gordon had, or Grace herself. The simplest explanation was probably the right one: Joe covered for his wife, and her guilt and mental illness ultimately killed her. And the police, lacking hard evidence—seeing, perhaps, in the wake of Donna's death that it was more a tragedy than a crime—let it go.

'Do you think whoever wrote the warning would actually harm a baby? If Dean said the hospital was to close down, or if jobs were to be lost?'

'Joe? I don't think so. Or do you mean Conor?' Grace attempted a smile and a shrug. Her quick look to Noah sent a wave of nausea through me. Not pity, I thought. Fear. For me and my child. Like she had feared for her own child all those years ago, even if she had denied it. The tightness in her smile made her look older. 'I'm sure there's nothing to worry about, Issy. Just be careful who you trust.'

She immediately changed the subject back to the upcoming fete and commenced a barrage of instructions: quilt-making, baking and what to volunteer for on the day of the fete. 'It's huge, everyone will be there, from miles around. You'll see the better side of Riley.'

It wasn't the better side of Riley I was left thinking about. I felt more uneasy than before—but whatever was behind it seemed to skid away from my thoughts every time I got close to it—a portent as ephemeral as the barking that kept starting up every evening in the trees beyond my veranda.

My meeting with Chris McCormack was scheduled for late morning. I had planned to have lunch with Dean afterwards but that was before we'd stopped talking. After Grace left, I thought briefly about cancelling but her departure made me feel the isolation intensely. Besides, it was time to fix things with Dean. I knew that he wanted to protect me and, remembering the state I had been in after Noah nearly died, I understood why he felt that way. It was up to me to show him I was better. I packed Noah up and put him in the car.

The huge grey kangaroo—the one who watched me most nights—appeared from the scrub to the left of me and watched us leave.

'I was about to give up on you,' Chris said with a smile. 'Want to join me for a bite to eat?'

I told Chris I was meeting Dean at one—I'd texted him to confirm when I got to town and he'd sent back a thumbs-up. And a smile emoji.

'Why don't we head there, then?' said Chris. 'I'll eat, and you'll get the insider knowledge on the lunch special.'

I would have preferred Dean, if he did turn up, not to

see me looking social with a man. Since his brother's wife had been caught *in flagrante* with another footballer, and a media frenzy and a messy divorce ensued, Dean was touchy about other men around me. Dean still couldn't make sense of why anyone would cheat on his brother, although, since I'd got to know Kieran, it seemed obvious enough to me.

Brian nodded. 'Morning docs.' I settled Noah into the playpen and took the table next to it while Chris ordered his lunch at the bar.

'Hope things have been a bit easier for you since we last met,' he said. For a moment I thought he knew about what had happened to Noah—but it was the heckler, Conor Rearden, he was referring to.

'I was just getting the flak from Dean's work.' I paused before adding, 'Whose idea was the postnatal group?' Dean had said Chris was on the hospital board; chances were he'd know where the push had come from, and whether it had been a sweetener to encourage Dean to come. No one else in his company had put their hand up.

'Mine.' Chris saw my surprise. 'When we heard Dean's wife and young child were coming I asked about you. When they said you were a psychologist, it seemed perfect to me.'

'Why?'

'You don't think they need help?' Chris laughed. He regarded me with amusement. I felt I could read his thoughts: *babe in the woods.* 'The town is spooked.'

'By what, that warning letter?'

Chris rubbed his chin. 'Hard to say,' he finally said. 'There's a scar from what happened years ago. Teagan being pregnant has kind of brought that back. She's certainly unsettled, but...I think women with young children are as well, generally. It doesn't take much. And anxiety and depression are so common after a baby.'

The sense I had had about my group hadn't been baseless then. Chris felt it too. 'Did Teagan's mother have postpartum psychosis?'

'Before my time,' said Chris, pouring me some water. 'Most people think she killed the baby. Zahra's husband, Massoud, was looking after Teagan, then there were some... issues. But she's only seen me twice, briefly, since. Haven't looked into her old notes.'

'Let me know if there's anything important. Does she talk about her past?'

'She's trying to look forward rather than back.'

'She off drugs?'

'Says so, and I believe her. She's focused on doing the right thing for this baby, being everything her mother wasn't able to be.'

'How about the baby's father?'

'Jed? He lives in Dubbo. I think his heart's in the right place, but he may still be using.'

So the drugs she'd tried to get from Zahra's husband probably were for him.

'Zahra is the other woman worrying me.'

Chris nodded. 'I'm keeping a close eye on her; this has been tough on her...and Massoud. It's been hard enough for them to be accepted here without this.'

I raised an eyebrow and he shrugged.

'The usual round of rumours. That they were suicide bombers or a terror cell for ISIS or whatever.'

I laughed, though it was a long way from funny. 'Right. Twin towers one day, Riley the next.'

Chris shrugged again. 'They don't trust easily here— hell, I'm still an outsider because I'm from Dubbo.'

'Zahra didn't make it to the last group so I did a home visit. Her mother thinks she isn't taking her medication, and I'm worried she's a risk to herself.'

Chris waited while the waitress put a burger in front of him, a coffee for me. He continued, more softly, though there was no one in earshot. 'I don't want to have to send her back to Sydney, but I will if it keeps her safe.'

I sipped my coffee. 'When did she stop seeing patients?'

If Chris thought it was a strange question he didn't show it. 'Late in the pregnancy—she was perfectly well until she went into labour. She's a hard worker, smart; and classy.'

So it was possible that she'd read my file. That she'd known about Noah's accident. And if she'd been seeing patients, perhaps one of them had told her something related to the Moretti kidnapping that had fed a later delusion. Just as she'd seen my history and blurred the boundaries, so might she have with some of her other patients.

'Do you know if Zahra was the GP for any of the women in the group, or their families?' I was thinking primarily of Joe Moretti.

Chris frowned. 'Why?'

'Something someone said has got her worried. I even wondered if she could have written the letter to the police.'

Chris's expression suggested he didn't think much of the idea. 'She wouldn't have seen Sophie, who sees Sydney specialists. Kate hardly goes to the doctor at all—I know Yvonne asked her to see Massoud but my secretary hasn't been able to convince her it's a good idea. Róisín maybe? She won't see a male doctor; she used to go to Dubbo when she was pregnant. Doubt her dad's seen a doctor since he was a baby, but I see most of the rest of the Rearden clan. I told you Teagan was seeing Massoud before me. And I see her dad.'

It sounded like neither of the Morettis had spoken to Zahra. Massoud surely wouldn't say anything to her unless it offered reassurance.

'Okay, your turn then. You said you had some ideas for me?'

'How are you with cognitive assessments? Not postpartum. We have a whole wing of oldies in the hospital and I imagine your husband is going to suggest they're staying too long.'

I didn't detect any bitterness, but I did think about the enemies Dean was making.

'Sure. I can do cognitive assessments.'

'It'd make my job a whole lot easier—and the hospital will be happy to pay, I think. Your appointment is through them already, so it should be straightforward.'

'As long as I can organise a sitter.'

'Great—let me know.' Chris looked pleased; I hoped I'd be able to justify his optimism.

'Country work suits you?' I said, thinking how relaxed he was.

'Definitely.' Chris looked at me as he mopped sauce off his chin. 'Tough at times, but the people need me, and I like that. It's why I stay. Even the parochialism…if you win their trust, they'll stand right behind you.' He winked. 'Give the place a chance, you might even stay yourself.'

'You reckon?' I said. I was counting down the days to our return to Melbourne for Christmas, and hoping I wouldn't need to come back afterwards. If Dean hadn't threatened me I would already be gone.

'A vibe I get.' This smile was more schoolboy grin. 'Patients here aren't the worried well. They have real problems, and they face them in such a way you can't help admiring them. Even Conor Rearden—I think he's wrong a lot of the time, but he has a vision. And he's a tough bastard.'

'I think you must be tough, too,' I said.

'More like stupid. Standing against Gordon Barclay's son.'

It wasn't what I meant, but I let him talk.

'I've been involved with Gordon and the party since I came here—not necessarily because I agree with them on everything, but the country needs a voice, and I'm not one to sit on my butt and complain—I want to do something active. Gordon and I often don't see eye to eye. I knew he wanted to drag Lachlan in, even though he knew I was running for preselection. Gordon thought I would see reason and drop out.'

'That's what democracy's all about, isn't it?'

'Yeah, but last time anyone opposed Gordon politically, their baby got killed.' Chris put his hand on my arm briefly. 'Sorry, I'm joking. Bad joke. But people talk about it seriously. Joe Moretti was an independent candidate when Gordon first stood.' This was the story Sophie and Grace had told me.

'Was Conor Rearden a suspect?'

'You've heard the theory that Gordon paid him to kidnap the baby?' Chris shook his head with an incredulous look. 'Living in small towns can be like a game of Chinese whispers. I can't blame the police for not taking that one seriously.' He grinned. 'Mind you, I wouldn't put it past Gordon to pay Conor under the counter to get something he wanted.'

'So some people do think Conor killed the child?'

'The theory—the one that involves Conor—says he was paid to kidnap the baby, which then died accidentally; they'd always intended to give him back. Joe didn't believe it, not at the time. Since then there's been bad blood and he says he'd like to see Gordon charged, but I don't think he really believes that's likely.'

'Actually,' I said, 'I wasn't thinking of politics. When I said you must be tough? It was about you saying you lost your wife.'

'Ah.' His expression softened. 'Yeah, it was hard. But these folks were sensational. Brought me enough casseroles to last a year. I didn't have the heart to tell them that I was the one who cooked; Evie couldn't boil eggs without them cracking and leaving a trail of white in the pot.'

'What happened?'

He looked down. Then he smiled. 'I don't talk about her much, and she deserves to be remembered. Hard when there's nothing left behind.'

'You don't have children?'

'No. Well, we'd been trying, and she was finally pregnant when she died. Subarachnoid haemorrhage. Bled into her brain.'

'Oh, God.'

'Only blessing was that it was quick—and too early for the baby to be viable. She'd have hated for either of them to survive and be...not been the way she wanted.'

'Could she...Was living so far away...?'

'You mean, would she have survived if I'd listened when she rang and said she had a headache, not just told her to take some paracetamol and lie down? Evie who never complained about anything? If we'd lived in Sydney and I'd taken her to emergency?'

I put my hand on his arm. My story of self-blame at least had a happy ending.

'I'll never know. I just tell myself we had a great life—or part of a life—and I'm trying to have one without her now.' He sounded like someone trying to convince himself he was okay.

'Hope you're not chatting up my wife, Doctor McCormack.'

Dean was standing behind me. It was his joking-not-joking voice. I felt myself stiffen as I withdrew my hand. I saw a question in Chris's glance at me, before he leaned back in his chair and smiled easily at my husband.

'I make it a rule,' Chris said, 'never to chat up an attractive married woman while I'm eating a hamburger— and she's waiting for her husband. It's good, by the way, the hamburger. I can recommend it.'

Dean plucked Noah out of the pen and held him in his arms.

'Chris was giving some background on my patients,' I said, trying to sound normal. 'And he's found me some work.'

'Great.' Dean was trying at least. 'Have you ordered?'

I hadn't, and by the time we did, Chris had finished eating and excused himself.

'So, what do you think about me working at the hospital?'

'Great idea. You'll enjoy it.' Dean looked at me carefully. 'Won't you?'

Yes, I would. But I could see Dean thought my agreement meant the argument was over and everything would be fine.

I checked the post-office box on the way to the next group: no faecal messages. This time someone had poured in a jar of treacle. Three days' mail would need to be opened carefully and messily. I blinked back tears, not sure if I was more unnerved or annoyed, and stormed inside. 'This,' I declared, 'has to stop.'

The postmaster followed me to see what the fuss was. 'Kids.'

'I don't care if it's bloody Martians,' I said. 'My mail's been tampered with and *you* are the one with the key.'

He looked alarmed. 'Key's there,' he said, pointing to a hook on the inside of the main door.

I took it off and thrust it at him. 'Find somewhere more secure.'

Maybe it was kids—it could have been anyone. There was no name on our box. Had someone been watching me? It was hard not to keep looking over my shoulder.

Yvonne had arrived at the health centre early. She'd taken the only shady parking spot—and today was already the hottest since I'd been in Riley. At least there was time to pick her brains before Róisín turned up. These women were her patients, and she'd lived here all her life.

She was still regarding me with a certain scepticism, but if I hadn't won her heart, Noah had.

'How's the little man going?' she asked him with a beam. He still had chocolate froth on his lips from our breakfast in the Railway Café.

'I'm going to be three,' he told her as he went to the toys that he was now familiar with, but not yet bored by.

'Can you tell me more about these women?' I asked as Yvonne jiggled a teabag and I took a slug from my water bottle. The air conditioner was off. The controller was now in place, but I had yet to see it operating.

'Most of the families here are battlers,' said Yvonne. 'Life out here...even if you're a townie, it isn't easy. But it's like a family, with all the bickering and alliances: at the end of the day, they'll cover each other's backs. Riley is where their loyalty lies.'

I thought this a rather idealised view, but then I was worse than a townie: I was an out-of-towner, a city girl.

'I sensed tension with Teagan,' I said. 'Maybe because of the past, what happened to Joshua and her mother.'

'You mean the kidnapping, or because they're Aboriginal?' Yvonne shrugged. 'Everyone tiptoes around it, but Donna and her family were dysfunctional, if you know what I mean.'

I looked at Yvonne; thought about letting it go, then thought about Olivia Doyle tormenting me. How no one stood up for me.

'No, actually. I don't.'

Yvonne looked at me. 'You live in the city. You wouldn't understand what it's like.'

I took a breath. 'You're right. *We* can't possibly

understand what it's like, can we?'

Yvonne looked at me, hard. Then she put her teabag in the bin and came and sat next to me. 'It was a tough time for all of us old enough to remember. I don't mean tough like it was for Donna and Joe...but we cared.' She made sure I looked at her, that I understood. 'I worked midwifery back then, so even though it was my day off, I was right at the coalface for the aftermath.'

'You looked after Donna when she went home?' I asked.

'Yes. She went home that day, but someone needed to do a home visit, help her with the breastmilk. She had her mob...but because she'd married Joe she wasn't living in the west of Riley with them. And her mother was up north.'

I thought of how hard it would be. Engorged breasts, bra cups packed with cabbage leaves...no baby to provide the milk to.

'I heard that maybe she had postpartum psychosis?'

'Nonsense,' she said firmly. Her lips pursed. 'People wanted to believe that. Easier that she was mad than someone else out there was bad, and might do it again.' She shook her head. 'That woman was as sane as you and me. Grieving, distressed. Drinking, later on, so she could sleep and not have to think about it. And who'd blame her?'

Donna Moretti would have been distressed whether or not she was the one who'd killed the child.

'Her story never changed. She put her baby down to sleep in the nursery. She didn't go back to check him after Joe went to take her stuff to the car because she was too upset. They'd had a row, and she didn't want the baby to pick up on her...being pissed off at his father. She wanted to calm down first. So Joe never saw him that day. And she was pissed off big time with the police taking the dogs to check her house out—thought they were wasting valuable time. She was still certain they'd find him alive.'

Didn't want the baby to pick up on her being pissed off. Angry at the police wasting time. The details had a ring of truth.

'How about after Teagan was born?' I asked. 'Was she depressed then?'

'I still feel bad about that. We should have seen it coming. Now? Yes, I think Donna was depressed. Anxious through the pregnancy and worse in the hospital, as you can imagine. But she didn't ask for help, and we thought once she got home, she'd settle. I don't think she'd thought beyond that first day. The reality of a baby overwhelmed her. No close family around. I think she was ashamed she was struggling—like why should she be, now she had a healthy baby?'

I now had three different versions of what had happened twenty-five years ago, all from people who had been close to the scene. Jeannie thought Donna had dropped Joshua and Joe helped hide the body. Grace thought Donna was mentally ill and Joe had covered up because of stigma. In Yvonne's version, Donna was completely innocent.

Was any one more plausible than the others? The simplest explanation was that Donna had suffered episodes of mental illness after the birth of both babies that played a part in both deaths; Joe probably had hidden the child's body. That gave him inside knowledge, but it didn't explain why he would send a warning to the police twenty-five years later.

Róisín settled her daughter in the nursery with Yvonne and Noah before coming into the kitchen, where I was waiting for our pre-group appointment. She was in a funereal black top over leggings, but there was a hint of make-up. With or without, she was pretty; she clearly kept her Irish complexion out of the Aussie sunshine. But she looked guarded.

I smiled and started on a safe topic. 'Bella is such a bright little girl. She seems very social.'

'Oh, um, yes, she is, isn't she? My grandmother used to say that about me.' There was a little of the uncertainty in Róisín's eyes that I saw in her daughter's. A fear of the world and what it might do to them. Today her hair wasn't tied back, and the streaks of grey were more noticeable.

'Your grandmother, not your mother?'

'Her too. Just, I was the eldest of six girls and I reckon Ma gets us mixed up. My grandmother brought me up as much as my mother did; all lived together, way out of town. My parents still rattle around there. My grandmother died when I was ten, and after that I helped with the young ones.'

As she talked about her childhood, it was clear that there hadn't been much time for Róisín—her mother cleaned to bring in some extra cash, and when her younger sisters were at school she had ended up helping with that too. Her father had worked long hours, both at his paid job in hospital maintenance and for the union. 'He had a temper. No one messed with him.' She still sounded scared.

'The only good thing, really good thing, I remember,' Róisín told me, 'was a book I was given by my grandma. No one else liked reading, and she told me I would be the smart one if I did. She was right—I was the only one that went to university.'

'What was the book?'

'Grimm's fairy tales. An old hardback copy.' Róisín forced a smile. 'I can still recite some passages, though I'm not sure I'd want to for Bella—they really are grim. But I loved them.' Her expression softened. For a moment I could see the child huddled under the blankets, lost in a world of magic.

I was starting to make some sense of Róisín. She had been neglected emotionally. When still a girl she had assumed a parenting role and had developed a prickly exterior to protect her inner child. It didn't mean she didn't want connection—she just wasn't very good at it. The fairy-tale book that had been her lifesaver as a child had perhaps been read too literally. The world was full of evil, there were no handsome princes and no one was good enough. Fairy tales were not just gruesome, they were black and white; one-dimensional. Her family cemented this view for her.

'Do you remember the kidnapping?' I asked. Róisín had been fifteen at the time. She was the only one in the group old enough to have been directly affected.

'It was horrible. Everyone seemed...excited by it. I spent most of my time avoiding the television crews.'

'A tough time.'

'I mean, how does it happen that a baby gets stolen? Right out of a nursery?' said Róisín. 'In a town this size it's probably someone you know. And it wasn't as if the police had a clue. They used it as an excuse to harass my father: it was all political.'

'I guess they were just trying to cover every possibility,' I said. 'Do you think it impacted on you? Now, I mean— made you more anxious as a mother?'

Róisín shrugged. 'I've *always* been anxious, Isabel. At the time everyone thought Donna did it and Joe knew. But...' She bit her lip. Wondering whether she should gossip? Or whether I'd believe her? 'The cops found porn magazines. *Kiddie* porn.'

I tried not to react, but Zahra's comments popped into my head—that Teagan's father shouldn't be helping her. Was this what Zahra had heard?

'Do you worry about Bella?'

'Always.' Róisín sighed. 'Bella is the centre of my life—I hate having her out of my sight. One of my sisters looks after her while I'm at work and I don't like that either, but at least she's with family. I know Bella has to make friends, but...'

'Do you worry about other things?'

'I worry about my work. I'm in nursing admin, so the staff come to ask what's going on. This whole hospital review—we're under a lot of stress. No one wants the hospital closed. Al, my partner, barely covers costs at the newsagents. He's not a good businessman.' She bit her lip. 'And when you think you know something...'

I waited.

'It's really hard,' Róisín said. 'I'm the union rep. I don't want anyone losing their job. But...things in the hospital kitchen...well they might be not exactly the way they should be. There's an issue with the contracts—I don't think they even got shown to the board.'

Nothing to do with the warning to police. This was Dean's job: he was a whiz at chasing money trails, but people like Róisín keeping secrets made his job a lot harder. And longer.

'I mean, too often the wrong person gets sacked and the real villain, the deputy in this case, gets off scot free.'

Villain. Too many Grimm's tales too young.

'Does Bella's father help out?' I asked after she told me she and Al had known each other since schooldays. They'd reconnected after she returned to Riley from working in Sydney.

Róisín nodded. 'He gets Bella's breakfast before he goes to work, dinner when he gets home. Gives her a bath, puts her to bed. Takes her to my sister's when I'm working.'

I was struggling to make sense of this. 'What do *you* do for her then?'

'Isabel, I love her. That's what I do. Love her more than life itself. It took six cycles on IVF. She's totally cherished.' Róisín drew Bella to her; the child looked dubiously up at me. More than Sophie's little boy, she seemed to have 'caught' some of her mother's anxiety.

'It seems...there's something paralysing for you about being a mother.'

'Hah. Life. It's not motherhood that paralyses me, Isabel. It's life'.

Róisín told me the story. Some of it, anyway. Before Bella, she was in Sydney working as a nurse. None of her siblings had made it to university but as well as her nursing degree she had a master's in health informatics. There was an affair with a doctor that ended badly; I guessed there was a termination, but she was not going to go there; problems with bullying in the workplace. She'd returned to hide in Riley nearly a decade ago.

'There's no fairness, is there?' Róisín concluded. 'People...There's no goodness in them.'

For a moment I was sucked into her bleak world. I wondered how long before Bella felt the same.

'Thinking...feeling that...must make it pretty hard to be Bella's mother.'

'That's why I'm at this group,' said Róisín. 'I want her to keep being like she is now. Happy, innocent. I don't want her to be...I want her to have things I didn't.'

'I guess that's what all good mothers want,' I said. 'But

it's about giving them the tools to deal with the world as it is, as well as trying to shape the world around them.'

A few days later Dean mentioned the kickbacks and the catering problem to me, complaining that it was hard to work out who was responsible for what. Not the chief caterer, if Róisín was to be believed. I thought about Róisín's story and how I couldn't breathe a word of it. How if I were to tell him that it might hurry things up so I could be home by Christmas.

Group three was about anxiety management. I knew how to teach people to manage their anxiety, even if I couldn't always manage my own; I'd been helping my mother with hers for years.

It was the symptom common to the group. Sophie was anxious about not being good enough. Róisín was anxious about Bella: she was probably worrying about her baby's future employment prospects, if not her retirement plan. Zahra's anxiety was in part a response to the warning the police had received, and in part the resolution of an illness that she was struggling to come to terms with. Kate appeared to fear anyone getting close, and Teagan's anxiety was mixed up with her childhood and with who she was. Her fears probably included everything from getting through an hour alone without getting back on the drugs to turning out to be like her mother—as well as a fear that the same thing might happen to her baby as happened to Joshua. Worrying about your baby was common; Teagan had more reason than most.

After tea and a slice of Róisín's cake—a manufactured sponge with bright white artificial cream—we began with a visualisation exercise. The aircon, which had finally been turned on, had to be switched off. It was too noisy for anyone to hear me, and shouting wouldn't have worked well for the exercise. I had them lying on warm sand, hearing a distant seagull call, gentle waves coming in and out, smelling the salt in the air. Then I asked them to concentrate on each part of their body starting with their toes, letting go of tightness in each muscle in turn—all to calming music. It would have worked better without the shrieks, banging and occasional cries from the children in the next room.

When I broke the spell and returned them to the main meeting room, they were all smiling: in a better space for the moment at least. Even Kate had allowed herself to go with the flow. Teagan said she'd been lying by the river and the seagulls were cockatoos. Despite her mother's story, the river didn't appear to hold any trepidation for her.

'Okay, now I want you to give me a list of any triggers you can think of, things that might set off that tight feeling in the stomach, the racing heart, the feeling of doom?'

'Cops knocking on the door.' That was Teagan; I was pretty sure she winked at Kate.

'Which could mean a whole range of things,' I said. 'Bad news, searching the house for contraband...or just looking for witnesses to a car getting dinged, right?'

'Yeah, right.'

'If Bella's sick.' Róisín—predictably.

Sophie nodded sympathetically. 'Stupid, but if I'm late for an appointment.'

'Guy with a gun on me,' said Kate, arms crossed.

'Being alone,' Zahra said softly. She still looked flat, but not quite as distracted and inward-focused as the previous week. There was a general murmur of support. I wasn't sure if it was because she was an immigrant, or because of her status as a doctor—and doctor's wife—or the severity of the psychosis, but I had a sense the women tiptoed around her. Even Teagan. Sophie was constantly asking her if she needed anything, and Róisín volunteered how well little Raha was looking. There was gratitude in Zahra's eyes for the mention of her daughter's progress.

The list of anxiety triggers kept growing: not being able to pay bills, not getting enough sleep, another pregnancy, not being able to settle their child. They could all identify with the anxieties common to motherhood, and there was palpable relief that they weren't alone.

'Something going wrong with the baby. When it's born, you know?' Teagan said.

'So,' I asked, 'what are we thinking when these things set off our anxiety? Teagan, when you worry something might be wrong, are you worried about something general or specific?'

'That the baby might die. I've seen the ultrasound, so I know Indiana's okay in there. Growing like she should.' She pointed to her bowling ball. 'But I'm afraid she'll die. Like last time.'

The last time? She was the youngest in the group—yet this wasn't her first pregnancy. Sophie's expression said *irresponsible single mother*. Teagan fortunately didn't see it.

'I'm sorry to hear about your first pregnancy loss, Teagan,' I said. 'It certainly gives you a reason for that trigger. If we want to control our anxiety, we need to look at how realistic it is. Has your doctor told you how likely that is to happen a second time?'

'Nothing was wrong with me then or now. They'll watch me real close, though. Booked me in for a caesarean 'cause the placenta's in the wrong place to have her normally.' Her look suggested that this was proof that nothing went smoothly for her and she really did have something to worry about.

'So, see you're already doing it—putting the trigger into perspective rather than catastrophising. There's a problem, but there's also a solution that will help keep her safe.'

'Being cut open sounds like a catastrophe to me. They reckoned I could be awake for it.' Teagan grinned. 'I said no fucking way, I'll take a good dose of that morphine and wake up after it's all over.'

I got them to all write down one anxiety they had, and then to see if they could think of rational answers that put their worry into the context of the likelihood of the risk occurring.

Róisín was going to find it hard to get past step one in managing anxiety.

'Bella might get rejected from school because she isn't vaccinated.' It was an anxiety she wouldn't need to confront for a few years or not at all if she went the homeschool route.

'So get her vaccinated,' said Kate.

'I know you all think that,' said Róisín, avoiding looking at anyone, 'and I don't care. I'm not getting sucked in by big pharma. They don't publish what they don't want us to see.'

'Jesus. Conspiracy theories, now.' Kate shook her head.

'Perhaps you should meet some polio victims,' said Zahra, as Sophie muttered darkly about what would happen if Tom got measles.

Mostly the mothers until now had seemed supportive of Róisín—but anything related to their children instantly trumped the bonds of the sisterhood.

'I guess this brings up a bigger issue, doesn't it?' I said. 'We all want what's best for our children, but what if we have different ideas from each other—the school, our community—about what best is?'

This at least broadened the discussion to controlled crying, breast versus bottle and how much to spend on children's birthday parties. Challenging, but by the time we finished they didn't seem to want to kill each other.

As they left, Zahra pulled me aside.

'I was told something about Teagan, remember? Something worrying...I said this to you?'

I nodded.

'It is about her pregnancy.'

I frowned.

'Perhaps not this one—but the earlier one.' Zahra shook her head and sighed. 'Maybe both...I am not sure.'

'Is this...something you were told, Zahra? Who by?'

'I...am not sure. The shock treatment affected my memory.'

'Could it be...part of your mind playing tricks?' Remnants of her psychosis—or its return.

Zahra met my eyes. I saw in hers the fear that I was right.

I watched her leave: head down, no small talk with the others. Zahra's psychosis could be behind her concerns about Teagan, but it added to my sense of unease. Even if the police warning seemed to be targeting Dean, Noah and me, there was no going past the fact that the baby killer was linked to the Morettis. I felt for Zahra—her isolation was not so different from my own. Even though I knew a lot about these women I was on the outer—therapist rather than friend. She had been their doctor.

I felt more anxious than when I had started.

Teagan was the last woman to have an individual interview. She was wearing another home-designed T-shirt, this one longer, over shorts. It was Disney themed— all villains. It made me think of Róisín and her morbid fairy tales; maybe Teagan could make her a matching shirt, but with heroes and heroines.

She made herself comfortable in a beanbag. 'Might need a crane to hoist me outta here.'

'You seem to have had a pretty eventful twenty-three years. Do you want to take me through it?'

'Has been, hasn't it? Right now, I seem to be, like, in the middle of it all for no good reason. Where do you want me to start?'

'Far back as you can go.'

'My mum? She's not so far back, not really. Been in my dreams ever since I was little.' Teagan paused and checked out my reaction. 'Always the same. She's smiling, but her eyes are sad.'

'Is it a good dream?' I said.

'Yeah. It's not as good as having her with me, but it helps. I go down to the river sometimes too. There's a real sense of her there. I know she's protecting me, like she doesn't want anything bad to happen to me, like what happened to her. It's our place, I guess. We were the first people to walk by the river and I reckon she's at peace there.'

This was why Teagan had gone to the river in the relaxation exercise, rather than the ocean. She went on: 'My auntie's great. She's told me all about our mob. And I've got people here in Riley. Auntie Jaz comes back when she can but she's up north now, looking after my nan. That's where my mum went after...Josh died.'

I had assumed—I suppose because it fitted with Grace's theory of postpartum psychosis—that Donna had been admitted to a psych ward in that period of lost time. But she had gone to her family. Maybe that was what Teagan needed, too: to be around women who knew what being a mother was about. Or perhaps the crowd I had seen her with gave her a strong enough sense of place. Having a child that belonged might help even more.

'Dad brought me up. He drank, and he got angry—at anyone and everyone.'

'Including at you?'

'Yeah. He had a real good backhander; lucky he never killed me.' She laughed. 'Think I must have nine lives or something. Same when I got into fights at school. Just kept bouncing back.'

'Scary, though?'

'Nah, there was nothing in it. He never hurt me; I was too quick.'

I wondered how much she was exaggerating...or covering up.

'How was school?'

'Better than home, at least when I was little. Didn't even

114

know we were blackfellas until Grade Two and someone called my mother a drunk Abo. Dad was furious. And sad.' She saw my expression. 'Not just about the shitheads and what they said, but 'cause he hadn't kept us in touch with Mum's mob. Started hanging out with them after that. And he took me up to Cairns for a holiday.' Teagan's eyes lit up, her whole body softened. 'It was great. Felt like I'd known them all my life.'

'How about in high school?'

Teagan shrugged. 'Wasn't really much for doing as I was told. Teachers really pissed me off. I was too white for the blackfellas and too black for the whiteys. They'd call me out to "special" Indigenous meetings and everyone'd be looking at me, snickering. "Going walkabout are you?" or "It's just the quarter of you that's going there, you can leave the other three-quarters behind."' She thought for a second. 'Art was good. I got the school prize for my pictures. But even then it was like, "you can thank the white part for that, otherwise you'd just be doing dot paintings".'

'When did you finish school?'

'Year Nine. Got a job in the supermarket, then Supré in Dubbo and decided I wanted to work in fashion. Go figure. Went to Sydney to stay with my auntie, studied to get the credits I needed.'

'What happened?'

'Shit happened, like it usually does. Found out I was pregnant.' Teagan picked at her nails. 'He didn't want it— we weren't like together or anything.'

Chris's referral letter about Teagan made no mention of the earlier pregnancy—because it had happened in Sydney.

'I didn't have an abortion, okay?' Teagan screwed her face up. 'Lost him halfway through. I don't want to talk about it.'

'Okay. Do you go to Sydney much now?'

'Nah, like, I don't know anyone there I want to see and Dad hates it.'

'You plan to stay locally after the baby?'

'Yeah. This is where my mob came from. It feels...I feel like I belong here. Reckon Auntie Jaz and my cousins'll be back, too. They can't go long without visiting. This area's ours, you know?'

Did I know? No, not really.

'Dad'll take us to my Italian grandma's after Christmas; he likes to see them every few months.'

'After the miscarriage. What happened next?'

'I lost it, I guess. Like for a year or two. Took anything I could get my hands on. Tried to get clean a couple of times but it wasn't easy—didn't know anyone 'cept other druggies. Auntie Jaz would have kept me, but I was too... shamed. Ended up running out of money and no choice but to come back here, about five years ago. I'm clean now, though. Ever since I found out I was pregnant this time. Not even weed.'

She sounded fierce, daring me to disbelieve her.

'I really want this kid, even if no one else does. I want to give it what my mother was never able to give me, you know?'

This time I did know. I also knew it wasn't easy when you didn't have a strong role model or much support.

'The baby's father?'

'Jed's okay. We're sorting out where we'll live. Like together, with Indiana, but it's tough 'cause he doesn't have a regular job.' She relaxed a little. 'I've been doing a correspondence course so I can look after my baby. Still want to be in fashion someday.'

Teagan nodded, smiling as she pictured her idealised family. She wouldn't be the first client I'd seen who held on to a fantasy. Wasn't I guilty of that too?

'Teagan, you were in the pub the other night. What do you make of that warning to the police?'

'Pissed me right off, some arsehole bringing up all that shit again. Bad enough I had to live my whole childhood with it. Indiana—do you like what I'm gonna call her?—doesn't need to grow up with it.'

'Indiana's a lovely name. Would you like to find out who killed your brother?'

'Once I would've, sure. Now I just want to get on with my life. The dreams I have with Mum? She isn't carrying him, and I figure it's 'cause she doesn't want me to worry. He's her responsibility, like Indiana will be mine.'

She sounded genuine, but her affect wasn't exactly stable. What she meant and felt now, she might not mean and feel tomorrow.

'I'm so scared I'm gonna be crap at this, but Dad says I'll be a great mum, and I'm gonna try. I mean, I haven't succeeded in anything before, but this...I have to.'

She did look scared, younger than her years. 'You don't think,' she said suddenly, 'that like, some things are doomed? Like the baby died because I really would have been crap?'

'No, Teagan, it seems to me you're doing fine on that front. What does your dad think about the warning?'

This got a reaction. She started rubbing her arm, pinching her skin. I could see old scars, but no recent track marks.

'Went a bit mental. Hadn't seen him like that for years— went on a bender.' She shrugged. 'He hates being reminded.

When I was about five, he went through the house and burned every photo of Mum. I've only got one of her and me because my auntie had it.' She looked glum. 'Maybe I could go and live in Cairns with Auntie Jaz, after the baby...I worry the baby killer might get her.'

It sounded like the letter to police had been a pretty big shock to Joe. That didn't rule him out of complicity in Joshua's death, though.

'Who does he think warned the police, then?' I asked.

'Think? Doesn't have to think. He knows. Same person who got rid of my brother—Gordon fucking Barclay. Wanted my dad out of the election back then, and now he wants us out of town.'

'Why would he want you out of town?'

Teagan shrugged. 'In case we mess things up for little *Lachie*.' She was looking down but her eyes flashed up through her fringe. 'Dad's working for Doctor McCormack's campaign.'

'Teagan, is there something you know?' I was firmer than I had been. 'This isn't just about you and your family. That tip suggested...other babies might be at risk. And the threat was tied to the hospital. I don't see how that would be directed at you or your father.'

Teagan rubbed her arms again. 'I know this sounds weird, but I just *know*. After that meeting at the pub? My mum sat on the end of my bed. She didn't like, say anything, but she's scared for me. I knew when I woke up, it was the fucking Barclays that she was trying to warn me about.' She shuddered. 'She's gonna try and protect me...but I'm afraid something's gonna go wrong.'

She was still only thirty-three weeks. Seven more weeks for her anxiety to ramp up. I didn't quite know what to make of the dreams. I hoped it wasn't incipient psychosis. She interpreted the images of her mother benignly but that could be because her mind didn't want to face up to something she knew deep down. Like it was her father that she should be afraid of.

I had to stay in town to see one of Chris McCormack's patients and Yvonne wasn't available to sit Noah. The car had been as hot as expected and he was beetroot by the time we got to the hospital, where he was reluctant to let me out of his sight and put a high-pitched scream into effect. It took an hour and, embarrassingly, ice-cream, before I could see the patient. She was an ex-nurse in her eighties whose memory loss was frustrating her. I managed to frustrate her further, and by the end I was feeling pretty useless as a psychologist as well as a mother.

'She doesn't have dementia, does she?' asked her daughter, who had been visiting. 'Dad died of dementia. I don't think I could bear it again.'

I had no reassurance to offer her.

I was ready to go home at five, but Dean told me apologetically that he was expecting a call at six-thirty. I could either wait or come back for him later. With Noah tired, dirty and irritable, neither option filled me with joy. We went to the small municipal park by the railway station where the heat was still fierce but there was shade at least, and I fed Noah stewed fruit and a milkshake for dinner.

A woman emerged from the Aboriginal Land Council—the one I had once thought might have been Teagan's mother, now dressed in blue rather than red, and again with matching glasses. She wandered over and offered me a cordial. It was cold and not too sweet and was as good as a small taste of heaven.

'Too bloody hot to be sitting in a park,' she said. Noah looked like he fully agreed. Her smile extended to the depths of her dark eyes. 'I'm Maggie. You know Teagan, right?'

I nodded. She knew exactly who I was.

'I'm born and bred Riley. That place'—Maggie's head indicated the Land Council office—'is pretty much my second home. You should come in some time. We've just extended and we're opening a drop-in centre. For our young people.' She looked at me and seemed to be making a decision whether to press on. 'Teagan…she's been judged all her life. Doesn't always do the right thing, but…' She hesitated. 'Don't go thinking she's stupid.'

I smiled. Seemed like Maggie was the leader of Team Teagan. 'I certainly won't make that mistake. She's obviously bright and talented.'

Maggie nodded. 'Some people underestimate what she's capable of. Don't do that, okay?' She didn't wait for an answer before she headed back indoors.

By seven, Dean still hadn't called. I strapped Noah into his pusher and started off down the street—hoping he wouldn't fall asleep, or he'd be impossible to put down when I finally got him home. The sky looked threatening, but I'd seen that before. Since we'd been in Riley the promise of a storm had not been delivered on.

On one of the lampposts on the edge of town, staring at me quizzically, perched a brown and white owl, maybe the same one we'd seen the first time we drove through Riley. He appeared to be frowning down at me. I thought of Teagan's dreams and my own sense of foreboding; the owl wasn't helping.

We turned and came back past the Riley Arms. As we passed the front bar, one of Gordon's posters, already ripped, was caught by a gust of wind and flew across the pusher. There was a noise behind me and I turned to see Joe Moretti stagger out the bar door. He had tripped on the step—but was also obviously drunk. As he steadied himself, he saw me; I turned quickly and kept walking.

'Hey. You. Yeah, you, I'm talking to you.'

I quickened my step. Even pushing Noah, I should be able to outwalk him, I thought, but I was wrong. He caught up and grabbed my arm, stubby nails digging in, his grip surprisingly strong.

I was worried I would start shaking, so I put one hand firmly on the pusher.

'Please let go. Now.'

I must have sounded firmer than I felt. He let go.

Standing there, he looked all burnt-out boxer: no heavyweight—too short and slight—but a good deal stronger than me. My heart was still racing as I squared my shoulders and took a deep breath.

'You should get out of Riley,' said Joe. Up close I could see the indentations in his bulbous red nose, and under a stubbled chin his parotid glands—like my father's—were squaring off his neck, blending it with his broad shoulders.

'Keep away from me and my son,' I said, taking a step backwards. There was no one around; above him a street sign shuddered in the gust of wind.

'You people need to keep your noses out of what doesn't

concern you,' Joe said, as if he hadn't heard me.

'I assure you I'll be getting out of this town just as soon as I can,' I said. I turned to walk away but he stepped in front of me. In front of the pusher, looking straight at Noah.

'It's not safe here,' he said. 'Already lost one baby, and I don't want anything happening to my grandkid 'cause things are being stirred up. Bad things sure to happen if you people keep—'

'Joe, that's the drink talking.'

Neither of us had noticed Chris come up behind me. The clinic was opposite. I yanked the pusher towards me and pulled back against the wall of the pub, grabbing Noah, who had started to whimper.

Chris put a hand gently on Joe's arm. 'I think you've had enough, mate. Time to go home.'

'She needs to know—'

'No, Joe, she doesn't. Now, are you going to be right to get home? Or do I need to call Sam?'

'Teagan's coming to get me. She's a good girl, you know.' He seemed to be talking to me rather than Chris. Joe shook his head wearily, looked at Chris, walked over to the corner street bench and slumped onto it.

'Are you okay?' Chris asked me, turning away so that Joe couldn't hear.

I nodded.

'Like a drink?'

Dean still hadn't called. I nodded again.

With Noah parked firmly in my line of sight in the pub playpen, I sat down and let Chris get me a glass of wine. My hand trembled as I took it.

'I don't think he meant any harm,' said Chris.

I knew he was trying to be reassuring, but I had no intention of putting my head in the sand and hoping bad things would go away. 'You don't think so—but you don't know. Someone in this town means to cause harm. Certainly psychologically, and maybe a lot more.'

Chris shifted awkwardly in his seat and took a sip of red. 'I've spoken to Zahra.'

I'd forgotten about sharing my suspicions that Zahra knew something she might have got from Joe. After what had just happened, I was even more inclined to believe that Joe was not only responsible for the warning but had covered up, or even caused, Joshua's death. As Grace had suggested, maybe he'd half-convinced himself someone else had done it. He'd been through a lot, and alcohol wouldn't have helped his reasoning.

'Look,' said Chris, 'I know Riley sometimes feel a bit incestuous...that is, too many people know each other's business. But I'm confident Zahra doesn't have any inside information about who wrote to the police. She's still a little paranoid, adds two and two and gets five. Teagan only saw her once, when Massoud was out on a home visit.'

Once might have been enough. 'What about Joe?'

I could see Chris was torn—this was confidential. I was treating Zahra and Teagan, but I had no clinical reason to ask about Joe.

'I've looked at Joe's notes. He's never been treated by Zahra, okay?'

It didn't stop me thinking that Joe could be involved. Grace had hinted that he might be dangerous. Teagan, for all her fantasies about how she wanted her life to be, had said there were times—including recently—when he hadn't been travelling well. Joe wasn't travelling well now. I couldn't discount the things he said when drunk. Alcohol decreased inhibitions, which meant he was saying what he wanted to say, whether it was wise to or not to do so. *Get out, stop messing in things* that didn't concern us. And *making things worse.*

'Is there anything in his medical notes,' I asked slowly, 'about what happened with Joshua?'

Chris wouldn't meet my eyes. He wasn't about to tell me even if there was. I took a different tack.

'If Zahra didn't write the warning to the police, who did?'

'No idea.'

I didn't believe him. He was hiding something, at any rate. I didn't feel like sitting and drinking wine with him anymore.

'I've got to go pick up Dean.'

'Wait.' Chris put his hand on my arm. 'I know you're worried, but I think you should leave it to the police.'

'The police? Because they're doing a whole heap—not.'

Chris glanced at Noah. 'Not that I want to see you go, but...Could you go back to Melbourne? No, no; I don't think you're in any danger. But for peace of mind?'

I smiled tightly, wishing it had been Dean who'd said it. 'I need to stay...with my husband. Not to be scared out of town. Is there something you know about Joe Moretti and just won't say?'

Chris hesitated. 'Nothing that's to do with this. Or at least nothing that would in any way mean he was dangerous...' He hesitated and added, 'To you.'

'Joe was pretty clear to me just before,' I said. 'Get out, you're making it worse, you're not safe. Someone delivered us crap—literally, an envelope full of dog excrement. And there was a hostile message on our car.'

Chris was silent. 'Maybe just…don't go walking alone.'

Walking alone I could avoid. I couldn't avoid simply *being* alone nearly as easily. No car, arse end of nowhere. I would have to drive into town every day and drop off and pick up Dean if I wanted a car—and I'd still be alone. Worse than alone, because I would have Noah to protect.

'Teagan talked about Joe going on benders, getting physical with her and her mum.'

Chris's look told me all I needed to know.

My phone chose that moment to ping. Finally. Dean was ready to be picked up. I turned, grabbed Noah and left without speaking.

But I spoke to Dean.

'You need to find out about Joe Moretti,' I said as soon as he was in the car.

'And hello to you too, darling.' He didn't look at me, turned and gave Noah a beam. 'G'day mate. Mother been driving you bonkers, has she?'

'Giddee mite,' Noah repeated with a giggle. My hands clenched on the steering wheel.

'Have you been drinking?'

'I had half a glass,' I said between gritted teeth. 'With Chris. Who saved me from being assaulted by Joe Moretti.'

Dean opened his mouth then closed it. 'Are you okay?'

He looked like he'd had a shit day, but I needed him to take me seriously.

'Joe warned me off. Said I needed to get out of town, that you were making things worse and Noah and I weren't safe. I think he wrote the note to the police, and put the stuff in our letter box to scare us off.'

Dean frowned. 'What's his motive?'

'I doubt he's rational. He drinks. He probably doesn't know what your review includes—but maybe he thinks it might look at what happened when his baby went missing. Maybe he's got a police record too.'

Dean brushed the hair off my cheek. 'I'll talk to the cops, okay?' I didn't think he believed me, but he was trying.

As I put Noah to bed, I promised my son I would find out, with or without help, just how dangerous Joe Moretti was and ensure Noah was safe. But as I looked out from the balcony to the plains that stretched to the horizon and beyond, I wondered if I had made a promise I couldn't keep.

I had a restless night, for all that I was exhausted. The distant barking came and went. A streak of moonlight flickered across the bed as the curtains shimmered and I saw any number of shapes move across the sheets. Just as I was dozing off, I heard noises in the distance and jerked awake, pulse racing. I lay waiting for the noise to come again, felt my stomach knot.

Were they gunshots? Roo shooters somewhere across the paddocks? I glanced at Dean, who didn't stir when I slipped out onto the veranda. I waited for half an hour, but there were only the sounds of the bush at night, even the sheep finally at rest. The air smelled crisp and clean, faint hints of eucalypt and something earthier.

I finally went back to bed and slept, but my dreams were of Joe Moretti floating in the river like Ophelia, an owl swooping overhead with piercing cries that echoed through my mind. When I woke, hyperventilating, it was an image of Teagan and her mother huddled together, crying, that was left to haunt me.

Sophie had brought a plate of cupcakes with Disney characters and some Mickey Mouse masks for the children, upstaging the pastries that Teagan had provided. Noah looked mystified and had no intention of letting Sophie put a mask on him. Go, Noah.

Kate had told Yvonne she wasn't coming—no explanation offered.

The session's theme was how the past might influence how we parent.

'What are some things you learned from your parents that you want to do yourself?' I asked, pen poised in front of the whiteboard.

'Everything.' Zahra might be the only one who could say this honestly.

'Encouragement,' said Sophie. I wrote it down as she added, 'to be whatever he wants to be.'

'Resilience,' said Zahra quietly. 'To never lose hope.'

'So how do we help our children gain resilience?'

'Love,' said Zahra.

'By example,' said Róisín.

'Sure. Good parents are role models—they aren't perfect,

and when they make mistakes, they fix them, and their child gets to see that.' I hoped Sophie was listening: Tom didn't need to be pushed to achieve in the way she had been.

There was a long silence. I had a feeling that when I reversed the question—things they wanted to do differently from their parents—they wouldn't be so reticent.

'Feeling safe,' Róisín finally said as I wrote it down. 'My parents were protective but...that could be scary, actually.' She shrugged. 'There were a lot of us.'

'I'm sure they did their best for you,' said Sophie.

'Really?' Róisín said. 'How would you know?'

'Oh, well, I meant...'

'I wasn't born into money. I used to help my mother clean houses—yours included. You probably never...' Róisín shut herself down. 'Sorry Sophie...Isabel. I'm not in a good place at the moment.'

Zahra got up and gave Róisín a hug. No one was more surprised than Róisín—but after hesitating she smiled and hugged Zahra back. Sophie offered them both a cupcake. Nine weeks probably wasn't going to be enough to change Róisín's ability to trust, but it was start.

I turned to Teagan. 'I know my mother loved me,' she said. 'But sometimes I wonder why she left me.'

'Her mind was not right,' said Zahra, before I could intervene. 'I know this, because I have been there.'

'She may have thought she was such a bad mother she was doing it to save you,' added Róisín.

'I can't imagine that she didn't love you,' Sophie said, with only the faintest hint of the difficulty she had accommodating someone she mostly disapproved of.

Teagan's eyes had filled with tears. I felt like going and hugging each woman in turn.

As I'd expected, the next question—'What don't you want to do that your parents did?'—was more productive. They didn't want their child to feel either unloved or unsafe, but none of them could quite work out how to balance the two messages.

I had them take a photo of the whiteboard to give them something to think about over the week, and felt like the session had gone okay. More than the previous week, I felt I had stayed on top of things. Which I never would have predicted, because I hadn't been able to stop thinking about Joe Moretti.

My next stop would be hospital medical records.

There's something about hospitals that makes me feel I don't belong; the whole emphasis on physical illness, the smells of disinfectant and empty corridors where everyone seems to know where they are going except me. Riley hospital was no different. Even though small by city standards, it was a rabbit warren of misplaced rooms, signs to places you didn't want to go and closed doors to the places you needed to be. I was careful to be on the lookout for Dean and Róisín but I'd forgotten Conor worked at the hospital; he was fixing a light in the corridor and made a point of watching me walk its length until I finally found the medical records office.

I'd been given a hospital badge and a password for the computer system—the clerk didn't question my right to be there. She gave me a seat at a corner screen and pulled up the record I'd asked for. 'You're lucky: all the old records have been scanned. This is the baby killer, right?'

'Her baby died,' I said firmly and focused on the screen. All of Donna's hospital records, including GP correspondence, and the coroner's report. Not the baby's report—hers. It had occurred to me that maybe it wasn't Joshua's death that Joe wanted to keep quiet. Was there something about *Donna's* death that he was worried might come out?

Noah wriggled in his pusher. No way was he going to sit through this. I hit *print* then checked for Joe's record— nothing. Ten minutes later I was leaving with a bag full of paperwork. Conor clocked me as I left; I resisted the urge to flip him the bird and wondered if this urge of rebellion was an improvement or a deterioration in my moral character. I was pretty sure what my mother would have said.

I drove back to our house, put Noah to bed for an afternoon nap, made myself a cup of tea and looked at the printouts. It hadn't seemed such a big thing flicking through a file at the hospital. Now, I no longer felt quite so certain of the ethics.

I reassured myself: Donna was dead and this was for my client, Teagan, who might be in danger. I spread the paper out, inexplicably thinking about guns. Male suicide rates were high in rural areas, and the favoured method was a firearm. Did Joe own one?

Prior to Joshua's birth, Donna had been admitted once, aged fifteen, for an appendectomy. Then a normal delivery, the nurse's notes barely legible. The doctor's scribbles were worse. Then there was a lot of...nothing. A summary that must have been written a lot later, on the same page with the admission notes. She was sent home with Temazepam and a few Valium. No antipsychotics that I could see, or the heavy sedation Grace had mentioned. No reference to a psychiatric admission.

Fast forward to Teagan's birth. Some careful notes; *postpartum loss* recorded under her risk factors. It referred, I assumed, to Joshua's death, but it could have been a bleed. The nurse had done a mental-state examination and noted *low risk* without elaborating. Donna was *quiet but loving towards her baby daughter.* I wished Teagan could see that. Then *discharged home with husband.*

After that there was only the coroner's report, which had been sent to the hospital and her doctor, Athol Broadbent.

I steeled myself to read it, skipped over the review of organs—all good condition given she was only thirty. There were cuts and bruises on her head, but the stated cause of death was drowning; she'd been alive when she'd entered the water. Alive but possibly unconscious; her blood alcohol had been 0.27. Death by misadventure: no suicide note. The location was noted to be where the body of Joshua had been found.

Racked by loss, by guilt about Joshua, visiting the site. Thinking she was not fit to be a mother to her new baby; that Teagan deserved better. Faulty thinking, I reminded myself, as guilt crept into the crevices of my own mind. You only had one biological mother. And statistically, your best chance of being loved unconditionally was by someone with a genetic link. Stepmothers undeniably got a bad rap in fairy tales, but there was some basis in fact. They tended to bring issues—baggage—that could create distance; then if they had a new baby there were torn loyalties. Although in Teagan's case there had been no stepmother, wicked or otherwise. Just a bereft and angry—and maybe guilty—father with a drinking problem.

I stared at the printout, looked over it again, resigned myself to finding nothing and packed up. Truth was, I didn't know what I was looking for. I had been sure this was what Joe was afraid I might see—but if it had been something obvious the coroner or Athol, as Donna's doctor, would have acted on it before. It had to be something that was only problematic when put together with something else: something Joe expected or thought I might know. From Teagan?

Noah woke and there was no chance to think about it further. But there was time for a drive before I picked up Dean. I wanted to see where Joshua had been found: where Donna had died.

The road didn't continue far along the river, but ended at a small park with picnic tables and benches. It was probably the highest point within a hundred or more kilometres, which still wasn't more than a slight rise. From the beer bottles on the ground and in the overflowing bin, I guessed this was the local teenagers' favourite site to hook up or do drugs. Or both.

I looked around. Listened. Thought of Chris suggesting I shouldn't go for walks alone—and how Dean had had a word with Sam Keller about Joe. There was no sign of life except for a magpie regarding me from a tree branch. I navigated the pusher around the litter and took the walking path that meandered along the ridge by the river, heading away from Riley. Fifteen minutes later it widened and split—I stuck to the river side, the trickle of water a few metres below.

I stopped, suddenly nervous. Had I heard something? I had a sense I was being watched.

You're being hysterical, I imagined Dean thinking.

Like my mother, I added to myself.

Ten minutes later the path stopped at another lookout. The foliage had thinned and I could see below. I shivered. A bit of water, and high enough to be dangerous to anyone who jumped or fell. There were a few large boulders and smaller rocks both in the water and on islands that separated different water courses that joined downstream. I felt certain it was here that Donna had died. It was a pretty enough place, but the drop from here was lethal. Right now it felt desolate.

Why would Joe bury Joshua's remains here? Was it just the first place he thought of, straight along the road from the hospital? I peered down, looking at the side. There were a few steep paths where people, kids, had most likely gone down to the river on their backsides.

In the bush behind me I heard a noise and whirled around. The undergrowth wasn't thick but there were bushes scattered among the gumtrees. It had sounded like a twig breaking. Like someone had stepped on it. My skin prickled. I yelled, 'My husband knows I'm here.'

'Dadda,' Noah added helpfully.

Silence. Then a rustling in the bush and a moment later a bird flew out. Was that all it had been? My skin still prickled with the certainty that I was being watched. I turned the pusher around and walked briskly back towards the car. Twenty minutes at least, even if I power-walked. I broke into a light jog, looking behind me as did. I caught the glimpse of a shadow at the moment I fell over a tree root and sprawled across the path, letting go of the pusher which shot ahead of me. There was a slight decline, so it continued on. I scrambled to my feet, one knee bleeding, and took off after Noah, grabbing the pusher, and then running as fast as I could with it in front of me.

I didn't look back until I could see the carpark ahead of me, with two cars—mine and a slightly battered silver Nissan. I had no idea what Joe's car looked like but if I'd had to guess, this might have been it. Panting, I slowed my pace to pull my keys out, thinking I could use them as a weapon if I didn't have time to open the car door and put Noah in. I caught sight of someone out of the corner of my eye, to the left, and realised there was another path there. Ahead, it joined the one I was on. I ran faster.

When I got to the car Noah had picked up my anxiety and was starting to whimper. The buckles of the pusher harness sprung open without issue and I grabbed him, whirling around to see how much time I had.

There was no one.

My heart was racing; had they had time to hide behind the other car? I put Noah into his car seat, jumped in and locked the doors. Hand trembling, I dropped the keys; started scrabbling around for them at my feet, eyes on the side window.

I saw no one. It didn't stop me, once I had the keys in my hand, accelerating out of the carpark at full speed.

The adrenaline had not just helped me run—it helped me think. The thought struck like a thunderbolt as I drove away. Donna had reconnected with her family and restored her sense of wellbeing before having Teagan—there was no suggestion at all that she had been mentally ill, other than Yvonne's and Grace's retrospective diagnoses. Joe might not have seen the coroner's report—in which case he wouldn't know if there had been any doubt, any signs of anything other than misadventure.

What if Donna hadn't jumped or fallen, but had been pushed?

Group five was about partners, about husbands becoming fathers and the change in dynamics when two became three—a dynamic I was still struggling with in my own life. My training had only superficially covered how the near-loss of a child can create a crevasse in a relationship: parents on different sides, without icepicks or crampons. I was usually too tired to feel like sex; Dean never pushed it. But we both missed the intimacy we had taken for granted.

'Honey, he's probably just stressed at work,' Angelica suggested over FaceTime.

'Make sure you look after him,' my mother said.

I had tried. I'd said we needed to talk.

But when we did, we seemed to go around in circles—never forward. I'd lost count of the phone calls he suddenly remembered he had to make, the urgent pull of the emails that popped up on his phone or the times he simply fell asleep. He was working hard, he was tired. Be patient, both my parents and my girlfriend had recommended. I knew that it wasn't just him, though. I had to forgive myself too.

•

My group seemed to have some good fathers among their partners.

'Lachlan's just a natural,' said Sophie.

'Massoud, too,' said Zahra. Today we were feasting on Iranian pastries and some kind of Turkish delight her mother had made.

'Give me a fucking break.' Teagan. This particular group was never going to be easy for someone who was probably going to be a single mother.

'Everyone has a different experience Teagan,' I said mildly. 'It's tough if your child's father isn't around. If it helps, research shows having no partner is better than an unsupportive one.'

'Jed's getting his shit together.' Teagan sounded like she wanted to believe this, but doubted it.

'What does everyone think a good father looks like?'

'Shares the load.' Kate. For all her depressive symptoms, I imagined Brian was the shining light for her and Ruby— and I'd seen Kate pitch in at the pub with him.

'Do you think men should have a different load? I don't mean quantity necessarily, but who does what?'

'Maybe it depends on who can do what,' said Róisín. Her partner did all the practical childcare. Róisín desperately desired the capacity to be able to do more: I caught her looking at Sophie sometimes, particularly after a cake triumph or when Sophie appeared especially well dressed, with a sense of awe.

'When Raha needs comfort, it is me she wants,' said Zahra.

'A baby needs their mother for comfort,' Sophie agreed.

'Bull. Ruby prefers her dad for everything.' Kate.

'I just think little girls go through that phase, don't you?'

Sophie was oblivious to Kate's internal narrative: terror that anyone would need her. Her parents had never been available to her emotionally and now it was hard for Kate to be there for her daughter. To love, it seemed, was to risk the grief of loss and to court the fear and loneliness she had as a child. Ruby hadn't given up on her mother, though; there was always a smile especially for her that came from a deeper place than the smiles for strangers.

'What I am hearing is children may turn to a particular parent for a particular need,' I said, 'and that there may be times when one parent is more able to do things than the other, and that working as a team is important.' For Teagan's sake I added, 'With whatever supports you have.'

There was some predictable discussion of who did the housecleaning, which seemed low on the men's list of preferred tasks.

'Does becoming a father change men?' I asked.

'Yeah,' said Teagan. 'They learn to run. Back to Mummy.'

I looked at her in surprise. This was at odds with her previous need to believe in Jed. Teagan avoided eye contact. 'What responsibility do you think they do take on?'

Kate laughed. 'Brian said he saw dollar signs in a halo above Ruby's head when she was born. Like how much it was going to cost to raise her. Started working harder than ever.'

Róisín nodded. 'We both worry about that. Money, school…Bella's an IVF baby so there's been a lot of outgoings. Luckily my partner's parents left him money when they died.'

'Well, the expense does put a lot of pressure on you and your partners,' I said. 'How do you guys deal with that?'

'Brian tells me not to worry. Anyway, we've got two wages.'

'Showing love is what is important. Keeping them safe.' Zahra spoke softly. 'Not money.'

'We talk about everything,' said Sophie.

'Really?' Teagan rolled her eyes and I could see Sophie pulling herself up for a fight. I interjected.

'How about play? Are dads good at that?'

'A little boisterous,' said Róisín.

'Ace,' said Kate.

'Lachlan's read up on the importance of bonding through play,' said Sophie, glaring at Teagan.

'That's right,' I said. 'In traditional families at least, that's how they fall in love with each other—oxytocin rises in fathers and babies when they play.'

'Figures,' said Teagan. 'Men get the fun stuff.' She looked distracted.

'And what about the oxytocin rush with their mothers?' said Kate.

'That comes when they comfort them, cuddle and soothe,' I said. 'And if for some reason the mother hasn't been there to do that, they'll get it from another carer. In your case, Teagan, your father probably did both roles for you.' Looking back at Kate I added, 'But they never give up on their mother. At least not until they're teenagers, when they see a wider world of alternatives.'

'Men,' said Teagan, getting up abruptly, 'are just fucking sperm donors. This baby's *mine*. I'm gonna do the comforting *and* the playing.'

She looked at each of the group, daring anyone to challenge her. Kate was the only one who didn't turn away. Teagan paused, then stormed out.

I hesitated, then took after her—without a baby to pick up she was out the door before I caught her.

'Teagan, a moment?'

Teagan glared at me. 'That lot are all bloody up themselves. Perfect families. You reckon I don't know they think I'm a no-good Abo?'

'None of them thinks that,' I said. 'And if you think they're perfect you haven't been listening. All of them—all mothers—struggle at times. Me included.'

'Doctor Know It All? Mrs Perfect Pollie's Wife? Constable Hardarse? Yeah, sure.' At least Róisín wasn't on her hit list.

'You reckon?' I said, arms folded. 'You can do better than that, Teagan.'

'Yeah?' She swiped at a tear that had dared to reveal her vulnerability. Teagan was annoying, childlike and manipulative. But she also had heart, some smarts and a sense of humour.

'Try again…and scratch below the surface.' I needed her to be able to do this—so she could do it with her child later. One day when Indiana said, 'I hate you' and meant 'I love you but you're being mean to me and I don't know what I did wrong.'

'Okay, Zahra. Doctor Crazy.'

'Teagan.'

'I guess she's had it tough, getting tortured or whatever by those mad bearded guys.'

'I don't think she got tortured,' I said, 'but you've got the general idea. Keep going.'

'She's not white, either. Probably gets a hard time around here.'

'Róisín?' I was going from easy to hard.

'She looks like she's terrified Bella might actually, like, have her own mind.' She thought a bit longer and grinned. 'Kate broke Matt Barclay's nose, so she isn't all bad.'

'Do you think she finds it easy, juggling being a cop and being a mother?'

Teagan shrugged. 'I guess not. But I'm not saying anything positive about fuckin' Snow White so don't even go there.'

I'd made my point—and reduced her anger to something more manageable.

'Are you worried about Jed?'

Teagan picked at a scab on the back of her hand. 'We had a fight.'

'About?'

'Nothing really. But he told me he wasn't even sure he was Indiana's father.' Teagan wiped a tear, and looked up, eyes fierce. '*I* know he is.'

'It was…probably just anger,' I said. 'You can always get a DNA test to prove it to him.'

Teagan looked away. 'Yeah, whatever. I don't need him anyway.'

I went back to make sure the other four women went home on a positive note. As they were packing up, Sophie turned to Kate.

'Any progress on finding who wrote the warning letter?'

'Like I could tell you if there was?' Kate's tone was mild.

'Maybe…' Sophie looked at me. 'Maybe we're the targets.'

'We don't think that's very likely.' Kate was on message.

How likely, I wondered, was not very? Ten per cent chance? Twenty? Forty-five?

'I heard,' said Zahra, 'that Joe Moretti threatened you last week, Issy?'

Great. I understood Chris might have mentioned it to Massoud, but I wished he'd had better sense than to pass it on to his wife.

Kate looked quickly at me—she already knew. Dean had reported it to Sam Keller thinking the police would do no more than keep an eye on Joe. But if Keller had shared the concern with his constable, he hadn't completely dismissed me as an hysteric.

'I suggest being alert but not alarmed,' Kate said.

Róisín looked at her. 'The police still think Joe was implicated in Joshua's death, right?'

'There was,' said Kate firmly, 'no evidence that the Morettis did anything wrong. Except taking their eyes off their baby for a few minutes, and if you're going to condemn them for that...' She looked at each of the mothers in turn. And, finally, at me.

But as she left Kate caught my eye again, and this time her look said something different. If I'd had to guess, I'd have said she was worried that I was in danger. If I put that together with her carefully phrased 'no evidence', it suggested in Joe a degree of calculation greater than I had given him credit for. I thought of Joshua's body being stuffed into a bag, of Donna being pushed drunk into the river. Of me being followed when I went there myself.

Maybe beneath the alcohol-soaked exterior there was a whole lot I wasn't seeing. Maybe Joe Moretti had conned everyone. Maybe he was a psychopath.

Dean was running late. I waited in the car, feeding Noah a snack, and thought about trust. About women sticking together. About the Morettis having run-ins with the law. About the look Kate had given me at the end of the group.

I drove to the pub and she didn't seem surprised to see me.

'I need to ask you something,' I said. 'Remember we talked about protective mothers? The lioness?'

'Yes,' said Kate cautiously, looking around; we were alone.

'You described yourself as a tortoise when it came to being a mother.' I watched her face: it was giving nothing away. 'But would you pull your head into your shell if someone was after Ruby?'

'I'd blow his fucking head off.' Kate had the grace to smile.

'I'll stick with the lioness metaphor. But in order to protect Noah I need to know, one mother to another. Does Joe Moretti have a police record?'

She only hesitated for a moment. 'Yes. I'm not saying

anything that isn't general knowledge. There were a few call-outs for DV prior to Joshua. Donna wouldn't press charges, and it was mostly the neighbours complaining about the language and noise. Pushing, yelling…no broken bones or black eyes. Not that the situation was great, but he always walked out if he felt he was going to hit her.'

I could sense there was more. Waited.

'There was a stoush with the Barclay boys a few years ago,' Kate added. 'Something to do with Teagan. But they didn't take it any further; Grace felt sorry for him and the boys gave as good as they got. Well, Matt did, anyway.'

Kate hadn't said enough to justify the worry I'd seen for me and Noah. I kept waiting.

'He wasn't charged with the other crime,' she said eventually.

I steeled myself.

'It was deemed a justifiable homicide; self-defence.'

Homicide.

'Who?' I finally asked.

'He was seventeen. He killed his father.'

'We talked last week about how men and women fall in love with their babies and vice versa,' I said. 'Today we're going to focus on how that love can make strong children. How does your child know you love them?'

There was a tension in the silence. Sophie shifted uncomfortably, Róisín coughed, Kate looked to the ceiling.

'Touch,' Zahra said finally. 'Being there.' She was avoiding eye contact. I wondered if she was unwell again.

'Do you tell them you love them?'

'I tell Indiana all the time,' said Teagan.

I wondered at their reluctance. Too much stepping on each other's toes, or just wary of Teagan's outburst from last week? 'Other ways?'

'Letting them know you're there…like, if needed.' Kate had occasional moments when she was really trying.

'How,' Sophie asked no one in particular, 'can we ever be sure anyone loves us?' She tried to laugh, but the ponytail wasn't bouncing.

'Little things,' said Zahra softly. She was sounding okay but still not looking at me. 'Many, many little things.'

I pressed on. 'Trickier question now. How do we know our children love us?'

I became conscious of the hum of the aircon as I waited.

'How Tom looks at me first thing in the morning.'

'Bella's smile. It fills my heart every time I see it.'

'Raha settles faster in my arms.'

I nodded. 'We want our children to love us—making them feel good makes us feel good. So how about when we say no to our children? Is that hard?'

'Sometimes it's easier to give in,' said Kate. 'The sisterhood's not exactly supportive when you're holding up the supermarket queue over whether your kid can have the pink lollypop.'

'Al does the shopping,' Róisín murmured.

'Ruby and Bella are at the age, like Noah,' I said, 'where "no" becomes a daily part of life. How do you guys handle it?'

'Valium.' Kate finally grinned, and it felt like a breakthrough. Maybe here, seeing other mothers were not so different, that they weren't perfect either, she could drop the armour she needed at the police station. Or maybe seeing my vulnerability had an upside.

'*Why* is it important to, at least sometimes, say no?' I looked at the group, each in turn, wanting an answer from them all.

'To prevent utter chaos,' said Kate—who, in her line of work, had probably seen her fair share of people without boundaries.

'To help them feel safe.' Zahra. Tentative eye contact—and something in her look I couldn't read. Damn. I wished I had a co-therapist to help with this; keeping across five women at once wasn't easy.

147

'To help them fit in.' I looked closer at Sophie. She was more anxious, more edgy than usual. Problems arising from Lachlan's preselection campaign? Normal living-with-in-laws issues?

'To show who's boss.' I pictured Teagan and Indiana fighting it out like sisters rather than mother and daughter. I could help her with that, except that I'd be long gone before Teagan's daughter was more than a newborn.

I turned to Róisín. She looked especially voluminous today in a full black skirt—she had her feet tucked up under it—and a loose white peasant shirt that she had to keep readjusting when it fell off one shoulder.

'You know, Isabel,' Róisín said, 'I don't need to say no to Bella. There's enough other people in the world to tell her that. From me she gets love.'

'Saying no doesn't mean you don't love your children,' said Sophie.

'In fact, it says you do love them,' added Kate. 'They need limits from you so they know how to say no to unsafe shit when they're teenagers.'

'I keep Bella safe by keeping her away from danger.' Róisín's voice tightened. 'My mother never stood up for me, not once, against my father. I'll never be like that.'

'But we can't always be there,' said Zahra. 'We must help them be confident themselves, so when they are hurt, they will stand strong like trees.'

Teagan looked like she wasn't listening.

'Perhaps, Róisín,' I suggested mildly, 'if you keep Bella away from the world, she gets the message that it's dangerous.'

'Well, it is,' said Róisín. 'Even here in Riley—we've had a murderer on the loose here for twenty-five years, apparently now planning to give it another go.'

Sophie picked up the thread. 'The police'—she gave a half-apologetic look at Kate—'aren't really able to do anything are they? It's the sitting and waiting...not knowing.'

Teagan's eyes were wide open. 'Fucking hell. I thought it was just me.'

'Okay,' I said. 'What you are all describing is feeling powerless. But let's put that into perspective. Are you really? You feel you can't leave, but could you? You are worried about your babies, but what is the real risk? Is your baby ever alone? If they are, can you change the environment, be proactive?'

The energy in the group had been low, but I saw them fire up with my little rant.

'Let's all buy Rottweilers,' suggested Teagan.

'Build the wall,' said Kate, deadpan.

'Is the rain not coming soon? How about an ark?' I wasn't sure if Zahra was being serious—they all looked at each other, then me, and in an extraordinary moment, they all, Róisín included, burst out laughing.

I let it settle. Then I said, 'Humour's one of the signs of resilience. A good sign. Before we go, let's think up one thing that each of us can do to help our children know that we are there for them, and that might help *them* build resilience.'

With a lot of encouragement they made a list, and I tried to orientate it to each individual:

Sophie to sit with Tom's irritability and frustration rather than trying to push him to perform.

Teagan to think of all the people she thought were good mothers—including celebrities she had mentioned—and why.

Zahra to go walking with Raha, to convey to her

that they were both free—and that Zahra was able to be independent again.

Kate to offer Ruby a cuddle while she read a night-time story—and relax into the pleasure of the moment.

And Róisín. Maybe Bella was already getting enough messages from her father to counteract Róisín's dour yet freaked-out narrative. I hoped so, but I doubted it. 'Next week,' I suggested, 'do you think you could leave her in the room with Yvonne and tell her you trust her to be good and to cope, and not check on her?'

Róisín looked at me as though I needed my own therapist.

'Can you stay back a minute, Teagan?'

Teagan's eyes were on the door. 'Why?'

'Just wanted to check in. How's the preparation for... Indiana?'

'Not much to do, really.' She moved from one foot to the other.

'How's Jed?' I asked.

'Okay,' said Teagan.

'Plans for after?'

'Never any point making plans,' said Teagan. 'Nothing I've ever planned worked out.'

'You mentioned an auntie.'

'Yeah. She wanted to come for Christmas but my nan's too sick. She can't travel.' *See?*

'What about your other grandmother? Your father's mother?'

'She lives in Griffith.'

'Has she lived there for a while?'

'Since she came out from Italy in like the fifties or sixties when my dad was a baby. She looked after me and Dad for a while after Mum died, but I don't remember that.'

'What happened to your grandfather?' I asked casually. Since Kate had told me about the murder—the justifiable homicide—I had searched the internet but hadn't turned up anything.

'He died before I was born.' She wasn't looking at me; the truth but not the whole truth.

'He must have been young.'

Teagan shrugged. 'Dad never talks about him.'

I bet he didn't. 'Teagan…' I paused. 'I am wondering… are you likely to be still living with your father after Indiana is born? With or without Jed?'

Teagan shrugged. 'Jed and I want to head up north—his mob are in Townsville and my nan's in Cairns. But we might need to wait till we've got some more money.' She sighed. 'Jed's trying but like I don't want to push him? For Indiana's sake, I'd like him around.'

'Sure. But if your dad's there…well you did mention he hit you as child. I wonder how…safe he will be?'

Teagan looked guarded. 'He's fine. It isn't like I expect he's going to suddenly be granddad of the year. But he'll try. And Jed *will* be there.' She smiled. 'And I'm having a girl, so it won't remind Dad of Joshua or anything.'

Teagan started picking at a loose thread on her baggy cotton trousers. 'I wasn't scared of him, not really. Not like Róisín was scared of her dad. Those times he hit me? I was pushing his buttons. I wasn't little. And when I was younger he tried to care for me. Brought me home presents, little things, 'cause it wasn't like he could afford much. Those Kinder eggs were my favourite, you know?'

I nodded. Her eyes were misting up. 'I loved my dad as a kid. He was all I had. I looked after him, and he called me his little Donna. Like I made up for Mum not being there.'

'But he had…girlfriends?'

'One or two. I don't really remember. He said he didn't need to,' she said forcefully. 'He had me.'

'What sort of work did he do?' I suddenly realised how little I knew about him—he had contested the seat that Gordon won, but what had he done since?

'When Mum was alive, they ran the greengrocers, but it was too much after she died. The shop closed.'

'After that?'

'Odd jobs for a while. He worked for the Barclays. Managed their property. He was pretty good then. We lived in a house there.' She looked at me. 'Place you've got now.'

Joe worked for the *Barclays*?

'What happened?'

'Shit happened. It always does.' She looked flushed, upset. A good memory interrupted by a bad one. It was what she had learnt to expect—I hoped becoming a mother might change the pattern.

'What happened?'

'It was all a long time ago.'

'How old were you?'

'I was a kid. Fifteen. Knew nothing. Thought I could go off to Sydney and become a fashion designer like I told you. But people like me don't do things like that. We stay in shitholes like Riley and become single mothers or get beaten up by drug-taking arseholes.'

She stood up. 'I meant it. I'll look after Indiana, and I don't need a bloke, not even Jed if he can't pull his finger out. Or my dad. Or interfering do-gooders. I listen to what you've been saying—I want to do it different.'

She picked up her backpack and took off, leaving me

thinking that she just might do what she said: be a good, or at least good-enough, mother.

Yvonne was still packing up and I paused halfway out the door. I looked up the street, almost expecting Joe Moretti to be walking down towards me.

'Yvonne, I need to run to the hospital. Could you stay with Noah for an hour?'

The medical records clerk barely looked at me as I sat down and logged in. Teagan's file was on the screen within a minute.

After Joe had warned me off, I had wondered. Was he concerned that I might review the hospital records from years earlier and join dots that hadn't been joined by the police? I had seen Donna's file, Joe didn't have one...so if he was worried about medical records, that left Teagan's. Records I was legitimately allowed to review.

Things Teagan said had made the hair on the back of my neck stand on end. 'Little Donna'; not needing girlfriends. The kiddie porn mention from Róisín. And the Barclays had given him a job after Joshua's death, and then had a falling out. The job could have been about pity or guilt, but I was curious about the falling out.

There was plenty of recent stuff in the file, most of it about Teagan's current pregnancy—ultrasounds, the date of her planned caesarean, sugar tests and blood pressure.

Nothing earlier. No prior pregnancy or miscarriage details. She had been in Sydney when she'd had her first child—and she'd never booked in at the Riley hospital. Would there be a record in Chris's file? He'd never got back to me about finding anything important; he was hardly likely to think a pregnancy test was worthy of mention.

I pulled out my mobile; Chris's receptionist put me through.

'Quick one,' I said. 'Did you know Teagan had a pregnancy before this one?'

'Yes.'

'So there are records?'

There was a pause. 'She was in Sydney.'

'But was anything sent back to you guys by her doctor there, when she returned? A courtesy letter?'

'Why does it matter?'

'It might not. Just seems strange that there's no record. She was so young—I would have thought she'd be mollycoddled and they'd want her to go back to her family.'

Another pause. 'Nothing I can see. She was using drugs rather than the health system, I think.'

'What's the usual cause of a late miscarriage?'

'Often unknown.'

'Could drugs and alcohol cause it?'

'Yes, I should think so. Any form of chemical poisoning, really.'

I hung up, frustrated. Would Teagan remember which hospital she went to in Sydney and give me permission to talk to them?

I clicked onto investigations and went through the tests for a second time. No pregnancy tests other than the recent one. I clicked on ultrasounds again. Eight weeks and eighteen weeks, pretty common times for an ultrasound. Except there was a nineteen-week scan as well.

When I checked the dates, it became obvious why. They were from different pregnancies. One—dated over seven years earlier, done in Sydney—showed abnormalities. Numerous. Foetus unlikely to survive—hence the miscarriage.

It was the last line of the report that had me shaking.

Multiple abnormalities of this kind suggest exposure to toxins or genetic conditions. Then the recommendations: *Suggest genetic testing for familial chromosomal abnormalities. Consanguinity?*

Teagan's first pregnancy could have been the result of incest.

Róisín was in the corridor as I came out of medical records. She didn't return my smile.

'Your husband. You told him.'

For a moment I didn't have a clue what she was talking about. She must have seen my confusion.

'You told your husband. About the catering. Even though it's Rachel's deputy who's doing the dodgy stuff.' Róisín crossed her arms. 'I thought I could trust you. I wanted to. Now she's out of a job. And she'll have to move because she'll never get any work here. She looks after her elderly mother with multiple sclerosis, and who knows what'll happen to her?'

Kate—and Dean—would have said, *She should have thought about that before she turned a blind eye to what was going on.*

'I didn't say anything to my husband.'

'Really, Isabel?' Withering disbelief.

My stomach tightened. So did my resolve. 'Róisín. Dean is interviewing whoever he needs to. I did not and would not discuss confidential information with him.' Information she should have told Dean in any case.

Róisín tucked the loose strands of black hair behind her ear. 'It's okay, Isabel. I'm just disappointed.'

Róisín spent her life being disappointed. A life pattern of subconsciously setting things up to reinforce her negative view of the world. I wanted to help her. How to get her to see people didn't always do the wrong thing. Or that even if they made mistakes sometimes, they weren't always malicious?

'I'm sorry if the wrong person got caught in the net. But if she knew and didn't do anything, then that's a problem too,' I said. 'You seem determined to blame me, though.'

Róisín looked uncertain.

'It's Dean's job,' I added. 'He's good at finding things that people try to hide. He can do it without any breaches of ethics on my part.'

Róisín pulled on the strands of hair that had missed being tucked into her ponytail. 'It just seems…well, it seems pretty minor compared to the overall mismanagement.'

'All the problems add up.'

'The hospital was run by the Barclays—one of their cronies—without supervision. That's where the problems come from.'

'What's your beef with the Barclay family? Sophie has been very supportive of you.'

'Just because you own things doesn't mean you can run a hospital.' She shook her head. 'Or other people's lives. Grace tried to help Joe Moretti out, after Donna died. Gave him a house, a job. Even organised for me to babysit Teagan.'

Róisín must have seen my puzzled expression.

'Well—that all blew up in everyone's face, didn't it? Teagan grew up and gave as good as she got—and her father had to take her side, didn't he?'

Then—either because of bitterness about a father who'd

protect his daughter, or to convince me (or herself) that humans were simply terrible—she added, 'Joe's always been a drunk. And violent. After he attacked Grace, that was the end of it.'

Shit happened, Teagan had said. Kate's version was that Joe had assaulted the Barclay boys on Teagan's behalf. Now, in Róisín's telling, they'd intervened when he assaulted their mother.

It was many years after the kidnapping—I couldn't see a connection, as much as I'd have liked things to hang together neatly.

As I was leaving, a dinged-up silver Nissan pulled out from the kerb opposite me. The car I'd seen when I was followed at the river.

It was not Joe driving it, but Chris.

It was the next night before I had a chance to talk to Dean. He was late, the day had dragged and the heat had left me irritable. I was making a patchwork quilt for Grace's fete, and when I realised I'd sewed the squares in the wrong order I snapped at Noah, and watched his wide eyes fill with tears. My mother rang with the usual litany of medical complaints and I snapped at her too.

'I'm sorry,' I said. 'I'm missing Melbourne, that's all.'

'I know you have more important things in your life than us.' Mum couldn't help herself.

Noah was asleep by the time Dean drove in, the sun lighting the horizon in shades of gold. The circling bird I had seen on previous evenings was joined by its mate. I was thinking how beautiful their graceful silhouettes were against the sunset, then only a minute later I heard the wild dogs start their barking, and longed to be home with my family and friends. Even Mum.

'Well. That was fun.' Dean sat down and poured us a glass of wine each.

'The board meeting?'

Dean nodded. 'That bunch are like the Addams Family.

With Grace Barclay as Morticia and your Saint Christopher as Gomez.'

'Was Athol Broadbent there? He does look a bit like Lurch,' I said. The wine had relaxed me.

'Yeah, Athol was on song. A lot of head-shaking and groaning about how much better things were in the good old days, if things worked in 1950 they still should now...Saint Christopher doesn't agree, so there was plenty of huffing and puffing about it.' Dean topped up his glass and put the bottle back in the fridge.

'Do you have a sense of where the financial problem is?'

'The hospital has a culture of corruption. The issue is how much is just bad management, and how much is crooked.'

'I heard the caterer was sacked.'

'Mmm-hmmm. Equal parts incompetence and greed there. She took off pretty much because I was asking questions. The rot with the union...that might go a good deal deeper.'

'Kickbacks? From the hospital?'

'Almost certainly. The lack of transparency...If there's something I can't see after spending seven weeks in the guts of the operation, that's a problem in itself. I've found some discrepancies and now I'm going back through all the records as far back as I can. It's slow and tedious because the records are...well, a lot are actually missing, others incomplete.'

'Whose responsibility is it?'

'The buck rests with the Board. They should all have a grip on the financials.' Dean shrugged. 'Trouble is, I don't know what I'm dealing with; it's not purely the financials, it's about due process.'

'So, who does know what's going on?'

Dean watched me. 'Your Saint Christopher maybe.'

I thought about his Nissan; the feeling of being followed. 'Why did you say he was Gomez? Because he's greasing up to Grace?'

We watched a flock of galahs screeching as they flew over the clump of trees by the creek while Dean thought about his answer. 'He certainly makes sure he keeps on her good side—he might be trying to blindside her.'

'Why would he want to do that?'

'Why do people ever do other people over? It's usually greed or power, regardless of what justifications they use.' Dean looked at me, his expression hard to read. 'But man, he's furious at the hospital for not upgrading their equipment. His wife died, did you know? Lot of feeling there.'

I tried to make sense of this—but it felt like I had two different jigsaws and the pieces had all been thrown together.

'Have the police been back in touch? Have you heard anything more about Joe Moretti?'

Dean tensed.

I went on: 'Like that he killed his own father?'

He knew, I could see it. Sam Keller had told him. Part of me wanted to scream at him, but I took a deep breath. 'Dean, you don't have to keep tiptoeing around me like I might break. I got help after Noah's accident. I'm better, okay?'

Dean took a sip of wine. He didn't look convinced. I leaned forward, put my hand over his.

'The way I see it, we've got...stuck. You don't talk to me about anything you think might upset me, and I get upset because I feel like you don't trust me. Thing is...'

Dean's fingers locked tentatively around mine.

'...I need to know. Otherwise my imagination starts

coming up with things that are worse than reality.' I took a breath. 'Joe grew up with domestic violence, significant enough that the police reckoned that he was justified in killing his father. Backgrounds don't come much worse than that, and then his baby and wife died, and there wasn't much to rule out his having killed one or both.'

'You still think he wrote the note?'

I nodded. 'He seems to care for Teagan—but...' this would still be consistent with him sexually abusing her; it would be his justification. I couldn't tell Dean that. 'I think he wanted...wants...to keep me away from her.'

Dean pulled me into my arms and just held me. For the first time in a long time I felt I had been heard. 'I'm doing my best to get us out of here,' he said softly into my hair. 'But if you really think you're in danger, go home.'

I blinked back tears thinking of his previous threat.

'I'm sorry babe,' Dean said, wiping them. 'I was just... look, no excuses, okay? I was being a shit. You're a great mum and Noah loves you to pieces.'

We made love that night—more than just having sex. Dean took his time, and waited for me. It wasn't quite the intimacy, free from worry and stress, that we'd had before Noah. But I felt, for the first time since the accident, like we were a team.

I thought we would sleep solidly in each other's arms until the alarm, but something woke me. Watching the steady beam of moonlight on the sheets I wasn't immediately sure what. Then the gunshots rang out again. I extricated myself from Dean's arms and slipped out onto the veranda. I couldn't see anything. The sounds were from the other side of the creek—if you could call it a creek when it had been dry when we arrived and hadn't seen any rain for two months.

I returned to bed. Lay awake picturing our local kangaroo mob scattering frantically in all directions, terrified as spotlights fell on them. I pictured them shot in the guts, writhing in agony. Joeys left to die in the pouches. Each shot felt like it went through my body, and when I finally fell asleep, the pillow was wet with my tears.

The next morning, like all the others, the sun rose in a hot blue sky and it was as if I had imagined the night shooting spree. I had a cup of tea but couldn't face food. I was just grateful that Noah's vegemite toast didn't make me feel sick.

The dead kangaroo did.

The big grey—the wise old man of the mob—was lying across the driveway just before the bridge. I could see the wound in his side, hear the buzz of the flies feasting on entrails that the crows had already picked over. Glassy eyes staring at the sky. Only a trickle of blood. He hadn't been killed here. The gunshots hadn't been this side of the creek.

'Someone dropped him here deliberately,' I said. My voice caught.

Dean got out of the car and looked at the body. Looked around.

'Bastards,' he muttered. He slammed the door when he got back in.

'I'll talk to Sam.' Dean looked at me. 'I meant it. About going home. I'd miss you both, but...I don't want you feeling anxious.' He took a breath. 'I mean, I want you to feel safe.'

He looked at Noah who had picked up the tension; his bottom lip was quivering.

The message the dead kangaroo was meant to give was clear—*next it's you or your child.*

'You know what?' I said, louder than I'd meant. Dean and Noah looked at me. 'No bloody way I'm going to be frightened off by some dickhead who thinks we're pissweak city slickers.'

Dean looked startled. But he was grinning all the way into town. So, to my surprise, was I.

None of my group attendees were there at 10 a.m. Not even Sophie.

'There was a party meeting last night in Dubbo,' Yvonne told me. 'Probably a late night for some.'

The preselection vote wouldn't be held until after Christmas, she went on; there would be grandstanding and tension between Chris and Lachlan and their supporters for a while yet.

I wondered if there was time to get a real coffee, but as I started to head towards the railway museum, Teagan drove past me and I could see Zahra walking in my direction. I turned back towards the health centre and as I did I caught sight of Dean walking towards the hospital—where I had dropped him less than an hour earlier. I wondered vaguely where he'd been as I ducked back into the building.

'Less than three weeks to go,' Teagan said as she flopped into a chair. She was wearing her owl T-shirt.

'Looks like you'll be pleased to be into the next stage,' I said.

'I am *so* over this. There's no God—she'd have let us lay eggs.'

'That why you like the owl?' I asked.

Teagan looked down. 'It's a local. We used to hear them barking down at the river when I was a kid.'

I stared. *'Barking?* You mean that's what I've been hearing?' *Owls!*

Teagan laughed. 'Had you fooled, did they?'

Sophie arrived five minutes later. Tom, in her arms, had tears running down his face.

'I nearly didn't come,' she announced. She looked close to tears herself. Yvonne swept in and tried to pry Tom away, but he cringed, holding tighter to his mother. She dumped several plates that had been taking up stroller space— sausage rolls, baby quiches and limp white bread wrapped around tinned asparagus. Party leftovers.

'Seems like you're both having a bad day,' I said.

'Tom won't let me out of his sight. I can't even go to the bathroom without him strapped on.'

Teagan rolled her eyes and mumbled, 'Frickin' nanny's day off, is it?' too low for Sophie to hear.

'When we have a bad day, what message do our children get?' I said as Zahra came in and slipped into her seat. She looked serene today; she even had make-up on. Róisín and Kate weren't far behind her. Tom remained in Sophie's arms. Róisín avoided eye contact. I rolled my shoulders and took a breath.

'What do you think Tom might be feeling?'

'Anxious? God knows why,' said Sophie.

'Children sense things, but it doesn't mean they come to the right conclusion.' I paused. 'And sometimes we give them mixed messages because of our own issues.'

'Like what?' asked Róisín. She was still checking on Bella as if there was a real possibility an alien might suck her into a black hole in front of Yvonne's eyes.

'The most common mixed message we give our children is about sleep. Like, you're really exhausted because your child hasn't been sleeping, and as you put them down, you tense because you fear they won't settle and it'll be another shocking night. How do you think your baby will interpret that tension?'

'Like they need to give their poor old mum a break?' Kate suggested and laughed.

'Like something's wrong,' I said. 'And when they're little, the fear button is a simple on and off switch. If you inadvertently turn it on, then they're likely to think they are in danger, and...'

'It's not about sleep.' Sophie shrugged. 'Things have been a bit...busy at home.'

Teagan's expression showed little sympathy—I wondered whether the imminent birth was heightening her antipathy to someone who had so much more support than she did, or if it was more about Joe. It was hard to look at her and not keep seeing that scan report. I reminded myself that incest wasn't the only possible cause of her first pregnancy abnormalities. Sophie was too preoccupied with her own issues to notice Teagan.

I nodded. 'Tom is very in tune with you. He'll pick up your stress but not know what it's about. He might think you're both about to be attacked by cannibals rather than just facing a pre-selection battle.'

'The whole family's pretty tense at the moment,' Sophie said, 'it's not just Lachlan's preselection. Grace is wound up about whether the hospital is going to close, Gordon's stressing about retirement...I'm looking forward to getting a few weeks in Sydney with my family in January.'

'I guess sometimes that can be hard too—living up to who they want you to be?' I was thinking as much about my own family as Sophie's, but she took a deep breath. I'd hit the mark. Her need to be perfect had started with a belief that it was the only way her parents would love her. The Barclays perpetuated it.

I asked the others to think about their own children picking up on their anxiety. Zahra gave a textbook account of what her child must have felt when she was unwell. 'It's better, though. She already senses that I am someone she can trust now.' Zahra's smile suggested she might even be trusting herself.

Kate was the only one who didn't buy in. 'Ruby's going to be the most chilled kid ever,' she said. 'She walked into the creche without even a "See ya, Mum". And she'll be in there now, bossing around Noah and Bella.'

'As children get older they can hide their anxiety,' I said, 'particularly if they know their mother wants them to be independent. We've talked before about secure attachments, being there; reading our children's cues. But what if our own stuff gets in the way?'

I showed a video about letting children play but allowing them to return to be comforted.

'Some children...some of us when we were young... learned that our mothers either wanted us to be mostly playing, or mostly close by.' I looked to Kate and Róisín. 'Either extreme can cause problems.'

Their expressions were remarkably similar: *noted and ignored*.

I turned to Sophie, holding on to a wriggling Tom as if he was a security blanket. 'How about you take him in next door to Yvonne and leave him. Pretend it's the first day of school, and he's going to go in and do really well, because he's checked the place out, feels comfortable, wants to have fun. Your manner has to show that you know he'll be fine.' This was something Sophie, unlike Róisín, could do just fine in normal circumstances.

She shrugged and did as I asked. We heard her encourage Tom to 'have fun', and he separated without fuss.

'He was ready to go.' I smiled. 'That's the challenge— picking when he needs comfort, when he's ready to go.'

I turned to Kate. 'Now Ruby's been having fun in there, but she'll also like knowing you're there for her. Could you go and tell her that if she wants to see you, she can come to you and show you what's she's been doing?'

'To prove what?'

'To remind her she can ask for comfort if she needs to, and that helps give her confidence. We're all going to watch—and it may be only a split second—but we're all going to look for a smile.'

In the next moment, I decided that this was the only work I ever wanted to do—because small children never give up on their mothers. When Kate stood in the door awkwardly shifting from one foot to the other, Ruby caught sight of her before she spoke. The smile was brief, and closed down quickly in case her mother saw it as being too needy, but unmistakeable.

'Oh my God, what a total I-love-my-mum smile,' said Sophie as Kate blushed, looking a little unsettled but not unhappy.

When we finished, I watched them leave. Sophie was picked up by Lachlan.

'Big meeting last night, I gather,' I said as Sophie strapped

Tom into his car seat.

Lachlan's mouth tightened before he smiled. 'Bit of a clusterfuck, actually.'

My jaw must have dropped open.

He laughed. 'Truth is, I don't think this is really my thing—politics I mean.' He looked down and shrugged.

'Did you say what I thought you said?' Sophie closed the back door of the car and looked horrified. I wasn't sure if it was the swearing or the sentiment.

'Sorry.' I wasn't sure if he was apologising to me or Sophie, or both of us, but I did see a flash of sadness—and worry—in Sophie's eyes as they got into the car.

I went to lunch with Chris, ostensibly to talk about the latest cognitive assessment I had completed for him.

'Howdy stranger,' he said, kissing me lightly on the cheek. 'Get you a drink?'

Noah was with Yvonne, and mostly I was dealing with the anxiety of him being out of my sight quite well, but a glass wouldn't hurt. 'White wine, please. The dry one.'

I brought him up to speed with the assessment then moved to what I really wanted to talk about.

'Was there really nothing about Teagan's first pregnancy in your file?'

Chris looked up. 'You don't need to worry about her.'

But I did worry. Teagan had stirred up the maternal instinct in me. Professionally, I hoped I could help her be the sort of mother she aspired to be and overcome some of the challenges she would face. At a personal level, I liked her. I admired her spunk.

Why was Chris trying—unconvincingly—to dissuade me?

He had nice eyes—more grey than blue; full of concern. I couldn't see him as a kingpin of corruption, whatever Dean thought. But I'd met psychopaths in my forensic term and not all of them had been leering maniacs. Some had been polite, even charming.

And I'd seen his car in the carpark that day at the river when I was so spooked.

'How's the hospital review going?' I watched him, looking for the Gomez behind the sympathetic eyes. 'Are the Barclays worried?'

'Grace feels she should have kept a better record of things. I gather...your husband seems to think there is a lot of jobs for the boys. Skimming off the top, too, maybe. Not that he tells us much.'

Dean was telling me even less.

'Who was behind bringing Dean here?' I asked, though suddenly I knew. 'It was you, right?'

Chris hesitated. 'Not officially. The place needed an overhaul. I was thinking the manager should retire. And Athol and I don't always see eye to eye. I know one of the government MPs, so...look, if it got out I was involved I'd have no hope of preselection, especially if there are job losses. I will admit I've got more than I bargained for. But it was necessary.'

Surely he wouldn't have called for an enquiry if he'd been involved in a jobs for mates scheme?

'Does Gordon know you're behind it?'

Chris shrugged, expression glum. 'I've a feeling he's waiting to drop the bomb at the final preselection vote next year. He wanted the hospital review too—just didn't want to take the fall politically. Everyone knows his own accounts are meticulous.'

Gordon hadn't managed to stay in power by luck.

'What's Athol's role?'

'When he retired he stayed on the board and handed over his practice to me; I brought in Massoud and Zahra. I've been trying to get a new operating theatre ever since; Athol doesn't seem to realise we've moved past chloroform.'

Chris had gone out of his way to befriend and help me. But there were things he wasn't telling me. Was it just confidentiality? Or was there something he didn't want me to know?

I had a date with Dean for lunch the next day at the Riley Arms. I was at the table when he phoned to cancel. He had to fly to Sydney, he said; he'd be gone for one, possibly two nights.

'Will you be okay? Sam said he's had a word to the Barclays—and the Reardens—about not shooting roos around our place.' Mostly Dean seemed reassured by my new sense of calm and purpose. But alone for two days? It would have been hard in Auckland or Melbourne...

'Absolutely,' I said, as much to convince myself as him. We hung up.

'Dry white wine?'

It was quiet—the only other customers were Conor Rearden and a younger man I didn't know, possibly his son—and Brian had come to get my order rather than wait for me to come to the bar. I had been thinking of leaving, but it wasn't like anyone was expecting me anywhere.

'Just two orange juices, thanks Brian. And the fish and chips.'

I was waiting for the meal and wiping Noah's OJ from down his front when Matt Barclay arrived, looking freckled and slightly sunburnt in a blue singlet and dusty shorts, and went to the bar to order a beer. He looked around; nodded at Conor and his younger companion before he saw me. I smiled and turned back to my phone, checking my friends' Facebook posts.

'Husband hard at work?' Matt wandered over and sat down at my table, ignoring my efforts to appear preoccupied.

'I imagine so,' I said. I looked at him warily, wondering what his agenda was. If he didn't have one, maybe he'd answer a few questions. Like why Joe tried to assault his mother. Or did he know anything about the messages in my PO box and the dead kangaroos?

'Gonna close the hospital, is he?'

I sat back in my chair and took a good look at him. He was twenty-three; looked older and acted younger. He took after his father, I decided; Lachlan followed the maternal line. Matt had Gordon's lighter complexion and beefy body shape, without the gut; and his arm muscles were more impressive. This was the son who was going to be the farmer. Looked like he was starting out at the hard end. My guess was Gordon didn't keep him informed—if he shared anything about the hospital, it would be with Lachlan.

'You tell me,' I said.

'What I'll tell you is no good ever came of suits coming here and messing in our business.'

'Well, thanks for the warning.' I was aware my heart was racing. Brian, I saw from the corner of my eye, was watching, which offered some reassurance. 'I don't have anything to do with that. I'm trying to help some of the women in the town. Maybe you can help too.'

'Yeah?' Matt took a swig of beer and leaned the chair back on two legs.

'Everyone's worried about the baby-killer threat. Who do you think sent it?'

Whatever Matt had thought I was going to ask, it wasn't this. His Adam's apple moved up and down. 'Morettis, probably. Been bad news around here for years,' he finally said.

'Seems Joe Moretti thought the same about you at one stage,' I said, thinking about the skirmish Joe and the Barclay boys had got into, possibly involving Grace and/or Teagan.

There was a look of bewilderment quickly followed by a flash of anger. The chair came down with a thud on all four legs and he leaned closer. 'What the fuck's he been saying?'

'What do you think he's been saying?'

'That little bitch...' Matt shook his head. 'It's got nothing to do with any anonymous letters. Also: none of your business.'

That little bitch? Teagan?

'So people keep telling me,' I said.

'Matt, me boy,' Conor called from the other side of the room. 'What you doing fraternising with the enemy?'

I stiffened.

Matt laughed. 'See? Really not welcome here, are you?'

I felt the heat of shame rising in my neck, the schoolgirl blush of being singled out and laughed at. Noah had stopped playing and was eyeing Matt nervously.

I heard Conor's chair scrape the ground and footsteps heading in my direction.

'Matt, come over and have a drink with me and Pat,' Conor said.

Brian emerged from behind the bar. 'As you were, Conor. Socialising with Matt ends in trouble. Let's keep it nice.'

'Matt's a grown boy,' said Conor. I could smell him

from where he stood behind me—beer breath, stale smoke and sweat. 'Think you can make your own mind up, Matt me boy, can't you?'

Matt stood up smirking: all teenager despite his actual age. 'Reckon I can. Another beer for me and my friends, Brian.'

'Well...' Brian hesitated. 'Just sit over with Conor, Matt, and leave Mrs Harris in peace.'

'Mrs *Harris*,' said Matt. 'Psychoanalysing us, are you?'

'I'm trying to have a quiet lunch, thank you.' I managed not to say *Doctor* Harris actually.

Conor made as if to walk away, waited until Brian was back behind the bar and then strode back and leaned into me. Now the smell was sour rather than stale, the anger in his eyes unmistakable.

'You're making things worse,' he said. Droplets of beer and spit sprayed my face. 'We don't need your sort around here, not you or your husband.'

'That's enough.' It was Chris standing beside us, arm on Conor's. 'Leave her alone.'

'Says who? You?' Conor let out a guffaw. 'Maybe her husband could look after his missus. But you?'

'If I need to.' Chris's voice was like ice, his stare at Conor leaving no doubt he meant business. Brian appeared on Conor's other side and Conor allowed Matt to pull him over to where he had been sitting.

I took a few deep breaths, too rattled to thank Chris. I hadn't really been threatened—but the attempt to intimidate was horribly effective.

It was a couple of minutes more before I'd collected myself enough to form the obvious question: what was Conor so worried about?

My hand was still shaking when I went to put the key into the ignition. I stopped and changed my mind. I wasn't going home—I needed the internet. I put Noah back in the pusher and headed to the hospital shop.

The computer was free, as always. And slow.

Conor Rearden wanted Dean to stop meddling with the hospital. No surprise there—Dean felt he was heavily involved in jobs for mates and union deals. I thought of how I had worried that Joe thought I might unearth something about the death of Joshua or his wife via my link to Teagan. Was Conor worried about my link with Róisín? And was Matt connected with them other than through his friendship with the youngest son? I could see him lining up with the Reardens in defence of the hospital—but Matt had some more specific issue with the Morettis. He felt strongly about them, that was certain.

Which took me back to the fight between Joe and the Barclays, if that's what it had been. When Joe had lost his job and *then* come to the conclusion that Gordon and the Reardens were behind Joshua going missing.

Google came up with nothing useful, which wasn't

surprising; my searches for *Barclay, Moretti, union, Rearden* were broad, to say the least. Jeannie brought over some children's books for Noah and looked over my shoulder. 'Anything particular you're looking for, dear?' She winced as she put down a coffee I hadn't ordered. 'Arthritis. I feel as sprightly as I did when I was thirty—until I move.'

There was nothing wrong with her eyesight, though. 'Interested in the Barclays?' she squinted at the screen and her eyes twinkled mischievously, rheumy though they were. 'Any one of them in particular? I remember Gordon's parents. His mother used to take off, you know—famous for it. She was found in the fish shop window once, squirming around among the fish.'

I stared. Jeannie started giggling. 'She was only three at the time, of course.'

'Oh. Well...'—I was struggling to think up a good reason for my Google search—'Lachlan's likely to be the local member isn't he?' I took a sip of the coffee without thinking. To my surprise it wasn't bad. Jeannie saw my expression. 'Your husband has supplied me with a plunger and beans for his morning constitutional along the river. Thought he wouldn't mind me sharing it with you.' She sighed. 'Myself, I don't see what's wrong with instant.'

I hadn't known about Dean's morning walk. He had to be missing the gym as much as me—country living wasn't as healthy as it was made out to be. I wondered if he got his coffee from Jeannie because he was afraid the admin workers would spit in it. 'The Barclays?'

'Oh yes. Sun shines out of young Lachlan's behind—as far as his mother's concerned, anyway.' Jeannie didn't look like she was quite as sure. 'Now the other one, Matt? Always thought Matt was too much like his dad, but without the brains.'

I smiled encouragingly.

'Likes a fight...underage drinking, that sort of thing. Cops just pick him up and drop him and the young Rearden boy home.'

I wondered if Pat and Matt also went roo shooting.

'I heard Matt got into a fight with Joe Moretti. A while back.'

'You could be right, dear. My memory isn't quite what it used to be—could be going the same way as my joints. Did it have something to do with Teagan?'

'Could be.'

'Teagan. Yes. She was a bit wild as a teenager. All that metal in her face, and the tattoos...I suppose she still is. I think,' she continued as if she'd read my mind, 'Grace was critical of Teagan and Joe stood up for her.'

People fought over smaller issues. But it was just small-town stuff—not in any way connected, as far as I could see, to writing a threatening letter to the police years later. Nor did it seem connected to why any of the three men—Joe, Matt and Conor—were trying to warn me off. All telling me the same thing: I was making things worse, and they wanted me out of town. I felt it was safe to conclude that Conor was motivated by my connection to Dean and the hospital review. The other two? Matt because he was mates with Pat Rearden, and Joe because of what I might find out about his daughter's first pregnancy. One of them was probably responsible for the petty messages; I suspected Matt, even though he had the least reason. It was too juvenile and required too much effort for Joe. Conor was the type of man that considered women weak, though; maybe he'd target me to get at Dean.

At least there were no more dead kangaroos on the

driveway on my way home, though I could still make out the leg of the grey grandad in the bushes where Dean had dragged it.

I ignored my mother's voicemails. Dean rang from Sydney to say he was talking to his firm's auditors. I gathered he wanted them to come to Riley and they were less than enthusiastic, especially so close to Christmas.

'Jeannie gave me some of your special coffee,' I said. 'You'd better get another supply in.'

There was a pause. 'Yeah. Sure. Got to go...love you.'

I stared at the phone. Had he sounded guilty—over coffee? Or was I getting paranoid?

I threw a salad together, doused myself in insect repellent and poured myself a glass of wine, taking my meal to eat outside as the sun set.

In a silence broken only by the calls of birds going home to roost—no sign of the barking owls—I allowed myself to just be. For once, I actually was able to do it—forget everything and enjoy the moment. Maybe it was the wine. The beauty of a pink and grey galah sitting for a moment on a dying branch of the gumtree closest to the house made me feel it was more than that. There really was a kind of peace in the country that you didn't get in the city.

I was finishing my second glass and dusk was on the edge of night when I heard the boards creak on the stock bridge. My first thought was *Dean's back*. But then I remembered: I had the car. And the only way out was across the same bridge this car was coming along.

It could be Grace—maybe she'd heard that Dean had been called away? But at nearly 9 p.m.?

It would be common knowledge that Dean was out of town. Was someone taking the opportunity to get me alone?

I jumped up, sending the bottle of wine clattering over and spilling onto the deck. The only light on in the house was in the kitchen. I turned it off, then realised they'd know someone was home. My mind was racing, but in circles. Did I get Noah? Should we hide? Would they go away if I didn't answer the door? What had been a remote idyllic landscape a moment ago had transformed in seconds—now the shadows looked ominous and the dark slash of the vegetation around the creek was a barrier as imposing as any wall.

This was why I had begged Dean to let us go home. I had no illusions about my capacity to defend myself and Noah. I was a hundred and seventy centimetres tall and weighed sixty kilos fully dressed, and the only time I had ever had to act under pressure, to save the most precious thing in my life, I had frozen. Now, for an instant, it happened again. As I stood watching the dust clouds come closer I had absolutely no idea what to do.

Then a little voice—my own, somewhere deep inside— said, *Noah* and I ran to the phone. After what felt like an hour looking up the number of the local police station, I called. Waited. Listened to an after-hours voicemail advising me to contact the police station at Narrowmine or *if it is an emergency* to call triple zero.

Shit. Should have done that in the first place. But the strange car had pulled up outside now—*no time no time no time…*

I ran to the kitchen, grabbed a knife and headed out the front door. Straight into a blinding headlight-glare that blocked out the vehicle itself. I held up the knife. The lights dimmed, a beaten-up blue ute was revealed—and a man got out. Much older than me, but with that toughness and strong musculature that stays into the sixties with men who've worked in physical jobs. I thought: Conor Rearden. My stomach turned over, remembering his belligerence in the pub earlier. Was the knife really a good idea? Would I be able to use it, or would he turn it on me? My palms were sweating.

But it wasn't Conor. It was Joe Moretti. Teagan's father.

Did this improve things? Joe was same age as Conor but not as well built, and probably diminished by years of drink. On the other hand I knew more about him and why he might want me gone.

A domestic abuser: loving dad one minute, backhanders the next. A man who had killed his own father, and who might have killed his child and wife. And who might be the father of one if not both of his daughter's children.

'What do you want, Joe?' My voice was louder than I had intended.

'I need to talk to you.' He was walking towards me and I stepped back involuntarily.

'This isn't the place, Joe,' I said. 'Go home. I can meet you tomorrow at the hospital.'

'Just a few minutes is all I need.' He stopped. Saw the knife in my hand and looked around as if Dean might suddenly materialise. I saw his tension ease when he realised there was no sign of him.

'Go home.'

'You don't need the knife. I just want to talk to you about Teagan.'

'What about Teagan?' As soon as I said it, I knew I'd lost my chance to run him off. And he knew it too.

'Look, let's sit. No reason we can't be civil.' He didn't wait for an answer; he walked to the veranda and sat on the chair opposite where I had been sitting, standing the wine bottle upright. That simple act made my skin crawl. He was in my space and I was powerless. I wasn't going to get rid of him until he'd said his piece. I took the other chair, pulling it back towards the kitchen door.

'Heard you'd been asking around.' Joe was looking directly at me. What little hair he had left didn't look like it had been cut in a while, and a shadow of stubble made his face look even darker in the shadows. He was probably smarter than Conor. The thought didn't give me any relief. Nor did the word *psychopath* that was running around in my mind. I was struggling to slow my breathing.

'Saw you out at the river, checking out where Donna died.'

'What, you were following me?' Had it been him, not Chris, I'd heard?

'Nah, I go out there sometimes. Wonder what I could have done different, you know?'

I could smell the beer on him, but he didn't appear drunk. Maybe just enough to disinhibit him. I swallowed. Regardless of whether he had killed Joshua or Donna—or both—he had killed his father. I gripped the knife tighter and he looked at it.

'Ever used one of those in anger?' he asked. He leaned back, eyes focused on my face which, I was quite sure, looked terrified. 'Where I grew up, we raised our own chickens. My father showed me—quick twist of the neck, then you need to draw them—slice them open and take out the guts. Rabbits too; Ma made a nice *ragu* with 'em.'

I could feel myself getting light-headed and tried to slow my breathing. *Focus.*

'Mr Moretti—say what you came to say and then please leave.'

185

'You're a psychologist, Teagan tells me. Do psychologists believe people can change?'

I was taken aback by the question—I had moved on in my mind from the chickens and rabbits to his father, wondering if he'd used a knife on him as well.

'I do Mr Moretti. Yes.' I did believe it, didn't I? Why else had I studied all those years? What was the point of my work without this belief? I sat up a little straighter. 'If they want to enough.'

'Teagan wants to enough. And she likes you.'

I stared at him.

'She needs help,' Joe continued. 'Not too many people willing to do that here in Riley, and fewer that actually can.' He leaned forward. 'If you're sticking around, then I'm holding you responsible for helping her. It's your job, I reckon. Help her, help the kid.'

'I...' I took a breath. 'Teagan's got a good heart,' I finally said. 'And she'll do okay.'

Joe leaned in, his elbow resting in the wine that had spilt on the table; he didn't seem to notice. 'You know she's not got a mum. I did my best but stuff she never got...woman stuff. You've got a kid, you're trained. Help her be a good mother, okay? Like Donna would have been if Joshua hadn't died.'

There were tears in the corner of his eyes.

All of the things I had thought about him...The words were out of my mouth before I had thought what impact they could have.

'What happened to Joshua?'

There was a long pause, but he held my gaze.

'Gordon Barclay wanted to win the seat. Back then, when he didn't own the whole fucking place, I could have won, and he wasn't going to risk it.'

'You think he took Joshua?'

'He wouldn't dirty his hands. He got someone to do it. Rearden, I reckon, or at least Rearden organised it. Joshua probably wasn't meant to die, maybe something went wrong.' He sighed. In the shrug of his shoulders he conveyed a lifetime of weary contemplation of where his life had gone wrong.

I didn't bother pointing out that Conor Rearden had an alibi. Joe was right: he or Gordon could well have paid someone else to do it. 'So why write to the police now?'

'That bit of poison? Same thing. Warning Chris McCormack to get out of his boy's way.'

Poison. That was what Grace had said. *Poison pen.* I thought of my old schoolmate Olivia Doyle and all the bitchy notes she'd written about me: it was stereotypically female behaviour. Had Teagan written it? I couldn't see it. And if Joe hadn't killed his son, then neither he nor Teagan would have the insider information the warning contained.

I pointed out the logical problem with Joe's theory. 'Why would that be directed at Chris? He doesn't have children.'

'You reckon he'd want the death of a child on his conscience? After he couldn't save his own?'

Joe was clutching at straws. No way Gordon was involved in alerting the police—his fury over the warning letter at the dinner had been real. And according to Chris, he had the ammunition he needed to ensure Lachlan was preselected, at least if the hospital review meant job losses—Gordon just had to let it out that Chris had been behind bringing Dean in. It felt like Joe *needed* to know who did it, and he wanted Gordon and Conor to fit. But I had no sense that Joe was covering up his own crime.

'If Conor did it for money, why's he still here in Riley?' Surely he would have bought a big house and car somewhere no one knew him.

Joe shrugged. 'Maybe he gave the money to his kids.'

'Róisín was left money by Al's parents.'

Joe snorted. 'Them? They were both on the disability pension.'

I opened and closed my mouth. Took a breath. 'Joe, you worked for the Barclays after Joshua died. You can't have thought they were responsible back then.' I watched his guard come up.

'It wasn't till I got a bit closer to them that I realised...' He stopped, shook his head. 'There isn't much they wouldn't do to get what they want.'

'What was the fight about? With Grace and her sons?'

Joe's fist came down so hard on the table that the empty bottle flew off and the wooden veranda shook. I pushed the chair backwards and the knife fell to the floor. We both looked down—but it was his foot that went over it first.

'Forget all that,' he said. His voice was ragged now, a man only just in control.

Had he been like this, I wondered, just before he'd killed his father?

'You said you believed people could change. I grew up watching my father beat my mother till she bled. Every damn week, new bruises, sometimes broken bones. I had to save my mother from him, because neither of them was ever going to change. And that was the day I decided I wasn't going to be like him. I wasn't a great husband or a perfect father, but I did my best. And I was—I was better than my father. The fucking Barclays? They aren't ever going to change.'

He was sweating. So was I. I could feel it in the creases of my neck. My legs were starting to shake and I wasn't sure how long I'd be able to stand, half up against the chair and leaning as far away from him as I could.

'So just do your fucking job,' said Joe. 'Look after Teagan.'

Dean was away for three nights. The evenings were no longer cooling below twenty degrees and there was a sameness to the days, all blue sky and dusty plains. I spent the evenings watching the sunset, drinking iced tea. Eventually I would sleep; when I woke I would stand over Noah, just taking in the deep, innocent sleep of early childhood.

The third night I fell asleep on a beanbag on the veranda and woke as the sun rose. Watching the light bring life to the landscape, I told myself that I had done this. I had stood sentinel over my child and we were all right. Despite Joe and Conor and the Barclays, and whoever had written the letter to the police and probably then sent the other warnings to us, nothing awful had happened.

Yet.

I spent most of those days reflecting on what Joe had told me—and what he hadn't. I had said I believed people could change, and it was true, they could. Their behaviour, anyway. Changing the core of what drove them was less likely. I didn't entirely believe in Grace's blank-slate theory; both genes and upbringing play a part in how we think, what our strengths and weaknesses are. I wasn't kidding myself that Joe was not a threat, or even that he'd been honest, but it occurred to me to focus on what expertise I could bring to the problem: the understanding of why people do things. People lie all the time—some little lies, some bigger. Behaviour, over years, tells a more reliable story.

What did I know about Joe?

I knew he had come from violence—and been violent himself. Teagan said, and Kate had confirmed, that he had mostly succeeded in getting that violence under control and been a reasonable single father. By his own account, killing his father had been what pulled him up and resulted in a decision to be someone different.

Whatever had happened with the Barclays years earlier, Jeannie and Róisín both agreed that Joe had been protecting, standing up for, his daughter: just as he had stood up for and protected his mother. Which meant he had a view of himself as a protector of women in his family. What if he'd seen Donna as a threat to Teagan? Would he have killed Donna to protect the baby? Maybe…but it would have been more consistent if he had protected Donna, because she accidentally killed Joshua. In that scenario, Donna's death was either an accident, or suicide fuelled by grief and maybe guilt, as the town assumed.

Rather than trying to hound me out of town, Joe was trying to persuade me to look out for Teagan. I just had to work out what had caused the argument with the Barclays— which seemed to have involved Teagan. If Joe had been responsible for Teagan's first pregnancy, I didn't think he'd have come to see me. Certainly not for the reason he did.

I started to consider an alternative narrative. If I was right, Joe wasn't a risk to Teagan after all.

I did a little reorganising of the postnatal-group program. This week we'd look at triggers from the past.

Teagan provided morning tea—'My nonna's recipe'—which was a buttery teacake with blue, pink and white swirls of icing and tiny figures from popular fairy tales. When Róisín saw it, she looked like she'd shed thirty years. For someone who claimed she couldn't cook, Teagan showed promise.

'There is a famous paper about how we become parents,' I began, 'called "Ghosts from the Nursery".'

'Our own ghosts,' said Zahra, finishing off a coffee she'd brought with her. Dean and I weren't the only coffee snobs in town. 'For me, I am more worried about cobwebs.' She smiled and looked radiant. 'But mostly I think I have brushed them out.'

Had the medication finally worked?

'Well I guess what I'm talking about is harder to brush out. Stuff that is about what makes us who we are—what we think and how we react.'

Five blank faces.

'Think about your hot-button issues. Things that your child or partner do that trigger a reaction.'

This produced ideas. I had to work hard to get beyond the level of towels on the bathroom floor, but we managed to boil it down to the way they criticised the child or partner if they didn't do something right—which led to discussion of criticism from their own parents when they were young. 'How might that make us feel as adults?'

'Makes us anxious,' said Róisín, with a haunted expression that also suggested 'unloved'.

'Pissed off.' Teagan gave a hint of a smile but there was steel in her voice.

'Needing to seek out approval from someone else,' said Zahra.

'Like you need a...a shell. Armour.' Kate crossed her arms: yeah, okay, I get it, just don't ask me anymore. I had to stop myself smiling.

Which left Sophie.

She stared at me. 'Like you have to appear...perfect. To be loved.'

'Mmm...interesting.' I resisted punching the air. 'Let's say your parents did criticise you a lot'—I avoided looking at Sophie but I could feel her gaze—'you can build a wall'—like Kate and Róisín—'or do your best to be like they want. But you'll always feel insecure, a fraud...If everything on the outside is an act because of your own issues, your children will be pretty confused. They'll think it's about them.'

'So you want us to just show we feel like shit and life is shit?' Kate was joking. Partially. Teagan looked amused.

'You need to *know* how you feel—and deal with it. Don't pretend it doesn't exist. And let your kid know that if you are feeling crap, it isn't because of them. They need to know they don't have to fix it.'

'All right, but some of us don't "feel like shit".' Sophie wasn't going down without a fight. 'I have a husband, a family I'm grateful for. I know how lucky...'

'Jesus, give me a break.' Teagan grabbed the Snow White figurine from the cake and flung it across the room.

Sophie straightened up, ready for a fight.

'Being a single mother—or waiting for the father of your child to commit—can be tough.' I looked at Sophie pointedly.

'Men are about one thing and one thing only,' Teagan said. 'We can probably blame their mothers. *I'm* grateful I'm having a girl.'

Sophie didn't look like she was going to back down.

'That's why you're here, isn't it?' I said quickly. 'To be the best mothers you can, and let go of things from the previous generation that have been unhelpful?'

Before there could be any more discussion, I gave them a homework task for their final group. Teagan announced she wouldn't be coming—she'd still be in hospital after having Indiana.

I finished the session off and the others, including Sophie, wished her well. While the women went to collect their children, I cornered Teagan and asked her to stay back.

'I suppose you're going to tell me off.'

'It wouldn't hurt to remember the group rules,' I said. 'Respecting each other makes everyone feel safe.'

'Yeah well, I don't respect the fucking Barclays and when she tries pushing them down my throat I'm gonna pull her off her fricking pedestal. She thinks she's so much better than me because she's married to money. I think I'm way smarter not tying myself to a pile of shit.'

'You're pretty upset about the Barclays.'

Teagan's expression was all *you reckon?* Her eyes hid behind her long fringe as she pulled at the chipped black nail polish on her thumb.

'So is your dad. Seemed worried about you too.'

Teagan shrugged.

'Is the issue you have with the Barclays something we need to deal with in this group?'

'They killed my brother.'

'None of that involves Sophie, does it?' I paused, gentler.

'Is there something else? Something more recent? Maybe eight years ago?'

Teagan peered up at me through a long section of hair that she appeared to be growing—I couldn't make her eyes out, so I doubt she could see me; maybe she heard something in my voice.

'Nothing happened eight years ago.' She didn't sound convincing, didn't sound like she was even trying to be.

I took a breath. This wasn't unravelling a mystery—this was dealing with a client I was worried about. 'Did you do a deal that said you weren't allowed to say anything?'

It was a guess—but an educated one. I kicked myself for taking so long. Doing the maths finally cemented it for me— eight years ago was when the fight between the Barclays and the Morettis had occurred. It was also when Teagan had her first pregnancy.

This time her head shot up and she stared at me. 'Who told you?'

I let out a breath. 'No one. And you're my client, Teagan. I can't talk to anyone about it.'

'I haven't told anyone, like they asked me to. And you can't either, ever.' She looked uneasy.

I nodded.

Teagan grimaced. 'I'm not stupid; I didn't expect to be taken home to Grace and Gordon. Boys like the Barclays marry girls like Sophie.' She crossed her arms over her belly, looked down at it for a moment. 'I was doing some holiday work for them. Lachlan and Matt were...around. We were young, and Matt got his hands on some dope and booze... It only happened a few times. We knew it wasn't going anywhere.'

'But you got pregnant.'

195

Teagan looked miserable, and still very young. 'Yeah.'

'What happened?'

'*Shit* happened—like it always does. My father went up there after he'd been on the grog. Gordon wasn't there, just Grace. And Lachlan and Matt. When Dad got angry, Matt punched him—and then they threatened to bring charges against *us*.'

Teagan looked out the window. 'Part of me knew I couldn't look after a baby. Dad kept saying he'd help, but…I was scared. Much more than I am now. I wasn't ready.'

'You were only a kid, Teagan.'

'Grace came to see me,' Teagan continued. 'Offered me five thousand dollars to get rid of it.'

I nodded, and waited.

'I took the money. She made me sign some shit, non-disclosure whatever. Couldn't be ruining her son's life, could we?' She chipped off the last flake of black polish from her thumb and started on another finger. 'And I went to Sydney. I had this great idea that somehow I could study fashion and still have the baby. No way was I having an abortion. Figured I'd use the money to pay for some baby gear.'

'So…?'

'Miscarriage,' said Teagan. 'Twenty-two weeks. They told me he wouldn't have survived even if it had been further on. Things weren't right with him, they said, but…his little face looked perfect to me.' There were tears in her eyes as she went on. 'And then I blew Grace's five grand on drugs. Pretty much hoped they'd kill me…I just wanted to feel nothing.'

So. The baby's abnormalities weren't down to Joe being the father of his own grandchild. This would be a mystery without a solution, according to Dr Google: mostly they never found out what caused multiple foetal abnormalities. And Teagan had been using alcohol and drugs—which she probably hadn't told the doctors.

'You survived.'

'And what doesn't kill you, makes you stronger, right?'

I smiled, nodded. 'It can. And you are strong.'

'Yeah well, not so strong that if beautiful-I've-got-it-all Sophie keeps talking about the fucking fabulous Barclays I won't chuck something at her.'

At least she hadn't sent the whole cake flying.

'She probably doesn't know anything about it.'

'I'm sure she doesn't; Grace has got her hands on the reins, least where those boys are concerned.'

'Sophie...has her own stuff to manage. Can you try and give her some space?'

Teagan got up to go. 'Can you ask her to do the same for me?' Teagan's irrepressible grin surfaced. 'Maybe also tell her that bloody frightening smile of hers isn't fooling anyone. If Tom can't learn to toe the line, he's gonna turn out like Matt. And I bet that'd take the smile off her face.'

I wouldn't be saying any of that to Sophie, but it did make me wonder. I doubted she knew any of the history—her superiority over Teagan came from unthinking privilege. But Sophie had seemed more stressed in the last couple of groups. Had there been tension in the Barclay household? Had she overheard conversations, perhaps? Things brought up again because the warning to the police had put the Morettis back in the spotlight?

Of course, there could be a totally different reason for Sophie to have heard conversations that made her uneasy. To do with who had fathered Teagan's current child. I thought of how Teagan had looked away when I suggested a DNA test; about Jed's accusation that he wasn't the father.

Teagan turned in the door as she left. 'My mum...she's coming to me most nights. She's trying to warn me.' Her hand went to her belly. 'Whoever wrote to the police knew something about Joshua—so however you look at it, this has some connection to Indiana.'

'Teagan...' I took a breath. 'I know you think...know... Jed is Indiana's father. But is there any chance...'

I could see her hackles rising.

'...any chance someone *other* than Jed could *think* he was the father?'

In the pause Teagan looked torn—to come clean or keep the defences shored up? What decided her in the end was that she liked me. And trusted me. And wanted to change.

'Look, it happened once, okay? I was drunk. I'd had a fight with Jed...wasn't like we were a real item then, still just working it out. It was too early for Matt to be her dad.'

'So Matt could *think* he was the father?'

Teagan nodded; she looked miserable.

'And you don't want to ask Jed to get a DNA test because you don't want to risk it?'

'Un-huh.'

Which left me wondering. Maybe it wasn't just Jed who was concerned about who Indiana's father was. If Matt thought that he was the baby's father, did that put Teagan and Indiana at risk?

The next week passed in a haze of humidity that made breathing a struggle. Nights were long, with the constant hum of the fan, the buzz of mosquitos and the sweet smell of mosquito coils burning. I sat on the veranda, keeping Noah in the shade, sprinkling him with water from a bucket when the heat made us both irritable. The tank was getting so low we couldn't drink the water; we were on bottled stuff now. The local birds had taken to visiting as fast as I could fill the bucket. I watched the horizon in the half-formed hope that it would bring me answers. Instead it brought shrieking galahs that landed in distant gumtrees, and a kookaburra couple that eyed me warily as they worked up the courage to swoop down and collect a prize of meat scraps.

'Kookas,' Noah would say and break out into giggles when I tried to mimic their call. I hadn't heard my barking owls for a couple of weeks.

Noah and I spent the afternoon putting up Christmas decorations, even if we would have little chance to enjoy them. He mostly understood that the angels and baubles were meant to go on the tree, but he wouldn't relinquish the striped candy sticks or the Santa that laughed when you pressed his belly. After we'd draped tinsel all over the house, he wanted to pull it down so we could start again.

Dean put him to bed and we ate dinner as usual on the veranda.

There had been something different about Dean this week. It was a long time since I'd seen him this happy. Perhaps things were healing between us, I'd thought; it seemed easier, anyway.

Now, as he poured himself a drink and sat down with me, I felt something was up. There was a nervous energy to him, a tension in the tendons of his arm that jiggled the beer. A hint of that boyish excitement he got when he was pleased with himself.

'So you want to tell me about why you're in such a good mood?'

'I'll be done soon,' he said with a grin.

I didn't feel like opening the champagne; my group wasn't finished yet. 'What does that mean for the hospital?'

Dean looked more serious. 'A good manager could save it, but I think the government will find it easier to cut their losses.' He shrugged. He cared more than he liked to show— the trouble was it would make doing his job too hard if he had to keep considering the personal and community costs. Easier to compartmentalise.

I could almost see the gears change as he focused on the positive. 'I convinced the government to pay for our auditors to come in.'

That would win him kudos at his company.

'Forensic guys,' he said. 'They'll be here before Christmas.' He grinned. 'Not that these are the types to celebrate Christmas. Halloween would be more their style.'

'Why?' I asked, puzzled. 'If you found something,

couldn't you just give it to them?'

'This needs every detail documented. I have lots of dodgy deals and corner cutting; frankly the culture is so corrupt everyone is either doing it, benefiting from it or turning a blind eye.' He laughed. 'Even Jeannie at the café.'

'Jeannie? No!'

Dean shrugged. 'Well I'm pretty sure there's money missing from the café takings, but honestly it's so minor in the grand scheme of things I doubt anyone will chase it too hard. The auditors will be focusing on the big numbers.'

'What's Gordon's reaction?'

'Cautious. The money boys report straight to their boss not me—and he's a big contributor to the Libs so my guess is Gordon will know what they find before I do.'

I must have looked as appalled as I felt.

Dean raised an eyebrow. 'It's not about letting the bad guys get away with it. More a courtesy call—Gordon is smart enough to have totally clean hands in all this.'

'What about the board?' Which included two Barclays.

'They should have known but I'm thinking not. Primarily a scam Conor has been leading. Nothing will give me more pleasure than seeing his union-flunkey arse in jail. Though of course no one, including Doctor McDreamy, is in the clear.'

It was a mild jibe, nothing more. But my reaction was immediate. 'Did you get any more coffee while you were in Sydney?'

'Won't need it much longer,' he said, without breaking stride.

I paused. I hadn't really allowed myself to think about this…but it must have been churning away in there.

'So I hear you go walking with a coffee every morning,'

I said. 'Do you go by yourself?'

This time there was a pause.

'Clears my head, walking down by the river,' he said.

I thought of his brother Kieran, and his wife's affair, and...

My God, I was being ridiculous. Who the hell was Dean going to have a fling with in Riley?

I spent the week cooking for Grace's Christmas Fete; having the oven on didn't make the house any more comfortable. Between the white chocolate meringue and the carrot and walnut cakes, the apricot jam had overflowed onto the stovetop and taken me twenty minutes to clean. And the gas bottle ran out. When Dean came home, I was less Nigella Lawson and more Gordon Ramsay's kitchen nightmare.

There was only one more group to go, and I had almost completed all the outstanding cognitive assessments—and then I'd be in Melbourne for Christmas, with probably no need to return.

I stopped in to see Chris and ended up having lunch with him at the Arms. It would have felt more celebratory if I wasn't still worried about Teagan. As I counted the days till we left, the mystery surrounding the threatening letter became less and less pressing for me. But it was linked to the fate of Joshua Moretti, and the associated secrets that would continue to hang over Teagan.

And—I had to face it—I wanted to know. I was curious.

'Teagan told me about her first pregnancy,' I said, after we had ordered.

There was a long pause. Then: 'Oh?'

This was where it got tricky, even if he was the treating medico. Teagan hadn't given me permission to divulge the information about Matt—the opposite in fact, thanks to Grace's non-disclosure agreement. Presumably that wouldn't cover her current pregnancy, but still: my promise was to Teagan.

'I'm leaving soon, but...I'm worried Teagan and her baby might be in danger.'

Chris frowned. 'From whoever wrote to the police? I don't think you need to be concerned; it didn't have anything to do with Teagan.'

'I *had* figured it was Conor creating havoc, but...'

Chris's expression was kind but there was a suggestion that he was humouring me.

'She's anxious. Maybe it's natural, after losing the first pregnancy...'

But.

Matt hung out with the Reardens. He was still number one on my suspect list for the harassments we'd suffered. Even if he'd only done it to help out his mates. But what if he had his own agenda?

The little bitch, he'd said.

What if Matt had written the letter to the police in order to send a message to Teagan? Subtly—in a way she would get but that wouldn't implicate him? He could have got the insider information about what Joshua was buried in from his father, in the same way Sophie had found out about the anonymous letter to the police.

Matt was an angry man. I could absolutely see him being pissed off at Teagan, and his parents, about what had happened eight years earlier. And if he had fathered this child too, maybe he was worried Teagan would ask for money. More money. Perhaps she already had.

I thought about Gordon's meticulous trail of receipts.

His family's income was probably well beyond anything I could contemplate, but if he had his hands on the reins, maybe they couldn't access it easily. Could Matt be tied in with Conor in the scams at the hospital? The café? Gordon might be squeaky clean but it didn't mean his son was. I could envisage him taking money ahead of Jeannie, if he had access to it.

'She's going to have the baby in a week,' I said slowly. 'Could you run a test?

'You mean for genetic abnormalities?'

'You *did* see the ultrasound report, then?'

Chris's eyes widened. He had been worried that Joe had fathered Teagan's child.

I could at least put his mind at rest on that. 'The father of the first child wasn't…who you might be thinking. I can't say more. But no; it wasn't a genetic test I was after. I meant a paternity test. Teagan doesn't want to ask Jed in case… Well, it's more to take someone else *out* of the frame.'

Chris looked like he'd lost me back at the first pregnancy. He finally said, 'Teagan can look after herself. It's her choice to ask for maintenance or involve the father, not yours. Isabel, this isn't your problem.'

Chris was right. By the time Indiana was born I was hoping I'd be in my last week here. I could leave Riley and its secrets and reclaim my own life. It didn't feel as good as it should. The lattes in cafés, the late-night political debates and gossip with friends…I missed those, yet I was reluctant to let Teagan and her baby go. She'd survived so much, yet refused to be cowed.

Chris saw my expression. He hesitated. 'Look, I'd need a sample from either Jed…or the other candidate. With their permission.'

Kind of what I'd thought. Which was why I'd ordered a kit from ancestry.com. Not that I was sure Teagan would use it, but at least it would give her the option.

I wondered how much Teagan could trust Chris. She'd need someone after I left. Dean hadn't cleared him regarding the hospital problem. And I still wondered...

'Do you ever go down to the river?' I said. 'Near where Donna died? I thought I saw your car there once.'

He frowned, then smiled. 'I haven't been for a while, but...yes, sometimes when I need to think. Not to where Donna died, I don't think. Just near the carpark. Evie loved the spot.' His voice caught and he forced a smile. 'I scattered her ashes there.'

'Seems the river is a bit of a magnet for everyone,' I said. 'Even Dean walks there.'

'Yes, Zahra seems to find him...' Chris saw my look. 'I mean, ah, she likes walking along the river too.' *Zahra?*

Nothing wrong with Dean and Zahra walking together. Except why hadn't he told me?

'I'm sure it's...well it's not...' Chris sighed. 'I've stuck my foot in it haven't I?'

I stared for a moment into my drink while I composed myself. 'Do you think they're having an affair?' A picture of Zahra looking radiant, wearing lipstick, flashed into my thoughts. She was insightful and attractive, and she had needed something—or someone—to increase her confidence after a severe illness.

'Look, I gather since...Noah's accident...things have been tough.'

'Is that from my medical records, or did Dean tell you I was fragile?'

Chris looked at me earnestly. 'I think he was just

worried the letter to the police would make you anxious. I had suggested he didn't bring you here, or that maybe you should get a place in Dubbo, but...well, none of us really thought it was a practical threat.'

'What...what do you mean you suggested he didn't bring me?' I thought of the email Dean showed me of the letter to the police, dated the day we arrived. Felt my heart thumping against my rib cage.

Chris took a long slow sip of his beer and drew in a breath. 'He didn't tell you.'

I waited.

'Whoever wrote the letter sent it to Dean. At his company address; at least two weeks before you arrived. It was them that sent it to the police.'

I have never found getting angry easy. In my house anger meant we might upset my mother, and I learned from a young age not to do that. But as my fury brewed at Dean, I knew there was more to it. As a child I was terrified by my mother's anger: unable to separate it from her mental illness. My existence had reminded her constantly of her own failures and, rather than try to repair the fragile bond between us, she found it easier to see me as the problem. And I had accepted that I was.

In my household, I had learnt not to be angry—because anger was murderous.

It was why Dean and I never discussed what happened with Noah. Not really. It wasn't just because I couldn't bear thinking I had been as bad as my own mother, but because I didn't want to find out that he couldn't forgive me—as she hadn't.

Now I had to decide: could I forgive him?

When Dean finally got home I'd eaten, Noah was in bed and the fridge stacked with wares to take to the fete the next morning. I was watching another sunset on another perfect horizon, the heat shimmering in the distance as dark settled across the plains. The owls were back—this time emitting an eerie howl rather than their dog impersonations. They circled the trees, the air currents taking them in and out of my field of vision until they finally disappeared into the darkness.

'Sorry to tell you, but the mozzies know you're out here.' Dean ran his hand through my hair and kissed my forehead.

I flinched. 'What's up?'

I lit the candle in front of me, steadying my hands as I did. I needed to see his face. He kept talking. 'My boss wants me to start in Perth in February. Which leaves us January for a break. Anywhere you want to go? Bali? Fiji, maybe? Lindeman Island has a kids' club.'

In the distance I could just make out the sound of a bark. 'Perth?'

'It'll be easier for you than here, Iz. Plenty of opportunities at the hospital psych ward running groups. We can probably stay a couple of years if you like.'

'We need to discuss if I'm even going with you Dean. Going anywhere.'

Dean looked at me warily. Waited. I couldn't make his eyes out in the shadows.

'Do you remember what you said to me, when we had out last argument?' My voice quavered. *Calm*.

'I said sorry, Iz.'

'I know you did, and I think you meant it—sort of. Just like you sort of meant it when you said I didn't even save him when I had the chance.' I looked at him, with a new resolve. Dean seemed uncertain what to make of it.

'Babe, I know you jumped in and did your best.'

'But my best wasn't good enough was it?' I was amazed at how steady my voice was. 'There's still a part of you that thinks I should have done better, that shit, hey, you deserve a wife that does a better job, right? Like you not being home a single night in the fortnight before it happened didn't affect the situation at all.'

'You want to blame me now?' Dean took a breath, the flickering of the candle making his expression more sinister. 'Like I was there when it actually happened? Rather than working to pay for the wine you were drinking?'

I blinked back the tears. 'I wasn't drunk, Dean. I was lonely. I didn't have a boss who told me I was doing a great job and provided a pay packet to prove it. I was home with our son, as we had both decided was best for him, and I was relying on you to give me support.'

Dean stood up and pushed the chair forcefully against the table. Walked a couple of steps, running his hand through his hair. 'You reckon the job I was doing was easy? You think—'

'I'm not criticising you Dean, I'm explaining. We both got it wrong. But I can't forgive myself until you forgive me. Or at least that's how it's been until now.'

'And now? You want to blame it on me? What, so you don't have to go to Perth? This is my job, Iz. You knew that when we got married.'

'I want you to understand how I felt. Every time we argue, the blame is just below the surface—I feel like it's waiting there for you to pull up and use against me.' I stood up. Looked at him. 'I know you got a copy of the threatening letter two weeks before we arrived here, Dean.' I let the anger, just a hint of it, out, in the tone of my voice. I wasn't used to it being anywhere but buried, was afraid if I unleashed it, I would scare not just Dean but myself.

'So here's the conundrum,' I said. 'Do I forgive you for

treating me like a child because you were worried about my anxiety and were being protective? Or do I never forgive you, never really trust you again, let it fester that you put our son in danger for the sake of your job—and don't fucking give me that I-know-better look because you could *not* have known how much of a risk there was. Do I hold it there in reserve against you?'

I gripped hold of the edge of the table. Slowed my breathing. 'I can't live like that Dean. I've done it already, with my mother. She couldn't face her own shame. I'm not living with mine. And I'm sure as hell not living with yours.'

Dean was still in bed the next morning when I needed to leave for the fete. I had slept in Noah's room and didn't bother waking him before I left. If he wanted to join us, he could walk.

The sky was a brilliant blue and by the time I had packed the car with Noah, five cakes, twenty jars of pickles and jams and the two patchwork quilts I'd painstakingly stitched and unpicked and stitched again, I could feel trickles of moisture down the back of my neck.

It was nearly nine by the time I got to the Barclays' and I was far from the first to arrive. Banners and stalls had been set up, lights, a stage for the band and what looked like a dance floor.

The fete was legendary. People came from hundreds of kilometres around for the footy carnival, the stalls and the kids' races, and then stayed around for the evening spit roast and dance. Grace had deputised Yvonne to organise a childcare centre, so I could leave Noah for at least some of the day. I had my doubts about how long into the evening we'd last.

What immediately struck me was how much work

Grace had put into the event. Did she know that some of the money she earned to support the hospital was going into someone's—Jeannie's? Teagan's? Conor's?—personal bank account? She looked tense, but as she had workmen and locals bustling around waiting for instructions, it was hardly a surprise.

'Would you mind sharing the cake stall with Sophie?' Grace asked.

I'd given up on not socialising with clients. Besides, I was nearly free of Riley. If going to Perth meant I'd be free.

'Your husband's auditors were at the hospital all week,' Sophie said as we stuck price tags on the array of baked goods.

Hence the talk of Perth. Dean was in the process of finishing up.

'Gordon's been locked in his office talking to accountants and lawyers ever since they arrived. Seems there's been some misunderstanding.' She looked at me sharply. 'Your husband doesn't really think Gordon's stealing, does he? He doesn't have anything to do with running the hospital. He's got millions in shares if he needed money.'

I shrugged. 'No idea. I gather everyone's being looked at. Especially the board—maybe it's Grace and Lachlan that Gordon is worried about.' I wondered if Gordon was being proactive or if he'd been given a heads-up, as Dean predicted.

'That's ridiculous. They don't need the money either. The rest of them are about a hundred years old, apart from Doctor McCormack—and since his wife died, he's been totally dedicated to the place.'

Since his wife died. Dean had said the same thing.

'Chris's wife. Was the hospital responsible for her death?'

Sophie sighed. 'Well, they didn't *cause* it, but...The

hospital just doesn't have modern equipment—that's what he's been campaigning for ever since. One board meeting I gather he came close to punching Athol Broadbent in the face.'

Sophie slapped the price tag on a Victoria sponge and nearly flattened it.

It was going to be a long day.

Sophie and I took it in turns to check on the children and to mind the stall. Mid-morning, I sat with Noah and Father Christmas for the obligatory photograph, then took him back to childcare.

We'd be gone in a week. But Teagan would still be here, and possibly still in danger.

All the same, I probably wouldn't have taken the sample if Tom—Matt's nephew—hadn't pretty much handed it to me as I was leaving. Part of the lollipop he'd been sucking broke off and caught in his throat. With my help he coughed it up, along with a fair amount of saliva. I stared at it, grateful I was wearing a multicoloured dress that hid just about everything, and then thought—why not? The kit from ancestry.com had arrived Friday and I still had it in my handbag. All we needed was a negative, then Teagan could be totally confident about Jed. More to the point, Matt could be shown that he wasn't Indiana's father.

One sample wasn't enough for that, of course. I'd need one from Indiana, due to be delivered the next day, as well. But by then it might even be academic. The auditors were doing all-nighters, trying to finish up before Christmas. If they found who was taking the money and why, the reason for the letter to the police—and who sent it—might become obvious.

I said as much to Kate as she perused the array of goodies I was flogging.

'Yeah,' she said with a grin 'Fireworks tonight could be more than a few crackers going off.'

Zahra and her mother and daughter were all in Christmas red and green; they wandered over to buy some biscuits, and I forced myself to smile, trying not to scrutinise Zahra's face for a sign of guilt. But I was proud that I'd managed to leave her and her walks with Dean out of last night's argument. It was already messy enough, God knew.

'Can I ask you something?' said Teagan when we found ourselves alone. Her latest long T-shirt had a dairy cow on it—with an engorged udder and patchworked buckets of milk and milk cartons along the bottom.

'Can I stop you?'

'No, but I guess I can't make you answer.'

We shared a smile.

'Okay: if you were me...No, if you felt someone had got away with something, like that they'd really hurt you and never said sorry, what would you do?'

'Sometimes it's best to look after yourself, and move on.'

'Yeah,' said Teagan, hands over her abdomen. 'But I'd like to sort it out and...kind of start fresh. So much I feel shit about, you know?'

I did. But...

'Focus on Indiana,' I said. 'She's the one who needs you now.'

I wasn't sure she was listening, let alone that she would follow my advice. Unlike me, she didn't run away from a fight. Maybe if I could get her that DNA test she'd move forward more freely.

The cake stall was popular and most of the town

dropped by. Those I didn't know introduced themselves. Some seemed to be sizing me up, and more than once I heard hushed references to the hospital and the auditors; Dean's name, then a quick look away.

Chris also stuck his head in.

'Are you okay? I really felt a jerk for putting my foot in it when we last met.'

I wasn't entirely sure he was as sorry as he was trying to sound.

'Not your problem.'

'I never thought you were fragile, or...'

'Nuts?' I wondered just what Dean had said to him.

'Not even a little barmy.' Chris smiled. '*That* would be the Riley Rogues—what men our age in their right minds would play footy on an afternoon when it's hit thirty-five in the shade? You coming to watch?'

'Probably. The stall should be sold out by then.'

'I gather your husband might save the day single-handed.'

I hadn't known Dean was meant to be playing. As far as I knew, he was still in bed.

'You know the auditors are looking at all of the hospital financials?'

Chris nodded. 'Grace let the board know before they came in. I have to say I'm relieved.'

'Because?'

'We need to get to the bottom of whatever's been happening, and have our names cleared.' He shrugged. 'I've never been on a board before. Truth is, I wouldn't know if someone had been doing dodgy accounting. You just believe what the treasurer and the auditors tell you.'

Were they all just naive? If I'd been responsible for a small-town hospital, I doubted it would have occurred to me that someone was stealing, but Dean sometimes said I lived in fairyland. 'Some people are just crooked through and through,' he told me often enough.

I still liked believing there was good in all people and that most of the time they were well-intentioned.

'You'll be there, won't you,' I said, 'when Teagan has her baby?'

Chris looked at me with a question in his eyes. 'Yes.'

'Obstetrician coming from Dubbo to do the caesar?'

Chris nodded. 'No insurer in the country would cover a GP picking up the knife themselves for an elective procedure. Besides, someone has to put her to sleep. She's refused a spinal and there's no routine surgery scheduled until after Christmas—the regular anaesthetist's already on his break—so I'm it.'

'You'll look after her. And her baby. The hospital…you have all the right equipment, don't you?'

Chris stepped forward. 'You're really worried about her, aren't you?'

I nodded. 'You'll tell me I'm stupid, but I just have…' A bad vibe because of what happened to her brother? Because of Teagan's mother appearing in her dreams? Because of the warning letter? Because if Donna had had postpartum psychosis, Teagan was at risk of it too? Because I was worried about her hinting about unfinished business and Matt was worried her baby might be his?

'I can't really explain it,' I finally said. 'Just too many things are slightly off…' I shrugged.

Chris, to my surprise, gave me a quick hug. 'I'll look after her, okay?' he said as he left.

Dean was standing outside, watching. Later, I found he'd got a lift with Chris and I wondered if he had followed him, wanting to catch me out. So he could feel justified about whatever happened with Zahra.

I stared at him and didn't look away. He mostly looked sad.

By 3 p.m. the cake stall had sold out and Sophie and I went to watch the football. Which, as I discovered, meant rugby. Thanks to Dean's family, I was familiar with AFL but I knew nothing about rugby. Dean was a pretty accomplished sportsman and probably knew the rules, but I doubted he had played: it wasn't a Melbourne thing. This was a 'friendly' between the Riley Rogues and the Dubbo Hotspurs to raise money for the hospital, but I doubted anyone would feel friendly after five minutes out on the field in this heat.

When Dean appeared in his football shorts, he had Noah. We didn't speak as he handed over our son and I took him to join Kate on the sidelines under the shade of several huge gums. I recognised most of the Riley team—many of whom weren't likely to be feeling friendly towards Dean. I squashed a deep sense of unease.

Unlike the Riley Rogues, the Dubbo Hotspurs were mostly under thirty. The captain, playing centre, was a redheaded guy with shoulder muscles like gridiron padding.

'You follow league?' asked Kate. I shook my head. 'He's going to attack.'

'Attack who?'

Kate grinned. 'I meant the Hotspurs won the toss and they get to kick off.'

The Hotspurs were lined in a formidable row. The ball— at least it was more or less the oval shape Dean was familiar with—was sent down the field by the redheaded captain. Matt Barclay caught it but was quickly tackled and had his face planted on the dustbowl under two of the Dubbo boys. After this, apparently the players were still able to play and I watched in bewilderment as whoever had the ball was promptly flattened.

'Are they getting a free kick for that?' I asked. Conor and his son, and Matt's mate, Patrick, had spear-tackled a Dubbo boy half Conor's age. One had hold of the kid's leg and the other looked to have him by the groin, if the amount of hip gyrating on the ground was anything to go by.

Kate laughed.

In between the tackles and an occasional scrum—Dean was always in the centre of these with Conor one side and Patrick the other—Kate gave me a run-down of the rules. It was all about getting the ball over the line and placing it in the dirt: that was a try. If you kicked a goal it didn't count for much. Still, when Matt ran half the field and scored a try thanks to a neat pass from Dean, and a goal kicker was needed, it was Dean's moment to shine. He duly slammed the ball over the crossbar. The group hug that followed suggested his skills on the field were currently more important than his work outside of the game. I breathed a little easier.

Fifteen minutes in the Hotspurs got their second try and then added two points by kicking a goal—twelve–six.

'Our boys are flagging,' Kate observed. 'Holes in the defence.'

She was being kind. I didn't think the Riley Rogues really knew where they were meant to be—apart from on top of any Dubbo man that had the ball. And more than once they were doing damage to each other—including an elbow from Dean that sent Chris sprawling.

'When the big boys play, *that'd* get penalised,' said Kate. 'Not the elbow—taking too long to get up.'

At half time the score was eighteen to six in Dubbo's favour and the Riley Rogues retreated sullenly to one end of the field. It looked like coach Brian McCormack was trying to suggest a change of strategy. I mentally wished him luck. All the men had grazed knees and skin missing from legs or forearms, Lachlan was limping and Chris had a beautiful shiner coming up.

'Those scums: why is Dean always between Conor and his son?'

'I could debate you about who's a scum,' said Kate grinning, 'but in this case I think you mean scrum.'

I laughed, realising that for a moment at least I actually felt close to Kate. Friend rather than therapist. Not a good idea perhaps…but it took away a bit of the sense of isolation.

'To answer your question, it's the positions they're playing. Dean's the hooker, I guess. Conor and his son are props.'

'And who decided that?'

'The captain. Chris.'

When the second half started, the Rogues struggled but soon the Hotspurs were flagging too. With twenty minutes left to go the Rogues were still twelve points behind. They all looked tired except Dean. He'd been taking it easy, barely involved in any of the tackles and even less the running up and down. It had to be for a reason. Sure enough, Chris passed to Matt who made a long kick—straight to Dean, well away from any of the Hotspurs who had forgotten about him. He ran almost the entire length of the field and was still a metre or more ahead of anyone when he touched the ball down. After a neat kick, it was eighteen to twelve. Kate was screaming in excitement; it was possible she thought there was a plan.

The Hotspurs came back hard. They got the ball to within a metre of the back line and the red-haired guy took a dive. I mentally cringed—this game was probably meant to be played on lush wet English pasture, not this dry cracked dirt. Several of the Riley Rogues descended on him—Conor, Patrick, Chris and Dean included. Without video it was impossible to say exactly what happened—there was a flurry of elbows and legs in the air and a sickening crunch as someone slammed into the goalpost. But when everyone scrambled up, Dean had blood pouring down his face.

'Oh my God.'

'It probably looks worse than it is,' said Kate, 'but, you know—it's a contact sport.'

I watched while Massoud, out on the ground, started winding a bandage around Dean's head and taped it on. It appeared the gash was over his eye. But his expression suggested grim determination to see this game through to the end.

No one was running fast anymore. The heat and over an hour of hard exercise was probably more than any of them were used to. The Rogues put in a good last-minute effort, getting the ball almost down to the line, before a scrum was called. With maybe only two minutes to go, victory—or at least a draw—was briefly within their grasp.

Dean was in the front row, between Conor and Patrick. The ball ended up spitting out between the legs of the Hotspur guys, and that was where everyone was looking.

When the men dispersed, someone tripped Dean. I imagine Conor got a punch in when no one could see; straight at the side of his head as he went down. Two of the others went straight over the top of Dean before a touch judge yelled and there was a murmur through the crowd.

Dean was still on the ground. Not moving.

'Take Noah, will you?' I asked Kate, not waiting for a reply.

Sam Keller was telling people to nick off, Chris was calling for a stretcher and Massoud was examining Dean's eyes with a torch, but he was out cold. I sank down to the ground next to him. The bandage had come off and blood covered his face. I could see the imprint of boot studs on his knee.

'Dean. Dean, wake up,' I said, shaking him.

He groaned. Massoud took out his torch again and this time Dean shook his head in protest, then moaned and clutched at it. A few moments later he opened his eyes—the one not covered in blood looked glazed.

'Careful,' said Massoud. 'We're getting a stretcher. All is fine.'

'Doesn't feel fucking fine,' Dean said, spraying blood as he spoke.

'The knee?' Massoud attempted to move it.

Dean winced. '*Fuck*.'

'We'll need a cerebral CAT scan, and X-rays,' Massoud told him. 'Jaw and knee—your jaw might be okay, but that knee looks like an anterior cruciate ligament.'

There was blood dripping from Dean's mouth as he scowled. I wondered if he'd lost a tooth.

'That was pretty scary,' I said, wiping the blood that covered his eye as fast as I wiped. 'Lucky Noah was asleep.'

Dean frowned at me. Too busy holding it together to play the family guy. He touched his jaw and winced. 'This town got a dentist?'

'We'll get the guy from Dubbo,' said Chris. 'We'll keep you in overnight anyway, so he can look over your teeth in the morning.'

'Bullshit. Iz, get the car. We're going home.'

'No,' said Chris, 'you are not. You lost consciousness.'

He was quietly firm, arms crossed. Dean looked at me.

'If he has a subdural,' Chris said to me, while still looking at Dean, 'then he could fit, fall—just not wake up. Think you'll be able to get him in the car in the middle of the night if that happens? The ambulance will take an hour. He'd be dead by then.'

I looked at Chris, then back to Dean. Wondered briefly about Chris's positioning of Dean in the match.

I made a decision. 'We need to listen to the doctors.'

Dean tried to stand, shaking Sam and Massoud's hands off him. His injured knee gave way and Massoud caught him as he fell; Dean's weight nearly pulled him over too. By this time the stretcher had arrived, along with two St John Ambulance workers barely old enough to drive, whose combined weight was probably less than Dean's.

Dean let them help him onto the stretcher, which took four of them to lift. He looked at me and for a moment I thought there were tears in his eyes. I didn't think it was from pain.

I was still shaken when I collected the sleeping Noah from Kate, uncertain if I should go to the hospital or home. I wasn't staying here, at any rate, so I went looking for Grace, to thank her and say my goodbyes.

I hadn't made it far when I heard a scream. *Everyone* heard a scream. An ear-piercing shriek that couldn't be anything other than one hundred per cent genuine.

Sophie came running out of the childcare tent looking like a ghost, her voice barely squeaking, like her vocal cords had no blood, her lungs no air. Her words, when she managed them, sent a wave of shock through me.

'Someone's taken Tom.'

Immediately people were all around her. Everyone was talking; now she'd found her voice, Sophie's high-pitched scream continued over the top of them all, not listening to anyone. 'He's gone, he's not there! Oh my God, someone's taken my baby!'

I pulled back from the milling crowd, looking with guilty relief at Noah, now stirring in his pusher.

'Get Gordon,' someone yelled.

Another said, 'Where's Sam Keller?'

Someone behind me, quieter: 'It's happened again.'

Lachlan came running. He folded Sophie into his arms, trying to calm her so he could make sense of what she was saying.

I looked over at the childcare tent. Mothers were rushing to grab their children. Yvonne was standing at the door, face grim. Beside her, a young childcare volunteer I didn't know was crying.

Someone fetched both Sam and Gordon. Kate had snapped into official mode.

No one was taking any notice of me.

I started walking. Looking. Not for Tom so much as the person I guessed had taken him. I thought of the odd conversation I had had earlier with Teagan—*if they'd really hurt you and never said sorry...*Matt didn't have a baby, but Lachlan did.

No, she couldn't have taken him. If she had, surely she wouldn't harm him?

I walked faster. Everyone was heading towards the ruckus at the childcare tent—I walked away. I knew what Joe's car looked like, and I knew Teagan didn't have one.

It took me five minutes to find it, to my relief, still there in the paddock. I turned back, mind racing. Where would Teagan take a six-month-old child, when she was too pregnant to walk far? I looked around. Plenty of temporary tents; sheds, barns and of course the main house. Circling the garden, I saw Matt, still in footy gear, sitting on a chair with his feet up, swilling beer with a couple of the other players.

'What's the shouting about?' he asked without any real interest in the answer.

I stopped and looked at him. 'Oh, nothing much,' I

said, wondering if I could add: *you piece of shit*? 'Just your ex-girlfriend has kidnapped your nephew, nothing serious or anything.'

Matt sat up so fast the chair his feet had been on went flying.

'What the fuck?'

'Teagan? Forgotten her I suppose, because they all blur into one?'

'Lady, you are nuts,' said Matt shaking his head. 'Totally fruit loops.' He glanced at the two men trying to pretend they weren't listening, then grabbed my arm and marched me away.

'I suppose you're going to deny that you even know Teagan Moretti? Never said anything to her, even though Joe Moretti laid into you when he found out?'

Matt's mouth dropped open. It would have looked comical in other circumstances. It was hard to know what was his most unattractive feature—his big nose or prominent ears. The nose was all Gordon; I didn't know who he could blame for the ears.

'That's none of your goddamn business.'

'It's about to be everyone's business if you don't find Teagan and Tom.'

'Me? How the hell would I know where they are?'

'Think,' I said. 'Did you guys used to meet somewhere?' I thought of what Teagan had told me. 'Where did you go to party?'

I could see him thinking—saw the moment he knew exactly what I was talking about.

'Yeah,' he said. 'The stables.'

'Well what are you waiting for? Let's go.'

'Why don't you get the cops?'

'You sure that's what you want?' I hoped I knew what I was doing.

Matt shrugged, put his beer down and led me around the side of the house and up behind where the band had been setting up. They were now looking uncertain whether to continue.

Several of the stable doors were opened at the top. One horse stuck its head over and looked at us with interest. Noah waved at it: 'Horsies, Mummy.'

Matt ignored them and continued around the back, where an open door revealed a ladder up to a loft. Matt nodded his head. I looked at the ladder, and at Noah, who was peering in, hoping undoubtedly for more horses. 'Neigh,' he added.

I looked up the ladder, climbed a couple of rungs and called out, 'Teagan, are you there?'

No one replied. I called a little louder. This time I heard a sound. So did Matt. It sounded like a child whimpering.

'Teagan, I'm coming up.' I took a couple of extra steps, looking back to Noah and whispering, 'Mummy will be back in a minute.'

Noah looked at me and then Matt, doubtful. He had good judgment—Matt wasn't the ideal babysitter. But I was only going to be a few metres away, and he was safely secured in the pusher.

Teagan was sitting with her back to a hay bale, holding Tom, whose tear-streaked face said he wanted to be anywhere but here. To her left there was a long drop into the stable below—and no barrier at all.

'Teagan,' I said carefully, 'I need you to let me take Tom.'

She looked at me, her expression hard to read. 'Hamish would have looked just like him,' she said.

Hamish?

She had named her stillborn child.

'But he isn't Hamish, Teagan. That's Tom. Hamish would be seven. Much older.'

'But he never had a chance to be older, did he?'

'That wasn't anyone's fault, Teagan. Certainly not Tom's. And he looks a little scared now; you wouldn't want Indiana to feel like that, would you? Teagan, I need to get him back to his mother.'

I edged forward, across the hay-strewn floor where, presumably, Hamish had been conceived years before.

Teagan clutched Tom tighter. He started to cry.

'Teagan, you asked my advice, remember? Listen to it now. You need to look ahead. Don't destroy your future, with Indiana, because of the past.'

Underneath the dairy-cow T-shirt that stretched across Teagan's abdomen, Indiana appeared to respond to her name. An extremity—an elbow, a foot—poked out through the cow's mouth.

It worked—Teagan felt her. She loosened her grip on Tom.

I leaned in and took him, and she didn't resist. 'We need to talk, Teagan, but right now I need to get Tom back to Sophie, okay?'

Teagan nodded, arms around her belly, a tear trickling down her cheek. Smiling and reassuring a distraught Tom, I went backwards down the ladder. Matt and Noah looked at us expectantly. I handed a whimpering Tom to his uncle. 'Take him back to his mum, okay? Right now.'

'What do I say?' Matt asked.

'I don't know,' I said. 'It's your family.'

He started to walk off and I looked at Noah, then at the ladder.

'And Matt,' I said.

'Yeah?'

'This needs closure. Get your butt back here to talk with Teagan. And bring Yvonne—the nurse?—I need someone to mind Noah.'

Yvonne arrived long before anyone else.

'What on earth is going on? Are you and Noah okay?'

'We're fine. What did Matt say?'

'Some story that sounded like complete bullshit to me,' said Yvonne. 'Sophie's too relieved to be questioning it but I can't say the same for anyone else. Sam Keller and Gordon carted Matt off to try and make sense of it. Why the hell would anyone think they needed to pick up Tom and then give him to Matt instead of his father? Particularly someone whose name Matt seems to have forgotten?'

'Keep Noah close, okay? I have to do some work here.' I automatically looked up to the hay loft. Yvonne followed my gaze and nodded. I felt like hugging her for knowing just what was happening and trusting me to do it.

'Oh, Teagan,' I said, as I slumped down beside her. 'You might be charged with kidnapping. You know that, don't you?'

'I didn't go far,' she said. She looked up. 'I would never have hurt him. You believe me, don't you?'

I nodded.

'I just wanted...I only have Hamish's picture. Indiana's coming tomorrow and...I just wanted to say goodbye to Hamish here. You know?' There was a pause. 'His dad...I felt there was something special between us. He even seemed to understand my loopy dreams, which is saying something for a whitefella; I thought he really got who I was and I thought...I felt I was worth something to someone.'

I heard a sound below. Surely Matt hadn't been able to offload Sam Keller and Gordon that fast? Teagan was too absorbed in her story to notice.

'I was really scared when I found I was pregnant. But he seemed...like he didn't judge me. I like, thought it might all work out. Stupid, right?'

'And then?' I prompted.

'Dad was furious. I told him it'd all be fine, that the Barclays would help me...I mean I didn't think he'd marry me or anything, but I thought, well maybe, he'd at least be around for the kid.'

'I would have been, Teagan. How dare you pay me back by threatening my child?'

We both looked up, startled. Teagan because she wasn't expecting anyone, and me because I wasn't expecting Lachlan. I stared at him in disbelief, my mind racing.

Lachlan, not Matt, had fathered her first child? Why hadn't I seen this?

No wonder Teagan had trouble being around Sophie. Jealous of their complete family unit, seething at how easy it was for him—his father's political seat, the silver spoon, the effortless transition between generations—while she struggled at every stage.

And now she was having a baby again. I looked at Lachlan, at the rage he could barely contain.

'I wasn't,' said Teagan. 'I wasn't threatening him. I just saw him there, and he looked so like how I thought Hamish would. I just wanted to have him. Just for a moment.'

Lachlan's expression didn't soften; I saw a moment of confusion, which he quickly covered up—he didn't know she'd named the lost baby. In fact, he would think she'd had the abortion his mother had pushed for.

'Teagan,' I said urgently, 'you need to tell Lachlan the truth. About Hamish.'

'What truth?' Lachlan had now come up into the loft and stood over us.

'I...couldn't do it,' Teagan said quietly. 'I took the money, but I never had the abortion.'

'Money?' Lachlan no longer sounded quite so sure of himself.

'The fucking hush money, Lachlan. So I'd go away and be a good girl, get rid of my baby and never bother the Barclays ever again.' She took a gulp of air. 'I didn't get rid of him. But I lost him anyway. Twenty-two weeks.' She held out the photo that had been in her hand, eyes meeting his. Slowly, he leaned over and took it. Stared at the picture.

'I...I never knew,' he said. 'You didn't tell me.'

He looked younger. For a moment, in the last trace of his youthful naivety, I could see what he and Teagan had seen in each other. Hope, maybe. A different way of being than either of their parents had shown them, before Lachlan had finally accepted the path that had been long mapped out for him.

Teagan snorted. 'Wasn't like you were keen to know.'

'But...' Lachlan faltered. 'I didn't know about any of it. My mother said...She said you'd had a miscarriage and didn't want to see me.'

'Your *mother*,' Teagan spat, 'came to our home with a chequebook.'

The two stared at each other.

'You didn't get my letter, did you,' he said.

'How did you send the letter, Lachlan?' I asked.

'By hand. I dropped it in Teagan's letterbox myself.'

So both Joe and Grace had conspired to keep them in the dark. Had Joe been paid for that service? I stared at Teagan. Was Joe still being paid?

'Lachlan,' I said, 'she wouldn't have hurt Tom. She's about to have her own baby. If she promises to leave you alone, keep away from Sophie and Tom, will you let this drop?'

Lachlan was still looking at Teagan. 'I didn't know, Teagan. I'm sorry.' There was sadness between them, for a moment. Despite everything, a lost baby united them. 'But you can't, I mean I will not let you, ever, threaten my family. Do you understand that?'

Teagan looked like a twelve-year-old getting a dressing-down from the headmaster—one she knew she deserved.

This was progress. Lachlan was making it crystal clear that he would protect his family, and that whatever had happened between them was no longer alive.

'Does Sophie know?' I asked softly.

Lachlan sat on a hay bale and put his head in his hands. 'No. She knew there had been a girl and a miscarriage. Just not who.'

Awkward.

'I won't tell her,' said Teagan. 'I'll do like Issy said. I won't bug you. You...I mean, I get it, it makes sense. It wasn't like your folks were ever going to open their arms to me.'

'Dad? No. But I thought my mother...' Lachlan shook his head. 'Not your problem. You can yell at your father on my behalf for not giving you my letter, okay? I have to tell Sophie; she needs to understand what just happened. And I can't promise she won't insist on criminal charges.'

Except then everyone would know about the pregnancy.

It wouldn't help his chances when the National Party came to vote in January. No, Sophie would be the perfect wife—she wouldn't want to harm his career. But he was going to have a lot of making up to do. I figured he'd have Grace and Gordon onside with this. And Sam Keller would toe the line, the same way the cops had probably done all those years ago, to keep Joe and Donna out of jail.

'Is...is your family worried about Teagan, about this baby?' I asked Lachlan. His puzzled expression appeared authentic; if Matt was worried, he hadn't shared it with his brother.

'Did you send that warning to the cops?' This time I was talking to Teagan.

'Me?' said Teagan. 'You think I don't have enough grief in my life without inviting in a shitload more?'

It was hard not to believe her.

Whatever Lachlan told Sophie and his family, no one detained Teagan or Joe. Joe had tears in his eyes when he hugged and thanked me.

While I still had phone reception, I rang the hospital and was told Dean was having a scan. I left a message that I'd be there in the morning and took Noah home.

By the time I had him settled, I was exhausted. Television seemed to be all bad news: natural disasters, American politics and the worst of human behaviour. I turned off the TV and sat outside on the balcony. As the sun went down, the heat shimmered on the horizon. Still no clouds to be seen. It had been relentlessly hot all day and I was aware of the dryness that sucked at each breath, the gritty dustiness that works its way into sticky body crevices and which no amount of washing ever seems to get rid of. Even the late breeze sweeping through the flywire front door and out the rear windows couldn't completely relieve the heat. There was a new edge to it, whispers of things to come.

I wondered at the sadness I was feeling. It wasn't the powerlessness of depression, the despair I'd had after Noah nearly died when I felt lost and wished I could sleep forever.

It was more accepting: as if I had opened my eyes and could see the future and no longer thought of it with dread, but rather, resolve.

Maybe it took someone else's tragedy to help me put my own life in perspective. I was never going to make my mother happy. I had no control over who my parents were or how they behaved, or who Dean wanted to be. But I did have choices about the sort of wife and mother I was. The sort of marriage I wanted. I had had that marriage once—it remained to be seen whether we could make it work again. But I realised with a jolt that I wasn't going to settle for second best.

I knew now what had caused Teagan's problems with the Barclays. Quite separately, the town had been scarred by Joshua's death. Joe and Teagan's lives had been shaped by it. My hope that solving that mystery would make it clear who had tipped the police off hadn't played out. I couldn't discount Matt, but it was a hard case to make.

What would happen to Riley now that Dean had made his move? The arrival of the auditors and all the talk of fraud had left little doubt in anyone's mind that the hospital was likely to close. If this was what the police tipster feared, would they give up now—or make one last attempt to prevent the closure or to exact revenge?

Despite the heat, a small shiver went through me. Someone cared enough to write a threatening letter. The hospital was a core part of Riley—without it, more than a hundred people would lose their jobs. That was enough to ensure the anger that had prompted the warning would continue to simmer. Or explode.

I set the alarm. Teagan was due to give birth to Indiana in the morning and I planned to be there. Even if her premonition and my unease were without basis, it wouldn't hurt to be cautious.

The next morning the sky was strewn with bleak grey clouds, scudding across with a sense of haste, more following in their wake. I wondered if, finally, there was some rain headed our way. For a moment I pictured the photos on the pub wall, and my sense of unease grew. As I crossed the river, there seemed no more water in it than there had been all summer. Overnight, the temperature hadn't got below twenty-five and by seven-thirty it was already sticky and humid but the wind was fractious, with sudden gusts whipping into mini-tornadoes, swirling and scattering dead leaves and dust.

Teagan was sitting on a gurney in the obstetric ward in a white gown, Joe beside her. She looked surprised to see me. Perhaps a little sheepish.

'Sorry,' she said before I spoke, ''bout yesterday.'

'It's Sophie you need to say sorry to,' I said. 'But let the fuss die down first.' I was hoping there would be no official fuss.

'I'm scared,' said Teagan; in the gown, earrings and nose-rings removed, she looked like a teenager. 'My mum… she came to me last night.'

'Yeah?' I thought of my own unease. I didn't quite know what to make of Teagan's dreams but whatever their base, her mum and I seemed to have similar intuition.

'She told me Indiana would be fine.' The tone of Teagan's voice suggested she wasn't reassured; as she met my eyes I knew she was holding something back.

'Your mum will keep an eye on you both.' I squeezed her hand.

'Lachie was telling the truth—Dad admitted he threw

away the letter.' Joe looked down at his feet. 'Probably should have known...' She trailed off, biting her lip. I had the sense she was deciding whether or not to tell me or ask me something, when Chris swept into the room with an officious-looking nurse. Chris smiled at me as he started manoeuvring Teagan's bed into the corridor.

'How long?' I asked him.

'Half an hour.'

'I'll be here when you and Indiana get out,' I told Teagan. Then she disappeared around the corner.

I'd already dropped by the ward to see Dean: the dentist had arrived, so I figured I had a bit of time.

The hospital shop was open, and Jeannie smiled when she saw me. 'Coffee, dear?'

'Tea, thanks,' I said. I couldn't help but feel that the coffee stash was tainted.

When she brought it over, she sat down with me.

'Everyone's anxious about the hospital,' said Jeannie, who didn't look that anxious herself. 'When you get to my age, you know there's nothing much for it but to just get on with things.'

'If they close the shop, what will you do?'

'Close the shop? Pfft. Over my dead body.' Jeannie might look like every-granny but she wasn't going to be a walkover. I nearly giggled, picturing her outside, chained to the hospital fence and waving a placard. An easier image to concoct than her as a thief. She added, 'I guess that'll happen before long regardless.'

'They're auditing the café,' I said. 'Do you think money has gone missing from here?'

Jeannie looked briefly unsettled. She rose to her full five feet. 'Never. Mrs Barclay would never have it. I wouldn't give her husband the time of day, but she works tirelessly. And she's very particular. Picks up the cash herself and takes it straight to the bank. Checks our receipts against it, too.' Jeannie hastily added, 'Not that she doesn't trust us, but "Jeannie," she said to me, "I don't want you to be worried." I've seen her do it every week for the past twenty-seven years.'

My skin started to prickle. 'She takes it herself? Never anyone else?'

Jeannie didn't seem to think the questions strange. 'Well, not always her; she's the one who always checks up on me, makes sure I'm okay. I meant her or her boys. These days the younger Mrs Barclay, too, of course.'

Matt and Sophie.

I was still sipping my tea, thinking, not noticing that Noah had tipped most of his milk into a large puddle in his pusher, when I became aware that it seemed unusually still. I looked at Noah's mess, and began to mop it up, but as I did my skin started to prickle. I looked up the corridor, saw nothing. Sat and listened. A door banging. Movement, somewhere. And then the announcement over the PA system.

Code blue. Theatre.

I was on my feet, running with the pusher in front of me, before I had given any thought to the fact that there was nothing I could do, that I wouldn't be allowed in, and that I would be more in the way than anything else.

I stopped myself before I got to the theatre, shrinking back against the wall so the nurses could pass me. The doors flew open as people came and went, with the sounds of short sharp urgent voices—I recognised Chris's—and metal crashing to the floor and banging on benches. I strained for the sound of a baby's cry. That first breath when the new infant was pulled from the gentle warmth and the muted sounds of the womb, to the taste of life and all its pains and joys. The cry that said I am alive and well, but not happy. The where's-my-mother-and-where's-my-food cry that announces a new arrival in the world. There was none. I felt sick.

Tears began streaming down my face; Noah looked at me with concern and I tried to smile and tell him Mummy was okay, but who was I kidding?

Was Teagan jinxed? Was the entire Moretti family?

I refused to believe that. A lot that happened in life might be luck, but I couldn't accept that there wasn't some control over destiny. Teagan had taken control; she'd stopped using drugs, she listened to everything we talked about in the groups; she was trying. Fate couldn't treat her this badly. Indiana had been alive and well yesterday—and it wasn't as if Teagan had been in labour, that the cord had got wrapped around the child's neck, that there had been no air for a baby stuck in the birth canal. Indiana *had* to be alive.

Nothing seemed to happen for what felt like forever. Then the door opened, slowly this time. The nurse emerging was dressed in scrubs. And in her arms was a bundle. I thought of all the cases of infanticide I had read for my thesis, about how I had pictured my mother standing over me with a pillow, wanting me dead. I wasn't good with dead anything, but a dead...

A picture of Noah, unconscious, underwater, bubbles slowly rising, made me retch. I wouldn't cope seeing a dead baby.

The nurse looked up, tears in her eyes. I vaguely recognised her and she seemed to know who I was. 'You okay?'

I shook my head, shrinking back against the wall. 'Is...
is that Indiana?'

'Do you want to see her?' the nurse asked.

I stared. Was this woman mad? I knew the protocol for
dealing with stillbirth: keeping the infant with the mother
if she desired, photos, farewells. But I was not this baby's
mother.

'I think,' said the nurse, 'she's got her mother's eyes.
What do you think?'

Before I could say I didn't care whose eyes this dead,
lost child had, the nurse had pulled back the blankets that
enclosed the bundle, and angled her so I could see.

At first I couldn't quite comprehend what I was looking
at. Inside the little bundle was a perfect little face—not the
elongated bone structure Noah had had, a result of the birth-
canal squeeze, nor his essentially bald head. The eyes were
Teagan's—large and luminous and knowing—a little girl
already wary of the world. And thick dark hair—Teagan's
and maybe Jed's as well. She blinked, looking right at me
and I wasn't sure whether I wanted to kiss her or kiss the
nurse.

'She's okay?' I whispered.

'She's...she's just fine.' The nurse's smile was forced and
I suddenly realised my fear had been for the wrong person.

'Teagan?'

The nurse flashed a look back to the closed doors. 'I'm...
they're doing their best.' She turned and disappeared along
the corridor into the nursery.

Teagan. I pictured her on the operating table, belly
open. I'd told her she was in good hands, but what the hell
did I know? The obstetrician could have been well past
retirement age; he could have been hustled out of Sydney to

avoid a scandal, or left because he wasn't good enough to get a job there. Rural Australia had its fair share of medical malpractice scandals involving inadequately trained or supervised doctors. Even frauds.

Teagan was young; that had to count for something, didn't it? Clean of drugs, not overweight. And a fighter. She didn't want to die, would do anything in her power to be there for Indiana. If it was in her power. I remembered, when I was pregnant, googling things that could go wrong in labour, and having to stop myself. Now I racked my memory for crises related to caesarean sections.

Infection? Not this soon. Blood pressure—it had to be. There were drugs for that, weren't there? Or bleeding. Did they know her blood group, did they have blood available? My hands were sweaty. I closed my eyes and offered a silent prayer to anyone prepared to listen. Save Teagan; she deserves a break. And Indiana deserves a mother.

I started walking the corridor as Noah became restless. I wondered about finding Dean and letting him take Noah home; I figured he wouldn't be allowed to drive. It was nine-thirty, but I didn't want to go until...until I knew.

I found Joe in the waiting room; he'd seen his granddaughter, but he looked like a ghost. He looked up when he heard me.

'Teagan?'

'I don't know. I'm so sorry.'

The man just nodded, staring at the wall. I sat next to him, rolling Noah's pusher to and fro.

'I feel like...like it's happening all over again,' he said, sounding like a dead man. 'I should have left, you know? After Joshua died. Should have taken Donna and Teagan and left this place and never returned.'

'She's a fighter,' I said.

'Yes, she is,' said Joe. 'More so than Donna. My wife lost part of herself with Joshua and never got it back. It tormented her, what the poor little thing went through. That they'd…abused him…and then burned him alive.' Joe shook his head.

'Burnt alive?' I asked, barely concealing my horror at the thought. Noah's near-drowning was bad enough a memory…but being burnt?

'The police felt certain he was already dead. Maybe an accident, that they were covering their tracks,' said Joe. 'But Donna got it into her head…' He started to choke up, past and current grief and fear mingled in his thoughts.

I let him sit and grieve, my hand on his. Jeannie was right—sometimes there wasn't anything to do. Other than sit and let someone know they're not alone.

I was still with Joe when the obstetrician came to find him. I explained who I was. Still in scrubs, gloves removed, she pulled her hat off to reveal short auburn hair, and sat on Joe's other side.

'Mr Moretti, I'm Doctor Jocelyn Jarvis. I'm sorry to say that there were some complications.' Her voice was calm and soothing; in her eyes I could see she was suffering. I admired how she held it together. And that she'd said the word sorry, even if she hadn't said whose fault it was, or if it had been anyone's. I thought of Chris and his attempts to update the theatre equipment. What was the chance that something waited for Teagan to come along before malfunctioning after all these years? That she was just in the wrong place at the wrong time.

'Is she…?' Joe's voice choked up.

'She's alive,' Dr Jarvis said crisply, and though I could

feel the relief pass through Joe, I remained tense. Something was coming.

'We're going to transfer her to ICU at the Dubbo hospital. She's going to need some tests and she'll have to remain there under observation.'

'She's going to be okay, isn't she?'

There was a fraction of a second's hesitation, but it was enough. Her eyes caught mine.

'We don't yet know exactly what happened,' said Dr Jarvis. 'But your daughter was without oxygen for...a period of time.'

Joe looked puzzled, unable to make sense of what he was being told.

'I'm sorry, Mr Moretti. I can't tell you more until she's had a scan, and even then...we won't know until she wakes up...if she wakes up...just what the situation is.'

What she was trying to say was that Teagan might have brain damage.

I managed to excuse myself and find a bathroom before I threw up.

It was ten-thirty before I organised for one of the administrators to drive Dean and Noah home.

'There's been a serious incident here,' I told her. 'I need to help debrief everyone.'

I told Dean I'd be home by dinner time. His knee was bandaged, jaw swollen, and he looked miserable. 'Iz, we need to talk.' I think that's what he said.

'I know, Dean, but for once it's my work that needs to come first.'

Teagan was still waiting for the ambulance when I got back to the obstetric ward. No one knew what the protocol was, but I was allowed into the theatre. The theatre nurses had left, but the place still looked chaotic—drapes on the floor, used surgical equipment on the stainless-steel benches. Chris was there, still in scrubs, fiddling with an IV. He looked shattered. A nurse came to collect a blood-filled tube and disappeared with it.

Joe was sitting on a draped stool, holding Teagan's hand. Covered to her chest in a white sheet, she looked even younger than she had before. No lines on her face, and a hint of a smile below her upturned nose, though it was probably the oxygen mask distorting the skin.

'She's going to be all right,' Joe said, as much to himself as me. 'She's a fighter, like you said.'

'She is, Joe,' I replied. Teagan looked too small and fragile to fight for anything. 'She might be able to hear you,' I added, 'so help her fight, let her know how much you love her.'

Joe sniffed. 'Never been good at that. She'll be right, she knows.'

When the ambulance arrived, we were asked to leave; the paramedics went into a huddle with Chris. Joe stood aimlessly, until I suggested he could organise going to see her in Dubbo.

Outside, I saw them open the ambulance doors and slide Teagan in. The nurse turned and went inside as it drove away, leaving Chris staring after the disappearing vehicle.

'How are you?' I asked quietly.

'What?' It was as if he had just woken. 'Ah. It isn't me you should be worried about.'

'Teagan?'

'Let's hope she'll pull through.' He forced a tight smile and headed back inside.

I went with him. 'What happened?'

'I can't talk about it, Issy.'

'Why?' When he said nothing, it occurred to me that it wasn't that he didn't want to talk about it—he really meant that he shouldn't. 'Hey. She's my patient too.'

'Yeah? Well I'm not.' He stopped abruptly and I nearly ran into him.

I stared at him. 'Did you...' I stopped, saw his face harden.

'Did I kill her? Did I fail her in every way possible? I've

been trying to get new equipment in that theatre for the last five years, and I failed—I should have refused to give the anaesthetic.' He shook his head. 'She suffered hypoxia, which may or may not kill her—and may or may not mean she has lost intellectual, sensory or motor function, so that she won't ever be able to be a mother to that baby.'

'Is there somewhere we can sit down and talk? We can call it a client relationship if you want. Keep it under professional privilege.'

Chris looked at me and shook his head.

'You need to talk,' I said, firmer this time, hand on his arm. 'Hanging on to it and blaming yourself won't help. I know that better than anyone.'

He hesitated. Looked at his watch. 'I need to get changed and cancel the afternoon patients. I'll meet you in the Arms in about half an hour.'

That left me just long enough to see the new baby for the second time. There was better security than there had been when Joshua was born. With no other newborns currently in residence, Indiana was in a cot in the nurses' station—and a staff member was with her at all times, said the nurse who had first shown her to me.

But the security wasn't so tight that I couldn't get a quick swab from inside Indiana's cheek while the nurse was talking on the phone. I slipped it into the envelope that already held Tom's sample and a completed form, addressed it to ancestry.com and took it straight to the post office.

It was just gone midday when Chris walked into the Riley Arms. I'd already bought him a beer, but he went straight to the bar and ordered a scotch.

'On the house, mate,' said Brian. News travelled fast.

For a minute he sat in silence, then took a second gulp,

and leaned back in his seat. 'There was no fucking oxygen in the canister.'

The swearing as much as the information took me aback. I hadn't seen Chris like this before.

'In theatre? Was there a backup?'

'There's two cylinders in theatre, plus one spare. First one had some oxygen, so I started with that. Second one—the gauge said it was full.' He put his head in his hands. 'I only checked two visually, didn't look for the third. I shouldn't have needed the spare, it's always there. Always. There's no reason for it not to be, no reason for anyone to move it.'

'Let me get this clear,' I said slowly. 'The spare oxygen canister was missing?'

'Yes.'

'When did you last see it?'

'We refilled one last week.'

'And the second one you started to use—it wasn't full?'

Chris ran his hands through his hair. 'I don't know. The gauge had to be faulty. She was under, it all seemed to be going fine, then just after Jocelyn delivered the baby, when I swapped canisters, Teagan's pulse started racing. I was adjusting her fluids, didn't notice. Then figured maybe she wasn't under enough, you know, that she was still feeling the pain, so I gave her some more anaesthetic. It took me another minute—two...three? Shit, I don't know how long—before I worked out something had gone seriously wrong. The gauge was still saying full, and I looked at her oxygen saturation and realised immediately. The second canister had drained and...there's supposed to be an automatic alarm that signals when it's empty, but that must have gone off *prior* to my ever using it. It hadn't been re-set.'

'So...she had no air...All that time?' I said faintly.

'As soon as I worked out the problem, I hand ventilated her. So, less than five. I'm certain it was less than five minutes without.' He sounded like he wanted to believe it but wasn't sure he did. 'She never arrested. The baby was delivered before any harm could have been done to her; Jocelyn was brilliant. But I...I couldn't bring Teagan out of it.'

'I can't imagine for a moment that you did anything—that you would hide or empty the oxygen canisters or tamper with the gauge. Right?'

'Of course not.'

'So you're guilty only of not checking the canisters more thoroughly,' I said carefully. 'Seems to me, everything else you did was textbook. Maybe a qualified anaesthetist could have done it better or faster, or maybe not, if they were old or hungover or just having a bad day at the office.'

'It should never have happened.'

'Agreed,' I said. 'But you're whipping yourself rather than addressing who's really to blame.'

Chris frowned. 'What do you mean?'

I thought of Teagan telling everyone she was having a caesarean, how long ago the date had been set, how everyone in the whole town would have known or could have found out. I thought of her strong sense of foreboding. The tip to the police and all that had happened subsequently. I also remembered how Chris was campaigning for new equipment and how it kept falling on deaf ears.

'It was deliberate,' I said. 'If the police haven't been called already, you should call them now.'

We didn't go home to Melbourne for Christmas: my decision. Dean was subdued and gave in without an argument. I had the impression he didn't know what to say to me. I wasn't sure if that was because he hadn't made up his mind what he wanted to say, or didn't know how to get me to hear. I thought about asking about Zahra, but in the end I decided not to force the issue. He needed to be sure what he wanted.

I already knew what my choice would be, and what it hung on.

The police were investigating the theatre accident. As the hospital psychologist, I had to be available to support the staff, Chris especially. Of course, apart from one group meeting I ran with Athol, none of them sought me out—they were country folk after all. But I kept turning up, offering an ear, allowing them to ventilate.

Then there was Teagan. She hadn't had many friends other than those at the Land Council, but now the women from our group were added to the tally. Our final meeting without her had turned into a debrief, and they said they wanted to meet again after Christmas. I hoped Teagan might have recovered and be able to attend, so I scheduled a meeting in January. More often than not, I bumped into one of the other women in the group when I was in visiting her. Róisín looked shaken; for all her world view that the worst could happen, she clearly didn't wish for it to be so. 'I'm going to leave this for her,' she said, putting a faded but grand-looking old book on Teagan's bedside table—Grimm's fairy tales. 'Perhaps when she gets back to designing her T-shirts she can get inspiration from some of the characters.'

On the next visit, Zahra was there to give Teagan a beautiful handwoven silk blanket for Indiana. I wondered whether I should ask her what I hadn't asked my husband, but she was the one to raise it.

'Isabel, your husband…Dean has been very troubled.'

I bristled.

'He needed someone to talk with,' said Zahra.

'And he chose someone in my group?' I asked, barely able to hide the bitterness.

'He did not know I was in your group, only that I was a doctor on maternity leave. We found each other—he knew nothing of my illness, and I found I could help him; and this helped me. It gave me the belief I could be a doctor again.'

Zahra put her hand on my arm. 'It is messy, yes. And…I must apologise for saying to you about your little boy, about his incident in the water. I would have been your doctor, had I not become ill; now I am your patient. And your husband needs to talk, some counselling. I have some experience in this, with couples; I did a lot of it in Iran.' A modest smile. 'It was good to feel needed, and I think it helped him.'

Counselling. Not an affair. I was surprised at how little this altered what I wanted—what I hoped the future would hold for me and Noah.

'He loves you, just...' She shrugged. 'Men are not so good with talking about feelings, no?'

Kate brought in some of Ruby's baby clothes for Indiana—a spectacular array of colour. 'I'd hate them to go to waste,' she said, blinking back tears.

'I hope you're not part of the investigation into what happened to Teagan,' I said. 'You're too close.'

Kate's mouth formed a firm line. 'I'm part of the team. Just doing the background checks.' She shook her head. 'I can't get my head around it—if someone really did try to kill her, it has to be connected to the warning. But I can't make it fit.'

I would have liked to ask questions, but I kept my mouth shut and let her talk.

'I mean, there was a...an item mentioned in the warning letter, right? And Joshua's remains—they were found inside this thing,' Kate said.

I looked at her, trying to appear receptive but not too avid.

'It seems kind of incongruous to me.' Kate looked like she was still uncertain what it was that didn't make sense for her. 'I can't tell you what it was, but let's just say it was... nice, this item, solidly made, and it had his rug in it. And I can't figure out why. Given they burned the body. I mean why, umm, lay him to rest like that? Why not just dump the remains?'

'Because they cared?' I was no profiler but I had studied criminology as a major. 'They were sorry for what they'd done, or at least sorry because Joshua had died unintentionally?'

'Exactly,' said Kate. 'Back then they sent a tip-off telling us where to find the remains—which I always thought implied some sympathy for the Morettis. So why try to kill Teagan now?'

For two days Teagan remained unconscious. The nurses encouraged us to believe she could hear us, and I spoke to her as if she could, but I never saw any response, and nor did Joe. He was there most days, and the nurses were pumping breastmilk for him to feed Indiana, who took whatever she was offered greedily, rarely crying. It was as if she knew she had to wait patiently before she could meet her mother.

Chris also visited, pale and still shaken.

'Will she make it?' I asked.

'I don't know.'

I hugged him. I sensed that he wanted to break down and let me hold him, but wouldn't let it happen.

I had wondered whether Chris could possibly have done this as a stunt to show how badly he needed new equipment. He might have been intending just to switch over to the spare canister after he'd made his point—then been devastated to realise some genuinely incompetent person had misplaced it. I couldn't see it, but I knew that was partly because I didn't want to. Still, I didn't think anyone could act as shattered as Chris unless it was real.

On the third day Teagan was semi-conscious.

On the fourth she woke up.

I t took two more days and a raft of scans for the doctors to be sure, but on Christmas Eve Teagan was discharged home. When I dropped in on Christmas Day with homemade shortbread, seeing her with Indiana in her arms was the best Christmas gift I could have imagined.

We went to Sydney for New Year. Dean had meetings in the first few days of January, and he was keen for me to come. He didn't bring up our argument; I sensed he was hoping it would go away. It wouldn't, but I didn't have the energy to address it again. Not yet.

In the week we returned, the Riley news was full of the cyclone that had hit central Queensland. The reports of torrential rain were accompanied by pictures of rivers breaking over sandbagged thresholds and random items of furniture disappearing downstream. Cars had been abandoned and people had taken to rowboats; some residents of Lismore, only a few hours from Riley, were homeless. The premier was filmed in gumboots, declaring a state of emergency. Three dead, two missing. The barking owls were behind our house each night, as if they were warning us of more trouble coming.

I had noticed as we drove back from Dubbo after our

flight from Sydney how different the Riley plains now looked to me. What had looked like hell two and a half months earlier now seemed to hold a gritty resilience in its grass tufts and spindly gum trees. Riley's river was less a dark scar in the landscape and more of an oasis, for all that the flow was still only a muddy trickle. There'd been a sprinkling of rain one evening but the drops had quickly disappeared into the parched cracks; the heat and dry persisted.

I arrived a few minutes early for the January group, which was going to focus on wrapping up. I expected there would also be a need to debrief, to share anxieties heightened by responsibility for an infant and ramped up further by Teagan's near-death experience.

I would also need to help them deal with the tension between Sophie and Teagan. I had bumped into the other three mothers visiting Teagan, and Grace had left flowers but Sophie hadn't been in contact. She hadn't attended the pre-Christmas group either; I had assumed she was in Sydney with her family and it was only later I heard she had stayed in Riley. If she boycotted this group, I thought, I would drop in on her afterwards. The town was too small to let this fester; I had visions of the feud playing out between Sophie and Teagan's babies, Tom and Indiana, as adolescents, and none of the ways I envisaged it ending were good.

Kate was first to arrive, with Ruby dressed in a remarkably practical outfit. Kate saw my look.

'She said no to the pink tutu, can you figure? I suggested to my mother-in-law that Ruby needed a little scope to decide what she wanted to look like.'

I grinned. 'I kind of enjoyed seeing what she'd turn up in next.'

'Yeah, well, I suspect she'll come up with some interesting ideas of her own.'

She dropped Ruby off in the room with Yvonne. Ruby started to protest at her mum leaving and I heard Kate's voice, low and firm: setting limits. I wished I could get Róisín to do the same. Kate closed with her usual gruff 'You'll be right,' then turned back and added, 'Love you, kiddo.'

I must have still been looking astonished when she joined me. 'I listen,' she said, sounding mildly affronted.

I wanted to hug her, but she probably hadn't changed *that* much.

Zahra was in gold and pink, and Raha in blue and crimson. There was a sense of calm in them both but Zahra looked serious.

She said to Kate, 'Have you found anything? About why there was no oxygen at the hospital?'

'We're investigating,' said Kate. She knew I was across the details, but the general public weren't, or at least weren't meant to be. She quietly added, mostly for my benefit, 'They found the missing canister in a broom cupboard.'

Stored in the wrong place, or deliberately hidden?

Róisín's arrival didn't lighten the feeling in the room. 'I suppose,' she said after settling Bella with Yvonne, 'that we don't know anything further. About what happened at the hospital?' She looked at me, sorrowful and slightly accusing.

'Only rumours,' I said.

'It will be the final straw as far as the hospital's concerned,' said Róisín. 'And that means all our jobs are on the line. My father...Conor's already met with the workers. It'll be them that get scapegoated.'

I thought of the oxygen canisters, empty, missing and with a faulty gauge. If it was due to incompetence then, yes, they might get the blame, along with Chris. Except I didn't think it was accidental.

I glanced out the window and saw Teagan pushing an oversized pram up the path. Maggie from the Land Council was with her—dressed today in yellow trousers, her glasses decorated with small smiling suns—as well as two younger children on tricycles.

'Here comes Teagan. Can I request that we don't bring this up unless she does?'

Teagan showed the usual signs of new motherhood—clumsily managing the steps, the door and the pram—but her friend grabbed her bag and Kate jumped up to help them. Teagan smiled and the shadows under her eyes deepened. Part sleep deprivation, part recovery from a significant trauma, I guessed; but her smile was radiant. She'd squeezed back into tiny tattered jeans and a crop top that said *I'm awesome*. Maggie nodded at me and told Teagan she'd be back after the group.

'I made it!' Teagan said to us, scooping Indiana up in her arms. The child was fast asleep. 'Isn't she perfect? She put on three hundred grams this week and oh my God you should see her smile at me even if Dad wants to say it's just because she's having a dump—' Teagan didn't draw breath. She sat down, Indiana still in her arms.

'Do you want to leave her with Yvonne?'

'No *way*. You reckon I'm letting anyone else take her after the hospital nearly killed us?'

Trust Teagan to go right to the heart of what was on everyone's mind.

'It was an accident,' said Róisín, her need for continued employment apparently overriding her need for conspiracy theories.

'Bullshit it was.' Teagan's eyebrows, plucked down to almost the last hair, disappeared under her fringe. 'Someone's gonna pay—my dad's talking to lawyers.'

'The hospital won't be there to sue,' Róisín said.

'It must be frightening for you Teagan,' I said. 'None of us can claim to be that traumatised, but I imagine we're all feeling some anxiety.'

'Anxiety? Not me.' Teagan shook head. 'Anger, maybe.'

I sensed Kate wanting to give her a thumbs-up as Róisín mumbled something about not ever being able to rely on anyone anyway, and Zahra shuffled her chair back a little.

'When I get angry I don't sit around navel gazing,' Kate said, looking at Teagan. 'If someone's to blame we'll find out.'

I suggested a calming exercise—useful for anger or anxiety—and no one objected. I also raised the idea of one last meeting, mainly social, by way of a break-up; I wanted to end things on some exclusively positive messages. Teagan enthusiastically suggested everybody come to her place, but in the end we agreed that we'd meet at the health centre as usual, and all bring a plate of food.

I had just decided Sophie wasn't going to turn up, when she came through the door.

'Sorry I'm late.' There was an edge to her voice; she cast a look at Teagan and kept walking with Tom to the kids' room.

The tension was palpable. Enough to shut even Teagan up—after she'd completed a long spiel about the diabolical cost of disposable nappies. I spoke into the tense silence that followed.

'Before you got here, Sophie, I was saying that it's only to be expected that we've all been a bit traumatised. The whole town is under a lot of pressure, but I'm thinking beyond that, at a personal level. Teagan'—I saw Sophie stiffen—'has obviously had a big scare. I know you also had a frightening time.' I caught Teagan's eyes and hoped she'd play along.

'Having Tom *kidnapped* you mean?' Sophie said, her voice higher than she normally spoke, as if the air had to fight its way through her larynx to make a sound at all.

'What happened to Tom was unacceptable,' I said firmly. 'I know Teagan hasn't had the chance—'

'The chance to apologise?' Sophie was sitting bolt upright in her chair. 'No need for that—I understand completely. It's perfectly all right for your husband's ex-girlfriend to waltz off with your child. I mean, no harm done, was there?'

Teagan looked warily at Sophie, then me.

'There wasn't any harm done to Tom,' I said, 'but that doesn't mean it was okay, or that there wasn't harm done to you.' I mouthed *say sorry* to Teagan.

'If it had been me,' said Kate without a hint of animosity, 'I'd have decked you, Teagan.'

Róisín shook her head in sorrow. 'You really can't trust anyone.'

Sophie looked like she was in total agreement with that. Why had she come today? From a sense of duty to the Barclays? To show that she wouldn't be cowed? Beneath the hysterical response she was probably feeling lost, the picture-perfect world she had constructed in ruins. Lachlan wasn't a knight in shining armour, her refuge from critical parents and a career that frightened her. He was human; he had flaws and, worse, they had been exposed in public. Sophie's world was built on image—I wasn't sure what, if anything, she had been able to retain of that in her own mind.

'I'm really sorry.' Teagan's voice was low, defensiveness

shelved for now. 'What I did was like totally fucked, Sophie.'

Sophie's grim expression didn't alter. 'Well I guess that's all fine, then,' she said.

'It isn't fine,' I said gently, 'but understanding can help you make sense of it. Remember when we talked about how we were parented, and the way it affects how we parent? It's not just parenting itself, but all the things that happen during your childhood that affect your parents, and then affect you.' I turned to the rest of the group. 'Can you all think of something big that happened when you were growing up? Something that changed your parents and maybe who you became?'

'My grandmother died before I was born,' said Kate. 'My mother was only young and I'm sure that's why she didn't like to get too close to us; you know—fear of loss. And I reckon my father dying sent me that message, too.'

'Leaving Iran,' said Zahra. 'I was not so young, but...it is as if my home is always out of reach. Like a small part of me must be in grief for ever.'

'When Teagan's brother was taken,' said Róisín.

I looked at her. She appeared a little unsettled, as if she wasn't quite sure why she had raised the topic.

'It's affected the whole town, not just the Morettis,' she said.

'It has,' I agreed.

'So, Teagan had a hard life,' said Sophie. She looked so brittle that she might break in two at any moment. 'So jolly good for her that she survived it.' She leaned forward, towards Teagan. 'It doesn't give you the right to make other people suffer too.'

'I know,' said Teagan quietly, looking down at Indiana, who hadn't stirred.

'Teagan can't take back what she did,' I said. 'But she can promise to pay things forward—to learn, to leave you alone, whatever. If you let her. You've got the power here, Sophie.'

Sophie was struggling. Was it more that Teagan had taken her child? Or that she'd had a relationship with her husband and, worse, had a baby to him; for all that Hamish hadn't survived?

'Stay away from us. Stay away from our house, from me, from my family. Walk away if you see us on the street. Don't ever ask us for anything. And stay right away from Lachlan.'

I watched them look at each other and tried to read what the look said. There was a warning, but was there more?

I was sure Sophie would protect the father of her child come hell or high water. But if it was Matt, fearing he was Indiana's father, who was behind Teagan's brush with death, would Sophie cover that up too?

The rain in the north continued relentlessly. As the weather band moved east, we were catching the tail end of it in the form of scattered showers. It was still hot, but for the first time in four months I had to turn the windscreen wipers on. The car was covered with a thick layer of Riley dust, so I was soon peering out across a dirt-streaked screen, mud dripping across my line of vision each time the wipers moved. Crossing the bridge on the way to town, I slowed. I could see water—another first. Riley now had a real river.

At the post office I paused to flick through the mail and found, with a sharp jolt of excitement, an envelope marked ancestry.com. I took Noah off to the Railway Café and ordered an iced coffee and a chocolate milk. While I was waiting, I opened the letter.

The test results were clear: Tom and Indiana were cousins. That meant Matt Barclay was Indiana's father—which was, of course, why I had wanted to do the test. Except that I'd been hoping to prove the opposite.

Maggie from the Land Council had told me not to underestimate Teagan. I had taken it then in a positive way, but…Could Teagan be blackmailing Matt? It didn't fit with anything I knew about her. Except she was a survivor. And it might explain where the café money had been going. No way could I see Jeannie taking it, and she'd told me Matt was now one of the people collecting it.

What the hell did I do now? Did I tell Teagan? Or just let Jed assume the child was his? If Matt had been worried, he had cause to be: his arithmetic was apparently better than Teagan's. But what did it mean for the danger she might still be in?

Noah started protesting that I'd left him in the pusher. I automatically unfastened him and put him down on the floor and he headed off to the ancient kayak sitting on the enclosed platform. The latest delivery, maybe for emergency use in any future flood.

I needed to talk to someone. My first thought was Chris. He was Teagan's doctor, after all, and although she had sworn me to secrecy over the identity of the first child's father, she hadn't extracted any assurances about Indiana's father.

I texted Chris. His surgery was only minutes away, but I knew he'd probably be flat out. As it was, he arrived just as I finished my coffee, and ordered us both another.

'You okay?' he asked.

'I should ask you that.'

A crooked smile. 'Taking one day at a time.'

'I want to run something past you…It may have some bearing on who tried to kill Teagan.'

Chris shook his head. 'I don't think the police—'

'Hear me out, okay?'

He nodded.

'Ever since I got to town,' I said slowly, 'there has

been a threat against a baby, a threat tied in with what happened to Teagan's brother, as well as to the hospital— its mismanagement, missing money and the politics around it.'

Chris's expression didn't give anything away.

'Too many things happening at the same time not to think there is some connection.'

Warnings, money, blackmail.

'I need to discuss it with Teagan,' I said slowly. 'But I happen to know Indiana is Matt's baby.'

Chris raised an eyebrow. I passed him over the ancestry. com results, explaining whose samples I had sent.

'My thinking is she may have been blackmailing Matt, and he could have written the warning to police to scare her, to get her to stop.' I didn't imagine she was getting much money from Matt, but enough to make him worry that his dad would find out.

Chris looked startled.

'If so, it also implies that when threats didn't work, he got serious: that it was Matt who tried to kill her by tampering with the oxygen.'

Chris frowned and shook his head. 'As attractive as it is to think I wasn't at fault, Matt doesn't have access to theatre.'

'What about at night? After hours?'

'Police have already checked. Not for him, especially, but they know who entered in the previous two weeks. And Matt was the only Barclay who didn't.'

'Back doors? Does CCTV cover everything?'

'Exits and entrances, yes.'

Could Matt have got Lachlan or Sophie to do it? They had their own beef with Teagan...

Chris interrupted my thoughts. 'So, what are you going to do now?'

I felt a little deflated. 'Good question. You and I know Matt's the father, but...I need to let Teagan decide what to do about it.'

As I left the café, Conor was heading towards it with a couple of fellow rugby players. I was still trying to think through the implications of the DNA test results, and how Sophie's anger, Lachlan's guilt, Joe's resentment and the possibility of blackmail might sit in the mix. I had been certain originally that the Reardens were involved, but at the moment it looked like the whole mess was between the Barclays and the Morettis.

'Hey,' Conor called out to me as I turned towards my car. 'When are you getting the fuck out of Riley?'

I looked down at Noah as I put him in his car seat. I rummaged in my bag and found a container of chopped cheese and apple, gave it to him and went to put the stroller in the boot.

Conor and his companions were now only metres away. I half-expected Chris to come to the rescue, but he'd headed in the opposite direction, to the hospital. I could have jumped in the car and left. Instead I turned to face them.

'See what your husband's done,' Conor said. He was holding a sheet of paper and his face was deeply flushed with anger.

'Mr Rearden,' I said. 'I am not responsible for what my husband may or may not have done.'

'Yeah? You come to this town all full of yourself, telling my daughter you're going to help her and those other women. So how's closing our hospital going to do that?'

He was now waving the piece of paper, which I had no hope of reading, right in front of my face. 'First *you* promise things to my daughter you can't deliver.'

I hadn't promised anything other than to help her re-think her life and her problems, some of which Conor had caused.

'Then *you* tell my daughter she's a bad mother.'

I wondered if that was Róisín's interpretation of something I'd said, or Conor's invention.

'And now *you* swan around town giving not one fuck that *your* husband is closing the hospital.'

He stopped waving the piece of paper long enough for me to read it. A notice of a union meeting. To protest against the imminent closure of Riley hospital.

'And throwing us out of work,' one of the men standing behind Conor added. He was more sullen than overtly angry.

'You know what?' I said, crossing my arms as I faced the three of them. 'If the hospital nearly killed someone'—I looked pointedly at Conor; he was in maintenance, he could easily have accessed the oxygen canisters—'then maybe it's not such a bad thing. I don't see your union signing up to protect a murderer, do you?'

Conor was still giving me a piece of his mind—the words *fucking bitch* hanging heavy in the air—as I drove away. I thumped the steering wheel instead of punching the air; Noah looked slightly alarmed.

Of all the people who could have tried to kill Teagan

by fixing the canisters, Conor Rearden had the most opportunity. The set-up needed cold-hearted planning, which he and Matt were both capable of, but it also needed access, which Matt did not have. Conor was an arrogant, angry bully who believed people were out to get the union. And he was no fan of Chris's; if he got caught in the firing line, then that would have been a bonus.

Question was: why? What was his motive?

Why would Conor need to get Teagan out of the way? If Matt had paid him to do it, it would have cost more than a few hundred filched here and there from Jeannie's cash drawer.

By the time I picked Dean up at 6 p.m. the rain had settled in. As we hurried to the car Dean was juggling his crutches and a briefcase stuffed with papers while I took a cardboard box filled with his belongings.

Conor was right. Dean was leaving. Which meant Perth was only weeks away, after the holiday we hadn't confirmed yet. Dean was still talking about Lindeman Island, where Noah could go to the kids' club…'and we can work on making him a little brother or sister'.

That probably meant he'd booked it. Queensland would be humid; with the stingers at this time of year, you couldn't swim in the sea. Given my relationship with water, this was fine by me. But Noah would want to be in the pool. My stomach tightened at the thought.

'You've officially finished?'

'Pretty much,' said Dean, throwing his stuff on the back seat next to Noah. He pulled out a paperweight that was as much kids' puzzle as desk adornment and offered it to our son before getting into the driver's seat.

'When's the hospital closing?'

'End of the week.'

I watched it recede in the side mirror, wondered at what would happen to the people who worked there, and to the town itself. Despite what I'd said to Conor Rearden, I wouldn't have closed it. I'd have fixed the problem and made it more economic. Safer, if that was a real issue.

'When do we leave?'

'Whenever you like.'

'I have my last group tomorrow.'

'Okay. We'll pack tomorrow and drive to Melbourne the next day.'

Dean slowed to go through a large puddle over the road before the bridge. The river, now only a few metres below, a strong tide of brown, swirled as it hit tree trunks that days earlier had been on the banks, well away from the water.

'Your auditors find what they needed?'

'You bet.' Dean's expression was that of a man satisfied with a job well done, and whatever issues I had with Dean, he certainly knew how to do his job.

'So can I ask...anything dodgy in the café?'

'I wasn't expecting much from that, to be honest,' said Dean. 'But the new boy is a bit of a cash-business whiz-kid and wanted to look. Nothing else did cash. And surprise, surprise, just before I hit town their profits went up. Pretty telling.'

'What sort of amounts are we talking?'

Dean looked briefly curious at my interest but was too tied up in the excitement of the grand finale to sit long with it. 'As I said, small fry. Maybe two hundred a week.'

Ten thousand a year. Over how many years? Enough to keep Teagan quiet, not enough to pay someone to commit murder. Yet I still couldn't see Teagan as a blackmailer. If she was going to do something to the Barclays it would be impulsive—like kidnapping Tom—and...spectacular, somehow. I could see her burning down their house. But waiting for a weekly handout? It just seemed too petty.

'We're winding up,' I said when everyone had poured themselves some tea or coffee and helped themselves to one of Sophie's oversized chocolate chip cookies or the leftover white Christmas that Kate's mother-in-law had probably made. 'It's the last group, and it's especially sad for me because I'll also be leaving Riley.'

Only Teagan looked surprised.

'Looks like a lot of things around here are closing down,' said Róisín.

'Well, you could keep meeting.' I saw Sophie's look. 'Not necessarily all of you...but some regular get-together for coffee. You're all learners when it comes to kids, and parenting is a bit like being on the Grand Prix circuit. So having other people who are on your team rather than against you can help.'

I went through the content we had covered, reminding them all of the mindfulness exercises and breathing techniques, and their own particular areas of struggle. For the most part, they were subdued. Róisín and Zahra had their minds elsewhere. Róisín was not checking Bella so frequently, I thought. Probably worrying about her job—I doubted it was due to any progress as a result of attending the group. Maybe Zahra was worrying about me and my marriage. Teagan was preoccupied with Indiana, who was unsettled, and Sophie seemed less brittle, more resigned; possibly depressed. Kate was watching them both. If I pulled them aside at the end, I suspected Kate would try to eavesdrop.

'I'm going to miss you all,' I said, and it was true. 'I thought to finish off, we could all go around and say one positive thing about each person, about what you think they've gained, or how they've changed.' This was a gamble, but it wasn't hard. Sophie could at least say Teagan was trying to be a good mother.

'I'll start,' I said. 'With Kate. Kate likes to think she's tough.'

'She's a cop,' Teagan said. *Derr*.

'Yes, and I'm sure she is tough. But she's also allowed herself to be a little more vulnerable. So Ruby can crawl under her skin and know she's loved.'

Kate looked at her feet. I could see there was a trace of a smile.

'Me next?' Sophie asked. 'I love what she's done with Ruby's outfits.'

'You mean what my mother-in-law's done.'

'No,' said Sophie. 'Ruby looks like a little girl now, not a mini version of her grandmother.'

Kate looked surprised, but pleased.

The others added their thoughts: 'She smiles a lot more at Ruby,' said Zahra; and 'Ruby smiles back a lot more,' Róisín put in.

'Never thought I'd actually think a cop was okay.' (Teagan).

'Zahra,' I said, 'has been kind enough to share with us her wisdom.' I might have been a bit happier if she hadn't shared it with Dean, but still. She was a lot better.

All the comments that followed were variations—there was a sense the women wanted to like her but found her puzzling. Zahra herself was puzzled by the comments.

'You all think I am wise?'

'Sure do,' said Teagan. 'You remind me of a book my Grade Three teacher read to us on Greek myths...well yours'd be Iranian myths I guess...but you know stuff, like how to *be*.'

Next was Róisín, and this was difficult. The truth was that I thought she needed another year or more of personal therapy. However: 'Róisín,' I said, 'what I am most impressed about you is how much you love Bella.'

'And though you don't trust the world, you still came here,' said Sophie.

'You're really trying to be different...umm, from your family. I mean in good ways,' said Teagan.

Róisín blushed self-consciously, couldn't look any of us in the eye.

'You try to be brave,' said Zahra.

'It's hard,' said Róisín softly.

'But you try,' Kate followed up.

Against the odds, it seemed there had been some bonds of sorts formed here. I hoped they'd extend to the remaining two participants.

'Sophie, you have very high expectations of yourself and others,' I said. 'You are trying to be kinder to everyone, even those who fall short, but it's tough.'

'I always try to do my best,' said Sophie.

Teagan caught my expression and curtailed her eye roll.

'I think that makes you exhausted,' said Kate. 'Come in for a drink occasionally when you want to wind down, okay?'

I looked at her in surprise, wondering how much this was Kate the cop; it sounded like Kate the fellow-mother, and Sophie's startled look of appreciation suggested that was what she heard.

'I think you're very forgiving,' said Róisín, who I was certain wouldn't have been.

'Hate kills those who hate,' said Zahra, living up to Teagan's assessment. 'Better to fill your heart with love. And forgive yourself if you fall short, too.'

'Um, yeah,' Teagan put in awkwardly. 'Thanks again, and I am sorry.'

Sophie nodded, face taut, not looking at her.

'So Teagan. You're last,' I said. 'You've had your share of challenges, yet you've stayed determined to focus on being a good mother.'

'You swear a lot less,' said Róisín.

'You're a fighter,' said Kate.

'A warrior.' Zahra beamed at her.

Which left Sophie. There was a pause. Sophie opened her mouth and closed it. Then got up and walked next door to get Tom.

'I'll be back,' I said to the others, and went after her.

'I can't,' she said as soon as she saw me. 'That...woman. She took my child.'

'I know, Sophie, and nobody's saying that's okay. Is that what this is really about?'

She looked at me warily.

'How you are seen is so important to you; image, how others see you. That's what your family taught you, and it's so tied up with being lovable that you can't tell the difference. Maybe you think Lachlan having a relationship with Teagan is humiliating. But it was eight years ago; and you know what? I think it speaks to Lachlan being a nicer, more human person. He didn't just write her off like half of Riley did: he saw her as a real person, and he cared about her. Then, not now. It's Gordon and Grace that should be humiliated for paying her off, not you.'

Sophie now knew Teagan had been paid to have a termination. If she thought Teagan had continued to blackmail the family, there was no way this speech would hit home. But what I saw—for a split second before her defences went up again—was her wondering about Lachlan. Was he perhaps the hero in this story?

'There is no reason she has to be part of your life, right?'

'No fucking way.'

I must have looked startled because she smiled. A genuine smile. 'Maybe I've caught her swearing habit.'

Head held high, she walked back into the room with a topped-up cup of tea and told Teagan she was every bit the lioness that, in an earlier group, we had all aspired to be. I'm not sure which of us was the most surprised—but it told me something else for sure. She didn't know Matt was Indiana's father.

It was a good place to finish. They all thanked me as we packed up the leftover food. Róisín and Kate had to go to work. Sophie and Zahra lingered, chatting to Yvonne about using the centre for group meetings and maybe having some of the newer mothers in Riley join them. Teagan stayed with me in the group room.

I still had unanswered questions. If I listened to my nagging doubts, rather than the half-formed theories I had come up with, Teagan almost certainly was still in danger.

Teagan for her part, did not appear to be concerned.

'Teagan, remember that time I suggested a paternity test?'

Teagan nodded as she attached Indiana to her breast for a feed.

'What if it showed Matt *was* the father.'

Teagan looked up through her fringe. 'It won't. Jesus, look at her! She's obviously Jed's.'

Not according to DNA, she wasn't.

'Okay,' I said slowly, 'but Matt could be worried he was. Would that...would he go after you?'

'Nah. He wouldn't believe it. Thinks I screw round. Only did it that one time with me to stick it up Lachlan, I reckon.'

That had the ring of truth. Teagan didn't want Matt to be Indiana's father. She clearly didn't intend to chase it.

So why would he be worried?

I left the DNA test results in my pocket and figured they were no help to anyone, least of all Indiana.

I couldn't let it go, though. The possibility had occurred to me that there was someone else who could know more about Joshua's disappearance. Noah was tetchy, so first we had to go to the playground to exhaust him. Eventually he allowed me to strap him into the pusher, and was asleep before I'd gone more than a hundred metres.

Jeannie, as usual, was sitting in the hospital shop, knitting. If she was worried about what she would do when the hospital closed, it wasn't obvious.

'Hello there, dear,' she said. 'Coffee?'

'No thanks,' I said. 'I'm actually wondering if you could help me.'

'Of course, dear.' Her pale blue-grey eyes looked up from under her snowy white curls. The purple tips were gone.

'I'm going to test your memory,' I said. 'But the test won't be too tough—you've been asked lots of times. That day you were here, twenty-five years ago, when Joshua went missing.'

'Remember like it was yesterday,' said Jeannie.

'Can you remember who came into the shop, anyone who you saw entering the hospital? Around the time Joshua disappeared.'

Jeannie frowned. 'Well, as I recall there were lots of people. Police of course, Eric the manager, Joe and poor Donna.'

'Anyone else?'

'Well I'm not sure, about earlier, you see. I was late, remember—I'd been with my daughter.'

So...someone else opened up the shop?' I asked.

'Oh yes, now you mention it. I was going to ring Mrs Barclay, because normally she would have opened up if I couldn't, but she'd just had a baby herself a month or so earlier. I'd had a young girl helping me, like for work experience, so I asked her.'

I realised I was holding my breath. 'Who?'

'Young Róisín Rearden,' said Jeannie. 'She was fifteen or sixteen at the time.'

'And Grace,' I asked. 'Did she come in that day?'

'Oh yes, it was a Friday, the day she collects the money. Always on a Friday, even after Lachlan. She had him with her, but with all the fuss with Donna and Joe...well she didn't stay around long. All the mothers back then were shaken up. My daughter wouldn't let her child sleep in his own room for months.'

'When did Grace come in? Relative to the baby going missing?'

'Oh, after. We were all in a tizz, as you can imagine.'

I thanked her, and she went back to her knitting.

I made my way to admin. Róisín, I was told, had the day off. 'We'll all be off by the end of the week,' the woman reminded me.

I had Róisín's address, though. She and her partner lived in a small weatherboard that looked like it needed repairs, only a few doors from the hospital. I knew Al worked long hours and Róisín had told me the newsagency was barely covering costs, so home maintenance didn't look like a priority. I presumed all the in-laws' money—if there had been any—had gone on the IVF.

I wondered if what I was doing was wise. I was no detective…but the long hours watching the sunset had given me plenty of time to think, to make use of my six years of study. The whos and whys had started to slip into place.

Róisín looked surprised to see me. I pushed into the doorway and she let me in. The blinds were down and in the living room there was a pile of clean clothes on the couch for sorting. Bella, playing quietly in the corner, regarded me warily.

'I'm hoping you can clear something up for me,' I said, pushing aside a pile of underwear to give me room to sit. Noah was still asleep—I left the pusher in the corridor.

Róisín's expression was impossible to interpret.

'I'm worried about what happened at the hospital, with Teagan,' I said.

'Well. It's not like any kind of accident's going to happen there again.'

'It was deliberate. Someone with access to the theatre messed with the oxygen canisters.' I watched her carefully; I didn't expect to be able to read her easily. Róisín lived her life guarding against potential assaults on all fronts. There was no reliable way to tell if someone was lying, but I knew that guilt and lies often had telling signs. Probably, I thought, she'd be more defensive than usual, and launch a verbal assault, turning it back on me. The thought no longer worried me.

'I think,' I said slowly, 'it was because someone thought Teagan was doing something she wasn't.'

Róisín looked confused.

'I think,' I continued, 'someone thought she was taking money to keep quiet.'

The tell was there: Róisín's mouth tightened ever so slightly. 'I wouldn't know about that. I'm not friendly with Teagan.'

I thought of the gift of the fairy-tale book. Wondered if it was part guilt, part apology. I hoped it meant there was some chance for Róisín to shift; to be the mother—the person—she wanted to be.

'Perhaps not,' I said. 'But would you want her harmed because someone mistook her for someone else?' I wasn't sure, not completely. But it was the only thing that made sense to me, why someone had tried to kill Teagan.

Róisín looked at me warily. 'I don't wish harm on anyone, Isabel. I look after myself and Bella; it's all I can do.'

I wondered where to go next.

I had to press on, not because I cared about who was extorting money from the café, but because as long as someone thought it was Teagan, she was in danger. I thought of Róisín setting me up with the information about the caterer and waiting for me to 'disappoint' her. Her life script. She hadn't been able to use it against me, but if I'd played into it, she would have. I was almost certain she had set up Zahra with some gossip, true or otherwise, about Teagan and Joe that was behind Zara's sense of something wrong in the Moretti family. Unlike Teagan, Róisín's life was small and petty. And she thought the worst of people.

'Did your father pay for the IVF? No, that was Al's parents, right? From their pension.'

I felt rather than saw her jolt. She was sitting on the couch and it vibrated through the springs, a sudden, clear panic that briefly touched her eyes before the shutters came down.

'How I pay bills is no business of yours. You need to leave.'

'You're right. And actually I don't care about that,' I said, not moving. 'I do care about what happens to Teagan; she's an innocent party in this. She's already lost a brother and a mother. She's suffered enough.' I looked over at Bella. 'And I care about you, too, the sort of mother you could be and want to be.' I put a hand over hers. 'You may think money helps free you, but it's keeping you prisoner, Róisín.'

'You know nothing,' said Róisín sharply, pulling her hand away. 'All I care about is Bella. Nothing. Else. Matters. Everything I do is for her.'

'Including having her in the first place. IVF bills are horrendous, aren't they? I imagine it just didn't seem fair that the Barclays had all that money and you didn't even have enough for a baby.'

Róisín sat in stony silence. I pushed on.

'Did you see something, that day when Joshua went missing? Something that didn't quite make sense until later? Did you tell your father?'

Still nothing.

'I don't think *you* tried to harm Teagan,' I said. 'But is it possible your father thought she might get in the way of the ongoing payments from the Barclays?'

'I don't know what you're talking about. I said you need to leave.'

'I will as soon as you convince me your father didn't have anything to do with what happened at the hospital.'

Róisín looked torn—how much to tell me without incriminating herself.

'No one can prove anything,' she said. She took a breath. 'Look, my father's a thug, okay? When I was growing up he was a brute sober and worse drunk. I put up with that my whole life. Could he have done something to the oxygen canisters? I guess.' She looked directly at me. 'But he didn't, because he knows nothing. Absolutely nothing.'

I rose, and at the door, turned to ask one more question. 'Did you write the letter to the police?'

There were no words spoken; the same tell, the tightening around her mouth gave me my answer.

'And the dog shit? The treacle? The message on my car?'

Róisín scowled; she didn't ask what I was talking about. 'Why didn't you just *leave*?'

There it was. I knew who had tipped off the police, who had issued those petty little threats (except the dead roo, which I still figured was Matt's way of expressing what he thought of city folk generally and Dean in particular). Presumably because she was afraid the audit would put an end to her little scheme. She was also the blackmailer; the few hundred from the café might well have been ongoing after a much larger initial instalment that covered the IVF. But I still didn't know who was paying her or why—and who had attempted to murder Teagan.

And then I remembered Róisín was not quite sixteen when she'd worked in the shop that morning. She couldn't drive. And in her interview she'd told me her family had lived quite a way out of town. So how did she get into town to open up the hospital café?

Over the last three months I had become used to sitting outside after settling Noah, winding down and letting the magic of the lowering sun on a harsh landscape soften me.

Dean had been called back into town for crisis talks—Maggie, supported by the Aboriginal Land Council and the shire, had rallied the locals into a last-ditch attempt to save the hospital. Dean was helping them.

'Truth is,' he'd said, 'they could operate quite efficiently if they ran a half-reasonable kitchen and didn't use the place as a nursing home. I had it in the recommendations but the state government indicated they weren't keen.' He'd shrugged. 'Be nice to see them make it work.'

The view from the veranda bore little resemblance now to the dust bowl that had greeted us three months ago. I could barely make out the tree line for the fine mist that had set in. The rain had been continuous for three days—long enough for the cracked land to become soaked. Puddles were spread across paddocks and the occasional sheep that ventured out from under a tree had muddy black socks and had to pick its way slowly to find a blade of grass.

The evening news featured the countryside up north, which was still faring badly: people stranded up trees and on rooftops, water lapping at their feet as they waited to be winched to safety. There were warnings out to evacuate various towns, and I thought one of them was about a hundred kilometres away—without internet I couldn't check a map.

I didn't fancy venturing out to see if the creek had broken its banks. It was hidden by trees where it passed behind the house, but as we'd crossed the bridge earlier, the water hadn't been far below.

I'd just put Noah to bed when I heard a car outside.

A twinge of anxiety—I didn't expect Dean for hours—but it disappeared as I stood on the veranda and watched Chris's Nissan pull up. He got out with flowers in hand and thrust them at me.

'Kind of a goodbye and thank-you present,' he said, kissing my cheek.

Did I hear regret in his voice, or was that my own sadness at leaving?

I didn't say anything, and he added: 'Kind of a stupid present I guess; flowers aren't easy to keep alive in a car.'

I took them and smiled. His hand lingered longer on my fingers than it should have. That wasn't my imagination; nor was it coincidence that he had come when Dean wasn't here.

'They're beautiful. Thank you.'

We stood for a moment looking awkwardly at each other.

'Would you like something to drink?' I said eventually. 'Iced tea?' The weather might have looked grim, but it was still warm.

'Thank you.' He cast a glance at the boxes I'd been packing. 'Looks like Riley didn't work its magic charms on you.'

'I wouldn't say that.' I hesitated. 'I would have liked to keep working with my group. Some at least. And I'd like to know what really happened with the oxygen bottle'—Chris winced—'and to Joshua Moretti.'

'You aren't alone there.'

We sat on the outside chairs and looked out across the sodden landscape.

'You still think it was sabotage?'

I nodded. 'I know someone was blackmailing the Barclays—she almost certainly saw something twenty-five years ago.'

Chris's eyes widened.

'What I can't work out is how Teagan came to be targeted. If it was linked to the hospital problems—especially the money missing from the coffee shop, the blackmailer should have been at risk, not her.'

Chris thought for a moment. 'From the Barclays?'

'I guess one of them *thought* they knew who was blackmailing them, but got it wrong.'

'Can you go to the police?'

'With that kind of half-baked theory? No proof? They'd think I was bonkers.'

'I—' Chris stopped himself. Shook his head. 'At least talk to them before you go. Can't do any harm.'

I wasn't so sure. Wasn't certain what I owed to Róisín.

Chris looked at me long and hard. 'If I stay here much longer, I'm in danger of saying—or doing—something I shouldn't.'

I felt myself blush.

We both stood. But it was him that stepped in closer, and kissed me. A soft kiss of what might have been, before he turned abruptly and left.

I was still sitting on the veranda, thinking about forgiveness and wondering about happy-ever-afters when I saw headlights in the distance. Another visitor: it was getting to be like peak hour out here.

I remembered the near-panic of Joe Moretti's visit. I thought about how totally isolated I still was—and also without transport. I thought for a moment there were two cars, another set of headlights; then as the first car turned over the rickety bridge to enter the cottage property, the other lights disappeared. I wondered if they had been some sort of reflection, or Chris turning back around for some reason...

As the car got closer, I saw it was Joe's car again. I felt a slight easing of tension. He had no reason to see me as a threat...But why did he want to see me at all?

The car pulled up and the driver started to get out. It wasn't Joe, it was Teagan, wrestling Indiana in one arm and a paper bag in the other, dashing towards me through the rain.

'I had to see you before you left,' she said as she dumped Indiana on one of the chairs, car seat and all. She shook her wet hair, sending water droplets flying. 'Wanted to say thanks for everything you've done.' She thrust the paper bag into my hand.

Teagan looked at me expectantly. 'Go on, open it.'

Inside was a T-shirt. A Teagan original. In Indigenous colours, it was a startling collage of fabric textures that at first glance made an instant association with the outback.

'It's my mob's land you've been living on,' she said with a grin. 'This is to remind you.'

'Teagan...it's beautiful.' I had to flick the tears back as I gave her a hug. 'Can I try it on?'

I poured us both iced tea and returned to model the T-shirt. 'I love it. You're extremely talented.'

Teagan looked awkward. 'Do you think I could do it, like make it work? An online business, maybe?'

'Yes Teagan,' I said. 'You can do anything you put your mind to.'

She smiled, drank some of the iced tea. 'I wasn't sure you'd still be here. You seen how close the water is to that excuse for a bridge?'

Not for some hours. I looked into the dark towards it. I thought I heard something, but Teagan didn't seem to notice. The owl barked; maybe it had been him, out there hunting.

'I reckon here's a lot lower than the rest of Riley,' she said. Grace had told me the same thing. 'Maybe you should spend the night with Dad and me? You'd be welcome.'

I was sure we could get a room at the Riley Arms, and there was a motel not far along the road to Sydney—that might be the sensible thing. I'd already packed. When Dean got home we'd leave, I decided—worrying about water levels would mean I wouldn't sleep at all.

'Can I ask you something?' Teagan said.

The real reason for the visit.

'Do you think people can change?'

The same question her father had asked. I wondered if she was asking this about herself...her father...or someone else.

'Yes,' I said. 'It might require some tough decisions, but yes.'

Teagan seemed happy enough with this. She gave me a farewell hug, and packed Indiana back in the car. I watched the tail-lights disappear down the driveway and turn left in the distance, to the bridge. Then the lights stopped. The driver's door opened and I could see a figure get out and, a minute later, back in. Then the lights reversed, and Teagan headed back towards me. I hadn't told her I was going to leave. She must be worried about the water, and returning to warn me.

It was worse. She jumped out of the car, pulled Indiana and the car seat out and ran to the veranda, ashen-faced.

'The bridge is down.'

What? Surely in one hour the river hadn't been able to wash the bridge away?

'Well, not down exactly,' said Teagan. 'I was bloody lucky I didn't drive over it. There's a dirty great hole—like two, maybe more, boards gone. Car would have nose-dived in.'

She was clearly shaken.

So was I. That bridge had creaked and groaned happily enough twice a day, minimum, every day for the last three months. They had had heavy rain here plenty of times in previous years. What was the chance it would choose this moment to fall apart, even with two cars one after another?

I didn't like the answer, not when combined with the lights I thought I had seen and the sound I thought I had heard.

'We need to call for help,' I said. 'Your father?' And Dean.

Teagan nodded and got out her mobile; realised before I told her that there was no coverage. I showed her the house phone, thinking I might call the police station as well.

Teagan moved the handset away from her ear and looked at it like it was an alien life form. 'Aren't landlines supposed to make a noise?' she said.

No dial tone. I had a few seconds to take this in, on top of what I'd already been worrying about. So when the lights went out, it was perhaps less of a shock to me than it was to Teagan.

'What the *fuck*?'
I froze. I was in the swimming pool again, knowing I had to act immediately or Noah would die. Still unable to move.

Then I heard a noise on the veranda and saw Teagan's puzzled look and it shook me out of my stupor. This time I didn't have a friend to dive in and save me and Noah. I had to save us all.

'Teagan,' I whispered, grabbing her arm. 'You'll have to trust me. Don't make a sound. Get Indiana out of the capsule.'

Teagan might not have had a clue what was going on, but she caught the urgency in my tone.

'Lioness,' I added, and I could see in her look she knew exactly what I expected of her. I pulled her towards Noah's room. It was pitch black, but Teagan had fired up her phone torch. I used it to find Noah's old carrier and gave it to Teagan. She was going to need it. I had a more basic sling I put on to help carry Noah. He was heavy and I had no idea how long I'd manage with it, but not managing wasn't an option. I eased Noah out of bed, putting in his dummy to keep him quiet. He was still half-asleep—I hoped he'd stay that way.

In the doorway of his bedroom I paused to listen. Nothing. Back or front door? Was our saboteur alone or did he have help? And, much more importantly, how far was he prepared to go to silence Teagan—and did he now think he had to silence us both?

Teagan followed me back to the kitchen and watched me haul the trapdoor open. I could see she wanted to ask a million questions but my index finger at my lips silenced her. She hesitated when I urged her to start descending—a sound on the veranda convinced her to scramble down, one arm around Indiana in the baby carry pouch. I was right after her, pulling the trap door down carefully behind me. Teagan flicked her torch on.

'You can have the torch on down here,' I whispered, aware that the dark shadows of old washing machines and screen doors made navigation too hard without it. 'But once we're out, we can't be seen.'

'Who is it?' she asked, a tremor in her voice.

'Conor Rearden, I think, and probably his son. But... maybe the Barclay boys.'

Teagan looked surprised; in the shadows her expression looked at once fearful and perplexed.

We slowly picked our way through the debris that had collected under the house over the years. When I got to the door I opened it, then waited. I heard voices—soft and urgent and male. More than one. Coming from the front of the house, where they would expect us to go. The bridge might not take a car, but I guessed it would take two women carrying babies. If we got past our home invaders and made it to the road, the chances of a car passing before we hit the main road—at least a kilometre away—was zero. At this time of the evening it wouldn't be much better even once we got to the main road. And if we had to walk ten kilometres undetected—which would mean walking in the scrub on the roadside—we wouldn't make it.

On the other hand, if we were able to cross the creek behind the house and head directly north, it would be less than two kilometres to the nearest house. The phones' GPS wouldn't need network coverage to navigate us there.

There were two problems with this plan.

One, the nearest house was the Barclays', so we might be heading into the lion's den. In which case I would have to rely on the Barclay women, one of whom had warned Teagan off from ever turning up there. But I couldn't believe they'd all condone cold-blooded murder. I couldn't even be sure that was what the Barclay boys, if it was them outside, intended.

Two, and a far bigger issue, was the creek. Before the floods it would have been simple. Now, in flood, it was flat-out dangerous—just the thought of it filled me with terror.

The decision was made for me. Behind us I heard a gush of air, and then an explosion. It probably wasn't a big one, but it was close: in the silence, the noise seemed to split the night.

I turned to see flames start to leap from the front of the house. They'd decided to smoke us out or burn us to death. The burning house would light up the night sky for hundreds of metres. The only place we could take cover was in the trees by the creek, and that's where we went.

To the lion's den, I told myself. Were we not lionesses?

I heard it before I saw it. The sound of nature in a hurry, silent currents driving water through everything in its path, trees and rocks causing small splashes and knocking as the water surged on, taking the debris with it. I risked a quick look back—ash and smoke rising to the sky, the glow lighting up a hazy mist that reminded me that it was still raining and that both Teagan and I were soaked.

I saw the outlines of two men roaming around the house and shivered, grateful it wasn't winter. Teagan cast a worried look down at Indiana, nestled against her. It didn't have to be especially cold to put a three-week-old infant at risk. Only two kilometres, I thought, ignoring the bigger challenge in front of us.

At first, we walked along the edge. The creek's borders were no longer clear, and with the moon behind clouds, there was only the light from the burning cottage to navigate by. We both slipped but managed not to fall, the mud squelching and sucking our feet down; I lost a sandal and had to fish it out. Teagan abandoned hers, stepping barefoot with more confidence than I. Noah was now wide awake. His eyes stared at me: fear in them, but trust, too.

I swallowed. 'We're having a bit of an adventure, aren't we sweetheart?'

He nodded doubtfully and I turned to check Teagan was doing okay.

She'd stopped. She was staring back towards the fire; I followed her glance. One of the men was heading in our direction, swinging a torch in a wide arc.

'We have to get across,' I said urgently. 'He hasn't seen us yet, and they won't think we'd risk it.'

Her look of fear suggested there was a good reason for that.

I walked back behind her. I'd been looking for a crossing point, and we'd just passed the best one so far. Not great, but we weren't going to have time to find anywhere better. A solo man was going to travel a lot faster than two women with babies.

I took stock. The best-case scenario was that the creek was about six metres wide. I thought more likely ten—the other side was thick with shadows. There were plenty of trees—the biggest distance between any two branches on opposite sides was not much more than a metre. If we missed, there were more trees downstream. Except I'd seen on the news what floodwaters did to people—the current would be too strong for us, without support, to stay on our feet. And once we were knocked over we'd be swept away. A memory of Noah's lifeless face at the bottom of the pool flashed before my eyes and a wave of nausea surged through me.

Could we stand and fight? They had already tried to kill Teagan. They had torched the house meaning to kill us both. I wasn't going to gamble my son's life on unarmed combat with two grown men.

Hide, then? That wasn't an option. There was almost no undergrowth and the trees were spindly.

The torch waved across the grass tops looking for us.

Instinct said run.

'I'm going to get Noah across and come back and get Indiana,' I said, with more resolve than I felt. I wasn't at all sure I could get across once, let alone three times.

I didn't wait for a response from Teagan. I grabbed a branch that hung over the river and stepped gingerly forwards. Immediately I felt the pressure of the water against me, a stray branch brushing against my leg. A step further and the bottom dropped. I pulled back in alarm, slipping as the mud pulled one shoe off; stepped back, panting, and only just stifled a scream as the current threw something towards me that looked like a rat. It took the opportunity to run along my arm and onto an overhead tree branch. I caught my breath, watching what was coming at me as I lowered myself.

The cold water was up around my waist. Noah whimpered.

'Hush, sweetheart,' I whispered.

I couldn't tell if it was him or me who gasped, but for a second the ground was gone and I was swimming. One second only—enough for a rush of terror at the thought of not being able to keep Noah's head out of the water—then in the next instant my outstretched arm was around the tree on the other side, debris in the dark, muddy water pushing relentlessly against my hand. God knows where I found the strength to haul us in: with one pull I moved us a metre, and my feet once again found the riverbed. Both arms on the branch, then the tree trunk; the last metre, wading up what had once been the creek bank.

We were across.

I looked back. Teagan was staring at me in horror. I untied the sling, ran ahead a metre and sat Noah down by a tree. 'Noah honey, you must not move. Do you understand?' He looked stunned—I used the sling to tie him to the tree and hoped it would last long enough. Then I ran back for Teagan.

She hadn't waited. She had started to cross further downstream than I had. It looked a shorter crossing—but it didn't have the advantage of a second tree well placed if the first was missed. Whether it was because she was not as strong as me, or less cautious or just unlucky, she slipped and went under.

I stifled a scream, then threw myself across the stream. I aimed for the tree branch and caught it. Teagan hadn't let go of it, and the two if us came up together, spitting water. Indiana, to my relief, spluttered and coughed.

'Let me take her,' I said.

Teagan had stepped back out of the main current, up to her waist in water. Her arms went protectively around her daughter. 'No way.'

'You can do it,' I told her. 'I'm going to hold on to that tree branch.' I pointed. 'And then all you have to do is grab my hand, okay?'

I didn't wait for an answer, couldn't afford to give myself time to think. I jumped, grabbing the tree branch on the other side, stabilised and stepped back as far into the main current as I dared. I was now starting to shiver, whether from shock or cold I didn't know. But the torchlight, though it had gone well west of where we were, was heading our way. Teagan's time was running out.

'Now,' I urged.

She didn't move, looking down instead at Indiana. The water running down her face was tears rather than rain or river water. 'I can't.'

'Yes, you can, Teagan,' I said. 'Hell, if I can anyone can. Teagan, you hear me? I'm phobic of water, haven't even been able to bathe Noah. *If I can get across you can.*'

It didn't resonate. I looked at the torchlight sweeping through the trees. It would pick us out in minutes. I took a gamble on the one thing I actually thought I was good at. I understood what motivated people. And with the possible exception of Kate, Teagan was the woman in the group I understood best. I thought about Maggie from Team Teagan, telling me that she had been judged all her life.

'No one in Riley's ever thought you'd amount to anything, Teagan,' I made my voice harsh.

I saw her look. A stirring of anger.

'Do you really want to prove them right?'

She jumped. Her response was so fast I wasn't ready for her. Her arm caught mine but she had gone under and I could feel her panic. I'd already used up a lot of strength rescuing myself, and now Teagan started to pull me down. I felt my other hand slip along the tree branch that was keeping me steady, and felt a certainty I was going to drown. I had to let go of Teagan, or we'd all die. And in that same instant, I heard a voice so soft I thought I was imagining it: 'Mummy!'

I pulled. I'm not especially tall or strong, but I had ten centimetres in height and twenty kilos on Teagan and with every fibre of every muscle I had, I pulled. I felt Teagan find her feet on the creek bed. Then she was beside me. Then we were falling into the bank, crawling and scrambling our way up as Teagan frantically checked Indiana.

We were still half-submerged when we saw the torchlight

and froze. To my right was a large fallen tree branch—I tipped my head and edged behind it, pulling Teagan with me. The torch swept across the water. I wondered whether they'd be able to see Noah. Was he still where I'd tethered him—and was it out of sight? I prayed that he would keep silent.

And then we heard the crunching of sticks and undergrowth and the light moved on. The sound of the rushing creek, and a pair of barking owls above us, covered any noise we might have made.

I took a slow breath.

I unzipped the baby carrier, edged myself further up the bank and pulled Indiana out of the carrier as I did. Teagan seemed too exhausted to protest. Indiana was soaked like the rest of us, but floppy and silent, too. Her face was in the shadows.

I crawled along the ground until I got to where I had left Noah and all but dropped Indiana on the ground: the sling tie was still there but Noah was not.

I whipped my head around frantically: nothing but darkness. Any flickers of light through the trees cast more shadows. I started crawling. Feeling around me, whispering Noah's name.

'Baby.' Was that Noah's voice?

I started shaking. Hallucinating, I thought, trying to sit up but so totally exhausted I couldn't seem to remember how to.

'Baby,' Noah repeated. He was sitting next to me and smiling at Indiana. Who was smiling back at him.

I really was hallucinating. Except Teagan, crawling towards me, seemed to be seeing the same thing.

'Is she…?'

I picked up Indiana gently and held her out, the urge to laugh bubbling up wildly inside me.

'I think she's going to be a swimmer,' I said.

Teagan smiled. 'That's what my mum told me just before I jumped.'

The two-kilometre walk was a blur. The burning cottage remained a reference point and offered enough light that we were never in danger of being lost. Between the fire and the moonlight I could see the dark edge of the river break its banks and edge further across the plains towards what had been our temporary home, the movement of storm debris more apparent than the water itself. Even if our attackers hadn't taken down the bridge, the flooding waters might well have.

I didn't think of the things I'd lost—only what I still had with me. Noah, Teagan and Indiana. And my T-shirt; after Teagan's calm recognition that her mother had come to her when she needed her, I felt that Teagan's people were protecting us. Something, at any rate, had given Teagan the confidence she needed—and was still giving her the energy to keep going.

My concern now was that if it had been the Barclay boys after us, they were going to find us as they returned home.

If.

I didn't think I'd got Lachlan so wrong. I didn't know him that well; but I did know Sophie, and I'd seen how

Lachlan behaved in the hay loft after I'd found Tom. That was the man Sophie had married—not a man who went around torching houses and terrorising women. Not one prepared to murder children.

But it could have been Matt with Conor.

The terrain was not hard and there were no hills between us and the Barclays' house. But although the moon was up now, it was behind cloud and we had no way of seeing what was underfoot. We stumbled continually, holding the children; both of us falling more than once. Teagan was shivering and any time I stopped to wait or to help her, my body started to shake too.

'It's cold, Mummy,' said Noah, who was way past thinking this was a fun thing to do. He'd wriggle and protest until I put him down, then walk a few steps and sit down until I coaxed him back into my arms, generally making it as difficult as he possibly could to carry him. He finally settled on being piggy-backed. He never heard a harsh word from me.

When we at last could see the lights of the Barclay house, I finally asked Teagan what had been nagging at me.

'Why does someone want to kill you?'

'Me?' I saw in her look she hadn't had time to think the events of the evening through.

'Is it because Indiana is Matt's kid?'

'Shit. What is it with everyone's obsession with Indiana's father? I told you it was bloody unlikely—and that was before I saw Indiana.'

Before I could get my thoughts clear, she went on.

'Is that what bloody Conor Rearden thinks too? He came to see me a month ago, just before the birth.'

My skin started to prickle.

'About?'

'Warned me off,' said Teagan. 'Even offered me money to get out of town. I mean. What the fuck?'

I stared at her. 'Did he say what for?'

'Nah, just I had to stay away from the Barclays and that there wasn't gonna be any more money.'

'To which you said?'

'That he could fuck off. When Hamish died I felt...like maybe he'd have been okay if I hadn't taken Grace's money. But why would Conor care, are the Barclays paying him? It was a bloody long time ago.'

For Conor, with a chip on his shoulder the size of a tree trunk, and facing a job loss, money would be important. Particularly if he thought he deserved it for some reason. All the pieces started to fall into place. I started laughing.

Teagan stumbled as she hurried to catch me. 'What's so funny?'

'Nothing really. Just that if the Reardens weren't such arseholes to each other and all got on a bit better, then none of this might have happened.'

'What?'

I stopped. The Barclay house was only fifty metres away.

'Teagan, I've got another question for you. If there was a secret that, let's say, your father had kept from you for your own good, about what happened to your mother or brother, would you want to know it?'

I remembered her answer to my question about wanting to know who had killed Joshua: *Once, sure. Now? I just want to get on with my life.*

Teagan looked at me curiously. 'Why wouldn't I?'

'The advantage of *not* knowing is it would make starting afresh easier. Right now, you could leave the past behind and not let it define you or Indiana. Letting out this secret means that all the past hurt will get stirred up—some people may go to jail, and they'd deserve to, but in all that legal process your own healing…well, it'll be like having a scab ripped off a wound the whole time. And…'

'And?'

'And you might gain a friend. But you both knowing this thing will hurt them and their family.'

'A secret about me,' she said. 'Something Dad didn't tell me 'cause he thought it would hurt me?'

It was hardly surprising that she looked at me like I was talking a different language.

'What would you do?' she asked simply. 'If you were me.'

The one thing I hadn't thought of. I was so tied up in solving the puzzle I hadn't actually stopped to really get inside Teagan and ask that question. If it was me in Teagan's position, would I want to know?

My first and fierce response to the question as a hypothetical was an emphatic *yes*. It was always better to be truthful. Deal with reality and move on. Don't let secrets fester.

But this wasn't hypothetical.

I thought of what I had grown up knowing—that my mother didn't want me, that she had tried to kill me and, rather than taking responsibility, had blamed me.

It was knowledge that had shaped me into who I was. It had caused me a lot of pain that, in the end, I had been forced to overcome and learn to live with. I was happy enough with who I was. Maybe a lot happier now: I realised some of the guilt surrounding Noah's accident had lifted. I had failed him then, but now I knew I'd been the lioness all mothers want to be.

If I could un-know what I grew up with? If my parents could have risen above their own failings and not projected their guilt onto me, would I choose that?

In a heartbeat.

Teagan's situation was the reverse. If the full story came out it would change the past version of the truth…More like me finding out I'd got it wrong, that all that agony I had suffered, feeling unloved and rejected, had been based on false evidence. But knowing wouldn't heal that scar: it had already shaped who I was. In this case, new people would be hurt.

'I think,' I said slowly, 'weighing everything up, I'd rather not know.'

I had no idea what she would make of that. We walked the last fifty metres in silence. If I was going to get at the truth, I had to think about protecting her from it. Chances were, she wouldn't get the opportunity to choose. Trying to kill us was something not even Gordon Barclay could get the police to sweep under the carpet.

To say we caused a fuss would be an understatement. The lights were out when we arrived—later I discovered it was not far short of midnight—and everyone had gone to bed. Teagan pushed hard against the doorbell and I banged the door. A woman I recognised from the dinner party—the property manager's wife—got to the door first, fully dressed.

She stared at us. 'What on…who…why…?'

I pushed past her. 'We have two hypothermic babies here. They need towels, blankets, whatever you can lay your hands on. A blanket for each of us wouldn't go astray, either.'

Teagan had sunk down onto an antique hallway chair.

I wondered what Grace would make of the wet stain on the cushion. To be fair, when she did arrive a moment later, dressed in a long white silk dressing-gown that made her look like Barbara Stanwyck in a 1940s melodrama, she was more worried about us than the furniture.

'Whatever has happened? Are you both all right? *Kelly!*'

Kelly arrived back with an armful of towels and ushered us into the living room as Grace took charge. When Sophie arrived and stood gaping in the doorway, she was sent off for blankets and Kelly for the hot drinks. I put in an order for a hot chocolate for Noah. Teagan quietly crawled onto the sofa and ignored us as she put Indiana to her breast.

Gordon arrived next on the scene. 'What's going on here?'

I hadn't answered Grace, so I replied now. 'I need you to call the police.'

Grace wrapped a big fluffy rug around Noah, who was beginning to relax. He imitated a police siren, to Gordon's bemusement.

I looked at Sophie, who was now sitting in a chair trying to make sense of the spectacle. 'Where's Lachlan?'

Sophie stiffened. 'What has that got to do with anything?'

Gordon interrupted. 'What the hell is going on here? It's nearly midnight and you two have been wandering around in the rain. Are you mad?'

'Chased around in the rain and through a river, would be more accurate. Please call the police. Someone set fire to my house and tried to kill us. Your cottage.'

Gordon gaped.

'I think Isabel is right, darling,' said Grace quietly. 'Getting Sam Keller out might be a good idea. Would you mind?'

Gordon looked at me, then Teagan. Nodded and disappeared.

'Where,' I asked again, 'are Lachlan and Matt?'

'At the Riley Arms, I should imagine,' said Grace, smiling tightly.

Kelly arrived with hot chocolates for us all and a plate of chocolate slice; Noah thought it was Christmas all over again. The innocence radiating out of him made me want to gather him in my arms and run away with him. I looked at Grace, who was regarding me warily. Did she know what I knew? Was she making a damage-control calculation?

'Sophie dear,' said Grace, 'there's no need for you to lose any more sleep. Why don't you let me deal with this?'

Sophie's expression showed she'd just been put in her place, and it wasn't an unfamiliar feeling. I thought she would protest, but she looked tired and frightened. The way Grace had put it suggested there had been problems— probably as much with Lachlan as with Tom—that kept her awake. Living with your in-laws wouldn't make marital arguments any easier.

She got up and left us without looking back.

We sat in silence and I watched Teagan's eyelids start to close. Indiana had already fallen asleep, nipple still in her mouth. I rose and covered them with a blanket. Indiana was tucked in beside the back of the sofa and wasn't likely to roll off. Teagan's eyes opened as I stood up and our eyes locked. 'I'm going to talk with Grace,' I said. 'About...all of this. About past secrets and why someone wanted to kill you. And Joshua. Do you understand what I'm saying?'

Teagan hesitated, frowned, then nodded.

I felt her eyes on me as we left.

Grace led me to what I supposed was her office. Noah waddled beside me. He was carrying one of Tom's sipping cups so at least the dribbles of hot chocolate on to the pristine carpet were likely to be minimal. There was an elegant polished desk; Grace switched on a small blue lamp fringed with glass beads and sat behind it, holding onto every bit of authority she could. In the shadows she looked younger and it struck me what a knockout she had once been. She could have had any man—or done anything else she wanted to—with that combination of looks and brains. Yet she'd chosen Gordon. And Riley.

'What happened?' she asked.

She didn't, I imagine, *know*. But she knew what might have happened. I could see in the way she held herself that she was afraid her sons were involved.

'Two men sabotaged the bridge, cut my phone line and power and then torched the place.'

The horror in her face was genuine.

'I think you might know what led up to it,' I said slowly, 'and I'm not sure how to handle it.'

Grace's expression changed. She thought she knew what

she was dealing with—and I'd just indicated I was willing to bargain.

That might be true; I wasn't sure. I wouldn't be sure until I knew the whole story. Any bargain we came to wouldn't be the sort she had negotiated before, anyway.

'This is the second time someone has tried to kill Teagan Moretti.'

Grace shifted in her chair. I sat back in my mine; Noah was tiring, and he began to wriggle into my arms to get comfortable.

'You heard about the oxygen canisters?'

I saw relief in her eyes. 'Terrible,' she said. 'But it was an accident, mismanagement. Poor Chris has been trying to get that theatre updated for years.'

'It wasn't Chris's fault. Everyone in this town knew Teagan was having a caesarean.'

Grace's benign look suggested she was going to humour me. It hadn't occurred to me that she might be firmly invested in believing it was an accident.

'Is it possible,' I asked, 'that someone thought it was Teagan who was blackmailing you, rather than Róisín?'

A flicker of abject horror. Covered up, but not quickly enough.

'Please don't insult me by saying you don't know what I'm talking about. I've already spoken to Róisín.' Which was true, even if she hadn't actually told me anything. 'And please don't be worried that you now have another blackmailer on your hands,' I added quickly. 'I'm out of Riley tomorrow. To be honest…I don't know if the truth coming out would serve anyone. I figure it's not my secret.'

This wasn't strictly true. Teagan hadn't actually told me she would take my advice and keep her head in the sand.

I was too tired to work out what I was allowed to tell and what I wasn't.

'Then what exactly is your concern, Doctor Harris?'

'Teagan's safety.'

I watched Grace think about this—unlike Róisín, she wasn't trapped into a pathological way of viewing the world; she was smart and resourceful. It didn't take her long to get to where I had.

'What if I assure you I will take care of...any risk?' Grace asked.

'I would be grateful.' She could do it, I thought. But only if she considered all the possibilities. 'What does Lachlan know?'

'No one knows.' Grace immediately saw the problem with this. 'If what you say is correct, anyone who sought to harm Teagan did so because they *thought* she was blackmailing me. I have to assume they believed it was to do with...the awkward events of some years ago when she had an abortion.'

'Lachlan knows she didn't. She miscarried.'

'Yes. My son has had that conversation with me.' From her expression, it hadn't been an easy one for her. I also saw that she was fearful. Was she worried Lachlan had tried to kill Teagan? I hoped, for Sophie and Tom's sake, she was wrong. She had to know him better than I did. But she was judging him by what she—or Gordon—had been prepared to do.

'I suppose I'll have to trust you to, ah, fix the situation,' I said. But I didn't. Not without leverage.

'Does she need money?'

'She wouldn't take it.'

'But...' Grace wanted to make things right—but some

things money didn't buy. 'I could organise that she didn't know. An inheritance.'

I thought of Teagan, perhaps starting her online fashion business and shrugged.

'Up to you. But I should warn you...'

Grace looked surprisingly calm.

'There's a DNA test linking Tom and Indiana.'

Grace looked as if she might faint.

'Teagan's child and Tom are cousins,' I said. 'I assumed that put Matt in the frame as Indiana's father...' I gave her a moment to process this. 'But we both know that's not how they're related, don't we?'

Grace stood up, appearing in that one moment to have aged years. She walked over to the window and looked out into the darkness, one hand at her throat and the other lightly on the glass. Her body sagged.

'I was about your age when I came here for the first time, a little younger perhaps. It was hard—a new country, hundreds of miles from anywhere, so little to do. I was excited by the challenge. Pleased, if I'm honest, to be rid of my family.' She turned to look at me. 'My father was a judge; he brought Gordon home for dinner one day—Gordon had been working on a Republican campaign—he was older than me, ambitious, busy networking and soaking in advice. He'd been married before, did you know that?'

I shook my head.

'She couldn't have children, so he left her, you see. Gordon is a man who needs a dynasty.'

She was lost in memories. For a moment I wondered if she had forgotten I was there. She started up again. 'What Gordon didn't know was that my father was about to be indicted for corruption. I got out just before it happened.

My father was flawed in many ways, but I found...I found I couldn't bear to see such a proud man brought down.' She took a breath. 'And then he killed himself.'

My mouth went dry. Grace really was tough.

'So here I was with nowhere else to go,' said Grace, 'and I didn't get pregnant. Not for two years. Each month the anxiety went up a notch—and the doctor told me that probably made it even less likely I'd conceive. Then...' She smiled. 'I did. And it worked like magic on me. My mood, my relationship. It gave me purpose and direction, and Gordon doted on me. It was probably the happiest time of my life.'

I wasn't sure I wanted to hear what happened next, but I was pretty sure I could have told the story myself, minus a few critical details.

'Grace, don't.'

We both swung around to see Gordon in the doorway. He was a big man. A big man used to getting what he wanted. I scooped Noah in closer.

'Sam's on his way.'

'What are you going to tell him, Gordon?' Grace asked.

He looked at me, then back at his wife, stony eyes surely trying to silence her.

'She knows more than you do, Gordon.' Grace moved back to the other side of her desk.

He stepped towards her. 'I've always known, Grace. How stupid do you think I am?'

If it was possible, in the midst of all the terror I had faced, in the midst of all the sordid lies and cover-ups, to see a pure motive, then for second I not only saw it, I felt it. The look between them was electric.

'You...love me that much?' Grace seemed overwhelmed

by what must have been staring her in the face for twenty-five years.

'You really don't know?'

She stood unsteadily, and he moved closer and embraced her.

'What on earth did you do?' I heard her whisper, which put the penultimate piece in the puzzle. With the warning to police, with the hospital review, Gordon had worked out—probably through his or his accountant's attention to detail—that Grace was being blackmailed, but hadn't known it was by Róisín. Because he knew about the abortion—and why it had been so critical for Teagan not to have the baby—he had thought Teagan was the blackmailer.

The only question left was—had he paid the Reardens to deal with it or come up with some story to get his sons to do so? I was betting on the former.

Conor: who must have driven Róisín to the hospital on the day Joshua Moretti disappeared. Who now didn't have an alibi for that day.

Which meant Grace didn't either.

'What,' Grace asked, 'are we going to tell Sam?' She was still clutching her husband; it was me she was looking at.

'I want to hear it. All of it,' I said.

Gordon's grip on her tightened. Grace rested her head on his chest before raising her eyes to look at him. 'Darling, why don't you call James Lucas?' Their lawyer, I was willing to bet.

Gordon was set to protest, but she whispered something and he withdrew. She may have said, 'Trust me.'

'Lachlan was a difficult baby,' Grace said as soon as the door closed softly behind him. 'Fussy, didn't eat or settle well. I worried I was doing something wrong, and the more

I fussed over him, the more it seemed to unsettle him.'

She got up, went back to the window. 'Then one day I went into his cot to check him—he'd had an unusually long sleep and that was like Christmas. I'd been able to have a shower, even breakfast. Gordon was in Sydney, so it was just me and the staff.'

'He was dead,' I said softly.

'Yes, he was dead. He was on his stomach. They tell you not to do that these days.'

'It must have been awful.'

'Yes,' said Grace. 'Awful...doesn't begin to touch how I felt. I sat there for what, an hour? Then I knew I had to do something, that it was pointless ringing an ambulance, so I bundled him up in his baby carrier and took him into the hospital. When I got there, I walked inside with him in the carrier. Did I say walked? I have no idea how I got inside. But when I did there was an argument going on.'

'The Morettis.'

Grace nodded. 'I knew Donna but I'd never met Joe, and he was so angry and so...ugly a person. Donna looked terrified. There were people intervening and no one really paid me any attention. I don't know how I ended up in the nursery, but I did, and there was this beautiful, perfect little baby boy, who just looked right at me. I felt he was saying take me home, look after me because they can't, they don't deserve me. Don't let them scare me.' She choked, took a moment to compose herself. 'And, God help me, that's exactly what I did.'

'Didn't anyone notice?'

'I had the baby in my arms and the carrier handles tucked along my arms—you couldn't see there was another baby, my beautiful Lachlan, underneath. I took them both out to the car and had Joshua in the car capsule before I remembered to come back and get the money from Jeannie.

'They'd worked out Joshua was gone by then…there was a fuss…and I left. I dropped the paperwork in to Conor on the way home. Later…when the police started to look at him, I said I'd cover him. He thought I was doing it to help him. Gordon had rung earlier, and I doubt I said anything. But I must have said yes, I was taking the papers to Conor. He didn't need to be asked to cover me—he wouldn't have allowed his wife to be interrogated.'

But she'd given herself an alibi. 'And Gordon didn't see the new Lachlan?'

'Gordon had barely seen the…our Lachlan. He was an old-style father; babies were women's business—and I used the excuse of fearing for Lachlan's life after the so-called kidnapping, to leave for Sydney just as he was coming back to Riley. By the time he saw Lachlan again a month had passed. I never thought…he never gave me any indication that he knew something was amiss. All these years.' She shook her head. 'And *this* Lachlan was a good eater, put on weight and blossomed. He could pass for being older, at least with Gordon, or so I thought. I managed not to go back to the same nurse for months, and by then—well it never occurred to anyone that Lachlan wasn't…Lachlan.'

'But he isn't, is he?'

'I've given him a good life. Far better than he would ever have had with Joe and Donna.' In her look she implored me to share her view. I could not. Her crime may have been without malice, seated entirely in pain, but it had a profound effect on all involved. It led to Donna's death. No wonder Grace was dedicated to charity—she must be consumed with guilt.

'And your baby?'

'I felt the least I could do was let Donna have closure. Not knowing…that would be worse.' She saw my expression. 'It was wrong, I know, all of it. But you see I loved him so much by then…I couldn't give him up, I just couldn't.'

Keeping the baby had also kept Gordon happy, and maintained her place in the Barclay world. Now she'd have to face the fact that Gordon would likely have stood by her. He would have found a way to cope with a cot death, and none of the subsequent tragedy would have unfolded.

'I loved my own child too. I needed…I cremated him. A ceremony to say goodbye, though I found I couldn't bear to watch. And as it turned out that helped everyone assume the remains were Joshua. DNA forensics were in their infancy still.…I buried his remains in his baby carrier, near the river, with Joshua's rug. A mistake, perhaps, but it seemed the right thing to do. I sent a letter to the police, a month later I made sure they found him. I gave the Morettis that, at least.'

I thought of Grace's belief in the tabula rasa: the theory that we all come into the world a blank slate. I wondered if it had made it easier for her to take on Joshua without hesitating about genetics. I remembered how Teagan had known intuitively that she and Lachlan—Joshua—were connected.

'So Róisín saw you at the hospital,' I said slowly. 'Why didn't she say something then?'

'Róisín saw me looking like a zombie. She probably thought it was odd that I'd come into the hospital and out, forgetting to pick up the money, but nothing more than that. Later, though…She came here to clean when her mother couldn't, and she was nosy. I used to wonder sometimes if she tried my clothes on. She saw Lachlan once, the real…

my Lachlan. And she saw that baby carrier—she noticed I had a different one later. When she came back to Riley in her thirties, she was still as nosy as ever. After Teagan disappeared to Sydney she looked up her medical records and whatever she saw there'—I figured it had to be the radiology report, plus maybe a covering letter she might even have removed—'she put it together with what she already knew. I guess she decided if I could pay Teagan off, I could pay her too. She needed money for IVF. I couldn't call her bluff, could I? A DNA test would show Lachlan...was actually Joshua Moretti.'

The timing explained why Gordon had assumed it was Teagan continuing to bleed his wife. Had he decided enough was enough? Or was he just tying up loose ends for Lachlan to start his career with a clean slate, free of his past?

'Róisín wanted the status quo to continue,' Grace went on. 'She panicked when she heard Dean was going to audit the hospital; thought she might lose her job, and she knew her whole family were likely to end up in trouble. When I told her the ongoing supplements she was receiving—so, as she put it, "Bella didn't go without"—were coming from the charity shop she was horrified. It enabled me to bring the payments to an end.' Grace's expression suggested that this had been a relief.

'So,' I said. 'What are you going to do now?'

'That is what I need to ask you.'

What could I tell Sam? That two men we hadn't seen tried to kill Teagan and me? That I'd done an illicit and inadmissible DNA test? That would be enough for him to get a real DNA test, though...

'Lachlan would never forgive me.' Grace murmured.

'No, I imagine he wouldn't.' There would be a lot for

Lachlan to adjust to—the discovery of a mother he would never know, a family he didn't know he had, a drunken, poorly educated father. An unsuspected Indigenous identity. Would Matt create problems regarding the Barclay inheritance? And that was before even starting to deal with the knowledge he'd had sex—had a *child*—with his sister. Or the reaction from Sophie, when their relationship was already under strain.

'It's what we give as mothers when they are young... that's what's really important. You've given that to Lachlan already. He is who he is. This would affect him, of course it would. But the love you raised him with has given him a solid base—and that holds up whether he's a Barclay or a Moretti.'

'Would you take that risk with your son?'

I looked down at the sleeping Noah—the thought that he would stop loving me or speaking to me felt like a sharp knife twisting inside. If he was living a good, happy life? Maybe I could live with it. It would be wrong to put my needs above his. But which course of action would hurt him more? Turning his world inside out? Or denying him the chance to find out who he really was? How could anyone judge what was right for someone else?

'I understand how Róisín became involved. But her father? I take it he was brought in by Gordon? Did he burn down the house, and try to kill Teagan twice under his order too? They don't deserve to get away with that.'

'No, they don't.' Grace turned, leaning her back against the window. 'We can tell the truth you know—just not all of it. Say Gordon *thought* I was being blackmailed—and *thought* it was Teagan because of the previous abortion money. That Gordon hired Conor—that man has always felt he deserved more than he was prepared to work for—to give her some money. Shut her up about the past affair, because it might damage Lachlan's bid for preselection. I'm quite certain Gordon never told Conor to kill anyone.'

Was I? I thought of the stony look Gordon had given me. No, I was not certain at all.

'Conor must have decided to keep all the money and get rid of her. Gordon might be charged, but we have a good lawyer, we'll take our chances.'

'And the blackmail? Won't you have to come clean about that? What reason can you give for that?'

'I won't have to. There was no blackmail.' She saw my surprised look. 'Nothing that anyone will ever be able to prove, whatever their suspicions. Cash is a wonderful medium. No one other than me ever tallied the books. It stopped before your husband arrived.'

She didn't know about Dean's whiz-kid on cash businesses. But given how much she had contributed to the charity I wasn't sure if there would be an appetite to chase this one. Their lawyer would undoubtedly do a deal.

'What about Lachlan's political career?'

There was a pause, a half-laugh. 'Lachlan has decided he doesn't want to stand. Ironic, isn't it? He wants to stay in farming. He has new ideas for the use of the land and the river he wants to test out; ideas for using the seasonal rains better. Matt and he both know they have different strengths. They're currently celebrating.'

I stared at her. 'Really?'

'Yes. Lachlan has always had a strong feeling for the land. The river. He wants to work at the university in Dubbo. He and Sophie are planning to move there.'

She smiled faintly, knowing what that said about his

heritage, which was also Teagan's: her sense of belonging to country, her tie to Riley and to the river that was part of her soul.

I thought of Donna appearing to Teagan in dreams, but without Joshua—Lachlan—in her arms.

I wondered if she appeared in her son's dreams and what he made of it.

'I won't reveal your secret,' I finally said.

Was it the right thing to do? I wasn't sure. It was an uncertainty I might have to live with.

I looked into Grace's eyes. 'Unless Teagan asks me.'

ACKNOWLEDGMENTS

Riley is a fictious town with completely fictious people in it. However, I stayed in a town called Nyngan, north of Dubbo, when researching this novel, and geographically this is where Riley sits. Nyngan did indeed have major floods in 1990, and there are pictures of it in the railway station museum. Many other aspects of Nyngan appear here, and I hope the locals won't mind too much my rescoping their town—the hotel that I reimagined as the Riley Arms is actually on the highway, and most of the Nyngan locals who want to eat out go to the RSL, not the pub (where you can't get shots or a Cosmopolitan). The Bogan River doesn't have the high banks I describe in one spot, which is part of the reason it floods. For the eighteen months I was writing this book, I was living mostly in another small town, in Victoria, and some of the experiences there have also been added to Issy's experience of country living.

Over thirty years I have worked with probably hundreds of nurses (psych, MCHN and midwives) as well as allied health from social work, OT and psychology in the field of perinatal mental health. They are a remarkable, dedicated lot who makes women's lives so much better. To Debra

Cass and Enas Ghabrial, I couldn't have written this book without the many years we ran Baby Love groups. It was a pleasure and an honour to have worked with you all.

A novel takes a lot of time writing alone but always relies, too, on a lot of support and help.

Thanks as always to my first readers (two lots: there was a second version of this story, and I needed to know if it still worked); Sue Hughes who fearlessly tells me like it is—in the first version I probably put her off psychologists for life; Dominique Simsion who is always astute on character, Daniel Simsion and Lahna Bradley who gave me the young-psychologist perspective; at least the story worked well enough that they were very forgiving of Issy's faults (some of which I was able to rectify). Angela Collie, Geri Walsh and Robin Baker helped with overall readability issues and, following on from other readers' comments, Dean ended up in quite a different place than he started. Karin Whitehead rounded the team off with her attention to detail. Thanks all!

A special thanks to Donna Stolzenberg and Ruth Wykes, who took on the sensitivity and cultural reading role with such good grace and encouragement. I am especially lucky that Ruth's mob come from the area this book is set. Both pushed me to have courage. Neither I nor they wanted to whitewash a region that has such a strong Indigenous presence and history. I hope I have done them justice.

As always the team at Text are a pleasure to work with; Mandy Brett (I've just recovered from chopping out 16,000 words at her request—sadly, she was right, it's better for it), Jane Watkins in publicity, who gets things done without fuss, Imogen Stubbs for the wonderful cover and Michael Heyward for his support and encouragement.

Finally, as always, thanks to my growing family—Daniel and Lahna, Dominique and her new husband Duncan—our MFDs put the important things in life up front and central. And to my husband Graeme, who not only reads and edits (and supports Mandy—'get rid of this shit...') but also cooks. Okay, he was writing a cookbook at the time, and I did occasionally have to time him at work, but it made the whole process so much more fun.